The Book of C

Chris Crockford

For Dave

And With Thanks to

Heather
Ginnie
Richard
Alex

Cover Design by Mike Smith

Find out more on Facebook.

Search for "Stones of Gunjai"

Also in the series

The Stones of Gunjai
The Crown of Gunjai

Chapter One

Ancient History
1301 AD

The knight nudged his tired steed forwards, his cuirass dented and dirty and face unshaven and scarred. Behind him lumbered a dozen soldiers, wearily trudging alongside a wooden wagon with solid wooden doors and roof. The heavy locks that adorned the door and sealed windows glittered in the light cast by the torches the men carried.

He held his hand up and the men stopped, fatigued hands automatically going to sword hilts as they scanned the darkness around them.

'Come out brother.' shouted the mounted knight, 'I know you're there.'

There was some shuffling in the shadows before an aging monk stepped into the ring of torchlight. He was almost bald on the top but with wispy grey hair stood at odd angles around the sides and large grey beard blossomed out from beneath his kind eyes. He bowed but straightened with a smile as the man dismounted.

'Matthew my boy!'

The grizzled knight stepped forward and gave the monk a bone-crunching hug.

'It's been too long.'

'That it has.'

They turned and began walking away with the soldiers and cart following.

'How goes the crusade? We get scant letters these days.'

The knight shook his head.

'Not good. We've lost Mamluk Sultanate. That was our last foothold in the Holy Land. I think we'll have to withdraw.'

The monk shook his head.

'That is terrible news, but then again, no one said doing the work of God was going to be easy.'

The knight didn't say anything. He'd seen too many good men die at the hands of the Arabs to have much to say about the glory of God's work.

They walked along in silence. A slight hill rose in front of them and atop that, was a high stone wall with lights visible through a large arched gate. The party passed under the gate and into a courtyard.

'It doesn't change.' said the knight, looking around.

'What doesn't?'

'The abbey. It looks exactly as I remember it.'

Across to the left was the main chapel with its tall stone tower, and to the right and in front the buildings where the monks lived and worked, all surrounded by the high wall.

'We have just begun work on building a new dormitory and refectory behind the main cloisters. I'll show you in the morning.'

The knight nodded.

'I'd like that.'

He took a lungful of air.

'It's good to be back. I've missed home.'

The older man turned to look at him.

'And it has missed you too. But we can save the reminiscing for later. I assume it's on the cart?'

The knight became serious.

'Yes. We have it. The fight to get it out of Jerusalem was not a pretty one.'

The old man nodded as a younger monk came hurrying out. He kept glancing nervously at the soldiers and knight and was wringing the hem of his robe in his hands.

'Are we ready?' the old man asked.

'Yuuuuhh... yuuuuhh... Yes.' he stammered.

'Good.'

The young monk nodded quickly and the old man turned to the knight.

'Everything is prepared.' he said, his companionable tone dropping to become serious.

'Bring it and follow me.'

The knight nodded once before turning to bellow orders at the soldiers.

Four of them quickly took out keys and unlocked the heavy door on the cart before they stepped back and drew their swords, as did all but two of the men around them. These donned heavy leather gloves before removing a large iron bound casket from the cart.

'Form up around the chest.' shouted the knight, drawing his own sword.

He turned back to the old man.

'Abbot.' he said, 'We, the Knights Templar, are entrusting you with this. Are you ready?'

The old man nodded with a sad smile.

'We are ready.'

They carried the chest into the chapel with the abbot in the lead. As they entered they were flanked by a score of robed monks, all chanting their praises to God. The abbot stopped in the centre of the building.

'Thomas!'

The young monk from outside scurried forward and was directed to a small hole in the floor at the far end, just large enough for him to get his hand in. The boy knelt and with a glance at the abbot, who nodded, he shoved his hand in the hole.

Thomas twisted his arm and with a dull thud, part of the chapel floor dropped away to reveal a narrow staircase leading down into the dark. Two monks appeared, carrying torches and they headed down, lighting more torches that were set into sconces on the walls.

The abbot nodded to the knight and went down with the soldiers following closely.

The tunnel below was roughly made and stretched downwards steeply. The procession stopped when they reached a large circular room with three branches. The monks headed down the centre, lighting torches to show the way.

'We've taken precautions. Just as you asked.' said the Abbot.

'Good. We're taking a risk with this but we couldn't let the Turkish bastards get their hands on it. God knows what horrors they would unleash.'

The Abbot nodded but didn't reply.

He led them down a maze of corridors until they reached a heavy wooden door, deeply carved with crosses and symbols and held in place by a stout wooden beam that fitted into two iron brackets, one at each side.

Thomas, the young monk, moved forward and took the beam out before swinging the door open. Beyond was a circular room with a high ceiling that looked to be naturally formed. In the centre was a solid stone plinth made of a dark rock, different to the sandstone of the walls.

The party moved inside, the soldiers setting the chest down on the floor near the stone block.

'Are we ready?' asked the knight, an unexpected nervousness in his voice.

With a nod from the abbot, the knight produced a key from beneath his armour. He knelt and with a silent prayer, unlocked the chest. The lid fell back with a bang as if something inside was trying to get out. The knight took a step back.

'This was a mistake.'

'No.' said the abbot. 'This is for the best.'

He moved to the chest and took out a book. It was two feet by one and at least six inches thick. The leather cover was dark and inscribed with concentric circles and overlapping five pointed stars.

Carefully he put it on the stone block in the centre of the room where it seemed to thrum with an inner energy. The old man was sure he could see traces of purple fire licking around the edges.

'Everyone out.' bellowed the knight.

The monks and soldiers hurried away.

'Thomas.'

The young monk stopped at the doorway and turned back.

'Yuuuh... Yes?'

The old man smiled kindly and beckoned him back.

'Is your faith strong Thomas?' he asked, resting his hands on the boys' shoulders.

'Yuuhh... Yuuhh... Yes. Of kkkk... kkkk... course.' he stammered.

'That's good Thomas. That's good. You've done well my son. Your faith will protect us all.'

'I ddd... dddd... don't underst... ssstt... stand.'

Suddenly the boys' eyes went wide in shock and pain. The abbot gathered him close and held him as the knight withdrew a dagger from the boys' back.

'I'm sorry Thomas. But it has to be this way.'

The abbot gently lowered the dying boy to the ground.

'Your faith will keep us safe. Trust in that and trust in the Lord.'

Thomas clutched at the abbots' robes for a second before his eyes rolled in his head and he was gone.

The knight laid a gentle hand on the old priests' shoulder.

'It had to be done. Carnothal needs to be held. Needs to remain imprisoned.'

'I know Matthew. I know.'

He muttered a small prayer and closed Thomas' wide eyes before he took the simple wooden crucifix from around the boys' neck. Softly muttering a prayer, the abbot dipped the end of the wood in the wet blood and drew a cross on the cover of the book. On the table, the book was visibly trembling and an awful malign presence permeated all around. They could feel it as a sick and bitter taste in their mouths.

'We must be vigilant, Matthew.' said the abbot as he began to draw two wavy lines on the book at the top, giving the effect of a chain.

The abbots' words were barely out of his mouth when two of the soldiers ran in with swords drawn and eyes filled with hate. They threw themselves at the knight with such ferocity that he was forced back.

'Hurry!' he shouted as the first of the attackers managed to catch him on the shoulder with the edge of his blade and cut him deeply. He parried a strike from the other before kicking the first hard in the knee. The man crumpled as the bone shattered and the knight ran him through.

At the table, the abbot finished drawing a chain at the bottom of the book and crossed himself. As the final link was drawn, they all flared with a brilliant white light. The soldier that had been attacking Matthew fell to his knees as if all the strength had left his body. The knight looked at him with pity before he drove the point of his sword into him.

'Is it done?'

The abbot nodded.

'Yes. I believe so. The power of blood and faith will hold. Thomas will protect us.'

They both looked at the book. A dull purple glow was throbbing from the pages.

'I hope you're right.'

'So do I.'

The knight called out and the rest of the soldiers came in. All looked dazed and were unsteady on their feet.

'Get these two out.' he ordered, pointing at the bodies of the men who had attacked him. 'Get them out and seal the door. Brick it up.'

He glanced back at the book and Thomas' body.

'This must never be opened again.'

Chapter Two

Nightmares

Molly Kane woke up suddenly, cramming her first into her mouth and biting down hard to stifle a scream. She was drenched in sweat and her heart was pounding. Next to her, her husband Marcus rolled over, oblivious in sleep.

Still breathing hard, she swung herself out of bed and softly padded to the door. In the coolness of the corridor she took a shaky breath and tried to push the nightmare from her mind. They were getting worse. Barely a night went past without one.

India. Malor. His dark eyes and laughter... Molly shuddered and ran a hand across her face. That was probably it for sleep tonight.

She moved to the window on the landing and glanced out. The cobbled street was empty and wet, with dawn a good few hours away. She sighed sadly and pushed her shoulder length, almost white blonde, hair out of her eyes and went downstairs. She was around five and a half feet tall and moved with a dancers' grace. Softly, silently, she hardly made a sound as she walked barefoot through the dark house.

The kitchen was empty, but the range had been banked for the night so it was nice and warm. She filled the old iron kettle and put it on. Mrs Kettering, the housekeeper, wouldn't be up for another couple of hours yet so Molly had the place to herself.

While the kettle boiled, she sat at the expansive kitchen table and rested her head on the cool wooden surface.

How had she got here?

A year ago, she had been hungry and homeless. Now she had a beautiful house, a husband, servants and more money than she could hope to spend in a dozen lifetimes.

She also had a title. Her Royal Highness, Lady Molly Kane of Sunjian. She smiled sadly. She didn't need a title. It had been a gift from Nareema. Her adopted sister. She was a real Princess. Princess Nareema Kareen Vashti.

She had been the daughter of the Maharajah of Sunjian and it was down to her that Molly had everything. They'd met when she saved Molly from a group of men who were going to hurt her. After that, well, they'd been on an adventure. First searching for the magical Stones of Gunjai and then journeying to India to look for the Crown of Gunjai.

The pair had grown close through their travels and adventures and become like family, even taking each other as sisters.

Molly had never had a family. She didn't know who her father was and her mother had died when she was young. She sighed sadly. She missed Nareema.

True, she had her husband Marcus, he'd been a Captain in the Army when they met but had now retired, and his love was another thing that she'd found in the last year, but it wasn't the same. She couldn't talk to him like she could Nareema and deep down she wished she had stayed in India.

She sighed again. On the range, the kettle was beginning to whistle. Molly got up, poured the water into a teapot and sat back down.

Mrs Alice Kettering walked to the kitchen. It was early, the sun just beginning to break the grip of night. She adjusted her mop cap and thought about how nice it was that the house had people in. It had been just her and Peter Simcox, the butler, for too long.

They'd kept Nareema's house in order but now things had changed. The girl Molly was the mistress of the house now, Nareema having written to Peter to explain, and that was just fine with her. It was a big house and needed to be lived in.

She and Peter only shared one bedroom and the kitchen really. The rest of the house was just a lot of empty rooms that gathered dust. Molly and Marcus made a lovely couple and secretly Alice hoped it wouldn't be too long until there was the pitter patter of tiny feet.

She smiled as she wondered what she would cook for breakfast. It was good to have someone to look after, she thought to herself. She opened the kitchen door to find Molly asleep with her head resting on the table with a teapot, cup and saucer next to her.

Quietly the housekeeper crept in. The pot was cold and the cup was half full of cold milky tea. She smiled and gently placed her hand on the girls' shoulder, feeling her tense under the touch. She murmured in her sleep.

'Molly?' she whispered.

The girl snapped awake suddenly and sat up with a sharp intake of breath. It took her a moment to realise where she was. She relaxed and rubbed her eyes.

'What're you doing in here? Wouldn't you rather be in bed?' asked the older woman.

Molly smiled sadly.

'I couldn't sleep.'

'Well why don't you go back there now?'

'No. I'm up.'

Mrs Kettering made a disapproving face.

'It doesn't do that a lady like you should be up so early. Or asleep in the kitchen for that matter.'

Molly looked at her with a wry smile.

'Mrs Kettering, you and I both know that I'm not a lady.'

'Yes you are. Nareema says so and that's good enough for me.'

Molly sighed.

'Do you need a hand with anything as I'm here?'

'No.' replied the housekeeper. 'Mr Simcox will be up

soon, as will the girl. We can manage.'

She saw the look of disappointment cross Molly's face so she sat down and took one of her hands before speaking softly.

'Look. I know this is new to you but please leave us to it. You pay us to do things for you, and I would lay money on the fact that no other lady of your standing offers to help make breakfast.'

'There are no ladies of my standing.' replied Molly sullenly.

The housekeeper patted her hand in a friendly manner.

'I'll go and get your maid. She can...'

Molly shook her head and stood up.

'No. Leave her be. I'll go to the summerhouse for a while.'

Mrs Kettering smiled in a kindly way.

'I'll send her up with some tea in a bit.'

Molly nodded sadly and went to the back door.

'I'm not completely useless you know.'

'I know dear. Just enjoy the gifts God has given you. You don't need to worry about anything.'

Molly nodded once more and headed out into the garden.

'What's the matter?'

Marcus Kane came into the drawing room. His wife was sat, staring out of the window, a cold pot of tea on the table next to her. She looked round and smiled sadly. Her hair framed her face and he couldn't help but smile at her.

'What?'

He shook his head.

'Nothing. You weren't there when I woke up.'

She looked away.

'No. I wanted to do some training.'

'Again? You should get some rest.'

'I promised Nareema that I would keep up with the things she taught me. Besides, it's the only thing I'm allowed to do around here.'

He came and sat next to her and took her hand.

'What's the matter?'

She looked up at him, her white pupil-less eyes boring deeply into his. They use to be blue but their adventures in India had taken their toll. She had lost her sight in the search for the Crown but it had been returned, in a manner of speaking, by otherworldly powers which had left them as dully glowing white orbs. Slowly she reached up and ran her hand across his cheek.

'You can tell me you know. I'm your husband.'

Molly smiled, more brightly this time as she looked at him. He had tousled brown hair and a strong chin. His brown eyes were soft but he had suffered too. Gently she ran her fingers down his arm to the stump where his right hand used to be. Now it was his turn to smile tightly. Their quest for the Stones and Crown of Gunjai had been hard on them both. She sighed heavily.

'I'm bored. I'm not used to doing nothing.'

Marcus smiled.

'What about these invitations?' he motioned to a small pile of cards on the table next to her.

'I'm not going.' she said sulkily. 'Not after last time.'

'It can't have been that bad.'

'They were all laughing at me. I was only there a freak. The lady with the white eyes. The one that doesn't know the proper etiquette for afternoon tea. The one that...'

'Alright.' said Marcus, interrupting her.

He knew how she felt about these things. Less than a year ago she was homeless, penniless and scratching around the dockyard for food. Now she was here, his wife, a lady with more money than she could ever hope to spend. She felt she didn't fit in. And truthfully, she didn't. But that was why he loved her so much.

'They just talk about nonsense. Who's going to marry who, what their daughters are reading, sewing, it's all so boring.'

Marcus smiled and changed the subject.

'How's the new girl fitting in?'

Molly looked at him. That was another thing she didn't like.

'I don't need a maid.'

'It's...'

'Don't you dare tell me it's the proper thing to do.'

'But it is.'

'Servants! I've never needed a servant before and I'm sure I don't need one now. I'm not an invalid. I can choose my own clothes and dress myself you know.'

Marcus sighed.

'And anyway,' continued Molly sullenly. 'her name is Gwen. not "the girl"'.

'I'm sorry. Look, I know how you feel about it but a lady of your standing...'

'I don't have a standing!'

'Yes, you do whether you like it or not.'

Molly made a dissatisfied noise and folded her arms.

'It's bad enough with Mrs Kettering and Simcox fussing about.'

'That's their job. They like it. Mrs Kettering told me yesterday. She hasn't felt more content for years. She likes looking after the house and the people in it.'

'I don't need looking after.'

'Now your just being stubborn.'

She made another fed up noise.

'They won't let me do anything!'

'You don't need to.'

'But I'm bored!'

Marcus sighed again.

'I've had a letter from mother and father.' he said, changing the subject once more. 'I told them that I was

back in the country and they've asked me to visit.'
 'Oh. What did they say about me?'
 Marcus looked down.
 'I haven't actually told them yet.'
 'Why not?'
 'I thought it'd be a nice surprise when we got there.'
 'Are you ashamed of me?'
 'What? No! Of course not.' protested Marcus as he took his wife's hand. 'They're going to love you. Trust me.'

Chapter Three

Introductions

The stone chamber was dark, lit only by candles and guttering torches. Censers swung from the ceiling, their incense heavy and sickly in the air, engulfing the ten black robed figures, that stood in a circle in the centre of the room.

In the middle of the circle was another figure stood before a heavy table made from dark stone in stark comparison to the sandstone of the chamber. On the table was laid a long-curved blade and a book. The hooded figure spoke from the depths of their deeply hooded robe.

'Bring her.'

His voice was soft but echoed around the room. The ten figures turned to see two more of their brethren dragging a struggling girl dressed in white. She fought them every step of the way, her struggles becoming more frantic as the circle parted and she caught a glimpse of the stone table.

The men dragging her tightened their grip and shoved her forwards. She begged for her release as they bent her over the table, fixing her wrists to the far side with heavy steel manacles.

Frantically she pulled at the bonds but there was no escape. Satisfied she was secure, the men withdrew to join the circle.

'Be still child.' whispered the central figure as he threw back his hood.

The girl screamed as she saw him. His face was pale with watery blue eyes and sandy brown hair. Concentric circles and awful symbols had been burnt into his skin, disfiguring him and giving him an air of darkness. Carefully he moved the book underneath her.

She was terrified and crying freely as he began to speak to

the assembled people.

'We are close. We have the book. The brotherhood searched for hundreds of years and have guarded this place once we had found it. Now the time is upon us. The lines of power that run through this place are due. With them, the book and the gifts of the blood, we will be able to summon Carnothal and his Heralds and with him bound to our will we will be unstoppable. All the power and wealth you can imagine and more will be yours.'

There was a tense silence and the man laid his hand on the girls' head.

'She is the first. With her blood, we will begin to unlock the gate. This book is the doorway. Through the parchment, we will free Carnothal and usher in a new era!' his voice rose to a shout as around the circle the others began to chant. It was a low murmur but filled the incense heavy air with an awful droning.

At the altar, the girl pulled at the manacles once more, desperate to get away but only succeeding in tearing her skin against the unforgiving metal. The central figure stepped forward and placed a hand on her head once more, stilling her instantly. He lent in and whispered in her ear.

'The more you struggle, the more I will make this hurt. That, I promise'

He wrapped his hand in her hair and yanked her head back sharply. She cried out and her eyes widened in terror as his other hand brought the long blade round and slashed at her exposed throat.

Blood spurted out of her neck, spraying the man with her life fluid and he laughed as he pushed her head back down.

The blood flooded from her neck, drowning the pages of the tome beneath her. It ran across the heavy parchment but instead of running off as it reached the edges, it turned back on itself and began to soak into the pages, almost as if the book were drinking the spilled blood. The man in the centre laughed loudly as spidery writing and disturbing images began to appear on the thick vellum.

  Molly sat in the coach as it rumbled along through the rain. Opposite was Marcus with his head resting against the window and was snoring lightly. Next to her sat Gwen. She was a short girl, only fifteen, with mousey brown hair and brown eyes.
  She'd left her parents to try to find some work in the city. The dressmaker Molly visited, Mrs Hopkins, had recommended her to Simcox when he had escorted her for a fitting.
  Molly hadn't had anything to do with it. The girl had been interviewed by Mrs Kettering and the first time she really knew there was another person in the house was when Gwen had served her afternoon tea, although served was probably a generous description.
  The girl had come into the drawing room, taken one look at Molly's eyes, jumped in shock, dropped the tray and then ran away in tears. Molly had caught up with her in the kitchen where she was trying to explain to Mrs Kettering why she had broken the china cups and teapot.
  Molly shook her head. That had been three weeks ago. Since then they had slowly gotten used got each other but still, having a servant grated on Molly's nerves.
  'Are you alright?' Molly asked her. The girl looked as sick with nerves as she felt.
  'Yes Your Ladyship.'
  And that was another thing! She insisted on calling her by a title. One that Molly secretly didn't like but knew it made Marcus proud.
  She'd asked Gwen not to call her that but the shocked look the girl has given her. Well it was like she'd asked her to run around the streets of London naked! In the end, she'd just let it go.
  The coach hit a pothole and Marcus jerked awake. He

rubbed his eyes and glanced out of the window.
'We'll be there soon.'

A few hours later the coach pulled up outside a sprawling country manor. It was set in expansive grounds with woodland all around. They even had a lake! The closer they got, the more scared Molly became. Marcus patted her knee as the coach stopped.
'It'll be fine. They'll love you.'
He smiled warmly but Molly didn't share his confidence. She let out a long breath and slipped on her glasses.
Thin wire frames held in place some smoked glass lenses. They didn't help with seeing anything but they hid her eyes. Molly got less stares and muttered comments when she wore them. They had been expensive but worth it.
A smartly dressed servant opened the door and Marcus climbed out before turning to help his wife. She stepped out into a light drizzle, feet crunching on a wide gravel driveway in front of the huge house.
Gwen jumped down behind them and followed them as the servant led them inside. The hall was huge, with a wide sweeping staircase in front of them and a multitude of doors leading off to the left and right.
They were led to a set of double doors which were opened to reveal a library.
'Wait here. I'll introduce you.'
Molly nodded and Marcus squeezed her hand.
'It's going to be fine.'
She smiled tightly and Marcus went into the room, leaving her and Gwen in the hallway.

'Father. Mother.'
His father, a large man with a heavy moustache that was greying at the edges, nodded cordially as his son came in. His mother stood and embraced him, but took a shocked breath when she saw his right arm.

'Marcus, what...'

'I'll tell you later.'

There were two other people in the room and Marcus recognised them instantly. Lady Samantha Banton and her daughter Jane. The girl had jumped up when Marcus had come in.

'Ah, Lady Samantha. Jane. How pleasant it is to see you.' he said.

Lady Samantha nodded and Jane stepped over to Marcus, lightly touching his arm. She was dressed to the nines in a floral print dress with matching hat. He could smell her perfume, heavy and intoxicating as she moved.

'Mr Kane. How terrible. You poor thing.'

Marcus smiled tightly.

'I wasn't expecting visitors...'

Jane smiled coyly.

'Your mother told us that you were returning home. Mother and I felt we should visit. After all, it has been nearly a year since we saw each other last.'

'Yes. It has been a little while.' replied Marcus, casting his mind back to the ball where he'd met Molly. That had been the last time he'd seen Jane or her mother. Back then a marriage between he and Jane had been all but arranged. Nothing had been officially said but the idea had been acceptable to both families.

'Where have you been hiding yourself?' she asked. 'You were sorely missed at Christmas. Your mother said you had been away.'

'Yes. To India.'

Jane put a hand to her mouth in mock surprise.

'India! My goodness.'

Marcus' mother spoke.

'Lady Samantha and Jane are staying with us for a few days. We thought it may be advantageous for you two to get re-acquainted. I believe that early next week, your aunt Sarah will be arriving with her daughters as well.'

'Mother…'
She gave him a pointed look.
'Is there a problem?'
'Well. Yes, there is.'
Marcus coughed politely and moved to the door, returning a moment later holding Molly's hand.
'Mother, father. Please may I introduce her Royal Highness, Lady Molly of Sunjian.' He looked down, embarrassedly. 'My, um my wife.'
He couldn't look at his parents as the words sank in. Eventually his father spoke, the shock evident in his voice.
'Your what?'
'My wife. We're married.'
'What?'
Jane looked between Molly and Marcus several times before bursting into tears and running from the room. Her mother stood and followed.
'Well I never!'
Marcus' mother sat down heavily on the chair, the colour draining from her face.
His father looked at them both in disbelief.
'You... You can't be married.'
'We are. I...'
Molly reached up and took the tinted glasses from her face and both of his parents gasped.
'My God! What's wrong with her eyes? Is she blind?' stuttered his father.
Molly resisted the urge to say something.
'No father. She isn't.'
The old man looked down at his wife who had a hand over her mouth, trying to suppress the shock.
'You were to be engaged to Lady Samantha's daughter.'
'I know father…'
'The poor girl! You can't just do that to her.'
Marcus bristled slightly.
'With respect father, that was a year ago. Things have

changed. I've changed.' he squeezed Molly's hand.
'Molly and I are married and that's an end to it. I'd hoped you be happy for us.'
'Nonsense. What about Jane?' the old man seemed angry and confused.
'When did you... Where...' began his mother.
'Last year. Aboard a ship.'
'A ship!'
'Oh my goodness. What will our friends say?' said his mother.
'Is she pregnant?' demanded his father.
'No. She's not.'
Molly stepped forward.
'I am here you know.'
The old man looked at her as if she were something distasteful and then back at his son.
'Well I've never heard the like. Married. To her!'
Marcus tensed.
'Father, mother, please excuse us. It has been a long trip and we would like to rest.'
He turned on his heel and walked off, with Molly and Gwen following close behind.

'Well that went well.' whispered Molly as another smartly dressed servant lead them upstairs.
'I thought they'd be happy for us.'
'I think it was a bit of a shock.' she looked down. 'I was a bit of a shock. And what about that poor girl? I think she was expecting you to pop the question as soon as you saw her.'
Marcus clenched his jaw.
'Nonsense.' he said eventually. 'They'll be alright. They just need to get used to the idea. That's all. And as for Lady Samantha and Jane? Well I expect there are men who would fall over themselves to be her husband.'
Molly frowned but didn't say anything else.

An hour later, Molly was in the room she would be sharing with Marcus. She was sat on the bed, staring into nothing, waiting for him to return. He'd gone to talk to his parents again, while she had decided that it was better to stay out of the way. It wasn't the welcome she'd had in mind.

But then again, she wasn't exactly sure what she had expected. Not to be welcomed with open arms but at least a bit more than she had got. And as for Lady Samantha and her daughter being here too, well it had all gotten complicated all of a sudden.

She looked around the large and well-furnished room. His family had money and Molly would have bet that they knew it. She sighed. This wasn't like home at all. There was a knock at the door and she stood.

'Come.'

Gwen opened it and came in.

'Do you need anything Your Ladyship?'

Molly shook her head.

'No. Thank you. What about you? Settling in?'

The girl nodded.

'Yes, Your Ladyship.'

The servants' quarters were downstairs, but Molly could summon her by pulling a bell rope. Molly had already decided that if she could manage to pull a rope then she could manage to do whatever it was that required Gwen.

'Mr Tanning said that he'd have your luggage brought up directly Your Ladyship.'

'Mr Tanning?'

'Lord Kane's butler.'

'Ah.'

Molly sat down.

'Are you sure you don't need anything?'

Molly smiled.

'No. I'm fine. Thank you.'

The girl turned to go but turned back. She looked at the floor and wrung her hands.

'What?' asked Molly.

The girl looked up then down again.

'I know I don't have no right to ask and now probably isn't a good time, but...'

'But what? Come on, out with it.'

'Um, would I be able to have a half day in July? My sister is getting married and...'

'Is that it?' said Molly more sharply than she intended.

The girl looked down, a mixture of guilt and fear plastered across her face.

'I shouldn't have asked. It was wrong to...'

Molly stood up and walked across to her.

'Of course you can. Take a whole day, take two. I'm sure I'll manage.'

Gwen looked up.

'Really?'

Molly smiled warmly and gave the girl a knowing wink.

'I've never known a proper family. It's important to spend time with those that you love. In fact, take anything you like from the pantry. I'll make sure it's very well stocked. You can even take the carriage to get you there. Does your sister need a ride to the church? She can use it for that too if she wants.'

Gwen smiled nervously.

'Thank you Your Ladyship.'

Molly smiled again.

'Is there anything else?'

'No, Your Ladyship. Are you sure you need anything.'

'No, thank you. Why don't you go on and get some rest? I think tomorrow we may take a trip to the village. I'd like you with me for that.'

'Very good, Your Ladyship.'

The girl bobbed a curtsey and left. Molly shook her head as she closed the door. Honestly, did she think that she'd have said no to a day off for her sisters' wedding? She'd make sure to send something nice as a gift.

She walked to the window and looked out across the estate. The sun was beginning to set and the drizzle was turning heavier. She shivered. India had been warm. Maybe she should have stayed. She missed Nareema.

There was another knock at the door. This time it was a couple of servants with their luggage, closely followed by Gwen.

'Put it over there please.' asked Molly, pointing to a spot near the wall.

The men nodded and hurriedly put it down, Molly sensing their eagerness to be out of the room. She also didn't miss the sideways looks they gave her or the fearful muttering as they left. Gwen quickly began to unpack. Molly went to help her.

'Don't worry Your Ladyship, I can do it.'

Molly frowned and took a long wooden box from one of the trunks. It was made of a heavy dark wood and inlaid with silver.

She gently placed it on the bed before opening it. Inside was a long, curved sword, it's hilt was studded with gems and silver, worn smooth through use. The fine blade was etched with swirling whorls and lines.

'Is that a gift for the master?' Gwen asked.

Molly took the sword and scabbard from the box, trying to ignore the irritation that she felt every time Gwen described Marcus as her "Master".

'No. It's mine. My best friend gave it to me. It belonged to someone who...'

Molly sighed again, as she remembered Aleena. The woman had hated her but still she had given her life to protect her. This had been her sword, and her mothers' before that. It was a special blade.

'... It belonged to a friend.'

She looked at the sword for a while before reaching a

decision. Snapping the blade into its scabbard she straightened.

'I'm going out for a while.'

'It's raining.'

'I know. Tell Marcus I'll see him later.'

'Do you want me to come with you?'

'No.'

Molly reached into the trunk once more and pulled out a black leather bag which she slung over her shoulder before striding out, sword in hand.

Rebecca Miller was scared. She'd been walking home from the village when someone had grabbed her from behind. They'd quickly bound her and when she tried to scream they'd crammed something in her mouth to stifle the noise before they bundled her into a cart.

Now she was alone.

She didn't know where she was apart from a small, cold, stone room with bars at the far end. A big man in a black robe had thrown her in here before uttering some guttural threats and leaving. Beyond the bars a small candle burnt in the corridor but its flickering shadows were doing little to light the space.

She crawled across to the bars, pulling a coarse weaved blanket around her shoulders.

'Hello?' she ventured quietly.

There was no answer.

Wiping away some tears, she hugged the blanket around her tightly and wished she were at home.

'Where have you been, I've been worried sick. Look at you, you're wet through.'

Molly was stood in the hallway. Sword in hand and soaked to the skin.

'I went for a walk.'

Marcus frowned as his father came out to see what was

going on.

'Why have you got a sword? Women shouldn't meddle with such things. You'll hurt yourself.'

'Father, please...'

Molly bit her lip.

'Please excuse me, I need to change.'

She strode off before she said anything to Marcus' father that she'd regret. On the way up the stairs she heard the man talking.

'Why'd you let her run about with a sword! It's bad enough that you've married a cripple let alone one that can't do as she's damn well told. Your mother…'

Molly shut out the rest of the conversation and quickly headed up to her room. So, it was going to be like that, was it? That's what they thought of her. She had hardly closed the door when Gwen came in, she looked nervous.

'The master was quite upset when you wasn't here when he came back. He's been pacing around ever since.'

'He'll get over it.' she said angrily.

Molly began to undress, stripping out of her wet clothes and into a long dressing gown.

'Shall I prepare you a bath Your Ladyship?'

Molly's reply was cut short as Marcus came in. He looked at the girl and then at his wife. Molly ignored him for a second and spoke to Gwen.

'Actually, that would be nice. Thank you.'

The girl bobbed a curtsey and left quickly, sensing the tension in the air.

'Where have you been?' he demanded.

'I went for a walk.'

'In the rain? With a sword?' he said, a touch of anger in his voice.

'I needed to think. I did a little training.'

'Think? What about?'

'Let me see.' she said dismissively, 'Why your parents hate me would be a good start.'

'They don't hate...'

'You married a cripple who can't do as she's told!' snapped Molly loudly.

Marcus looked down.

'He needs to get to know you.'

'It won't change a thing.'

'It will. Trust me. Maybe I should have told them.'

'Maybe you should.' she replied with a sniff.

'You're not helping though.'

'Me? Why is it my fault?'

'It's not, but you missed dinner. Mother was quite put out.'

'Really.' her tone told him exactly what she thought of that.

'Yes. Really.'

'Well I expect Jane was more than attentive to your needs.'

Marcus was shocked.

'What? How could you think that?'

'I heard the way she was fawning over you when we arrived. I was only stood waiting in the hallway, remember?' she put on a sing song voice. 'Oh, my dear Mr Kane. How terrible that you weren't around at Christmas. What must you have been doing?'

'Molly. That's not fair. Jane…'

'Jane what?'

Marcus turned to leave.

'I can't talk to you like this. I can't believe that you're jealous.'

'Jealous! Angry more like. Your parents almost had a fit when they found out you'd married a freak!'

He sighed.

'Please Molly. You're not a freak. Give them a chance to get to know you. Let them see the woman I love. I'll sort out Jane and Lady Samantha.'

'Really?'

'Yes really. Please Molly.'

Molly sighed.

'Alright. I'll try. I don't know I'll be what they expect though. I'm not the obedient little wife they think you should have.'

'And I wouldn't have it any other way.'

She sighed again.

'Look, I'm sorry. I've been scared they won't like me for ages and now we're here it looks like I was right.'

'They'll love you. You might want to leave the sword and training alone though.'

She shot him a hard look.

'Please. Just until we leave.'

Molly held his gaze for a second before nodding.

'Fine. But I want them to know that it's something I do.'

Now it was Marcus turn to nod.

'Alright.'

Molly left Marcus and wandered to the bathroom. A huge enamel tub was rapidly filling from some brightly polished brass taps. Gwen was stood nearby, checking the water.

'I can manage from here. You go to bed if you want.'

The girl looked at her as if she were going to protest but thought better of it.

'Yes, Your Ladyship. Good night.'

Molly watched her go and shook her head. She really would have to get her to stop calling her that. She didn't consider herself to be a lady. It implied that she was better than Gwen and she didn't like it.

She sighed once more and turned off the taps before slipping her dressing gown off her shoulders. It fell to the floor as behind her, the door burst open.

Molly snatched up the gown and covered herself as she turned around to look straight at a horrified looking maid clutching an armful of towels.

The girl was about the same age as Gwen but was wearing an immaculate black dress with spotless white pinafore and matching cap. The girl gave a little squeak of surprise as she saw Molly's eyes.

'Oh I'm sorry Your Ladyship. I'm sorry I...'

Molly shook her head.

'No harm done. What are you doing?'

'Brought clean towels.' she said, holding them up as if they were evidence. 'I din't know you were here yet. I saw your maid leave and thought she was going to get you. I thought I'd have time to...'

'It doesn't matter. I can manage without Gwen you know.'

The girl nodded but still looked scared.

'Please don't tell his Lordship. I was supposed to do this earlier but I got behind on the washing and...'

'It doesn't matter.' repeated Molly. 'I won't tell a soul.'

'Thank you Your Ladyship.'

'What's your name?'

'Elsie Williams.' she replied, bobbing a curtsey. 'I'm one of the maids.'

'You're about the same age as Gwen. Could you keep an eye on her for me? She's alone in a strange place and...'

'Of course Your Ladyship. No problem.'

'Thank you.'

Elsie put the towels in a cupboard, leaving two out for Molly. She went to go, but turned back as she reached the door.

'Beggin' your pardon Your Ladyship but what happened to your eyes?'

'I hurt them. While I was in India.'

'India? That's a long ways' away.'

'It is.'

The girl bit her lip and Molly knew what she was going to ask.

'Yes. I can still see. It's a long story. Is there anything else?'

'Is that a tattoo. On your back?'
Molly smiled.
'My mark. Yes, it is.'
Elsie smiled nervously.
'May I... Um. Can I have a look?'
Molly nodded and turned around. Across almost her entire back was a tattoo of a huge eagle, its wings curving up over her shoulders and upper arms. Elsie made an impressed noise.
'I ain't never seen a lady with a tattoo before. My granddad had a couple but then he was a sailor. Did it hurt? Why'd you get it?'
Molly pulled her dressing gown back on.
'It hurt more than you can imagine and I got it... Well that's another long story. Now if there's nothing else then I'd like to have my bath.'
'I'm sorry Your Ladyship. I'll be going. Thank you.'
The girl curtseyed once more.
'Don't worry,' Molly said. 'I won't say anything.'
The girl smiled nervously.
'Thank you, Your Ladyship. I'll look in on your maid.'
'Thank you.'

Molly returned to her room after a luxurious soak in the bath, felling quite relaxed. Marcus was already in bed and she smiled to herself as she found a plate of sandwiches and some spiced wine on the table next to the bed. Marcus rolled over.
'Gwen brought them. She thought you might be hungry.'
'She didn't have to do that.'
'No. But she did. You need to let other people look after you.'
'I don't need looking after.'
'I know that. But still, a lady...'
Molly held up her hand
'Don't say it.' she said playfully.

Marcus grinned.

'Alright. Mother would like to meet you. She's not had a chance yet.'

Molly looked down, her happy and relaxed mood dropping away quickly. Marcus took her hand.

'Please. They just need to get to know you.'

She took a deep breath and let it out as a long sigh.

'I'm scared.'

'What of?' he asked.

She shrugged and Marcus smiled.

'You've faced things that would turn most people's hair white! My mother isn't going to try and kill you.'

'I know but…'

'Please?'

Molly smiled tightly.

'I'll see her in the morning.'

'Thank you.'

She picked up a sandwich and sat back on the bed. It was roast beef with horseradish.

'So what's the plan while we're here?' she asked taking a bite.

'Well, there's the spring fair at the weekend in the village and the week after that mother has arranged a ball.'

'A ball? Marcus…'

'It'll be fine. We'll be the guests of honour. It won't be like last time.'

'I hope not.'

'What else are we doing?'

'I don't know. What do you want to do?'

Molly shrugged.

'Don't know.' she said with a mischievous grin. 'But I'm sure we can find something to do.'

Chapter Four

Tall Tales

The next day Molly and Marcus went downstairs and after a quiet breakfast, and a trip around the ornamental gardens, Marcus escorted his wife to the drawing room where his mother was taking tea. Gwen hovered nervously behind them.
Marcus pushed the door open and led her inside. Marcus' mother was there, sat stiffly in a leather armchair. Beside her was a low table and next to that, a matching armchair. Stood just to one side was the maid Elsie. She smiled nervously and bobbed a curtsey.
Molly looked at her.
'I don't think I'll need you for the moment Gwen,' said Molly without turning around. 'Please take the morning, no, the day off.' she turned to her husband who was holding a grimaced smile.
'Marcus, I'm sure you have things to do too? Perhaps Gwen might like an escort to the village?'
Marcus glanced at his wife and then at his mother whose face was stern.
'Molly...' he whispered through clenched teeth.
She smiled, raised her eyebrows and gave him a wink. He smiled tightly back before nodding.
'Of course.'
'Thank you Your Ladyship.' said Gwen before quickly heading out with Marcus following.
There was a tense silence in the room for a moment.
'Shall I serve tea?' asked Elsie nervously.
Molly smiled at her.
'I'll do it.'
Both Marcus' mother and Elsie spoke at the same time.

'You can't possibly...'
'I couldn't let you...'
Molly looked at Elsie.
'I'm sure you have other duties to attend? Or maybe you could go with Gwen?'

The girl looked sick as Marcus mother opened and closed her mouth a few times in surprise. Eventually she found her voice.

'Be away with you girl. I'm sure Mrs Baddock has something for you to do.'

'Yes ma'am.' she curtseyed before turning to Molly and dipping again. 'Your Ladyship.'

The girl quickly headed towards the door but was stopped by another word from the older woman. She gave Molly a calculating stare.

'Actually, ask Mrs Baddock to come and see me then you may have the day to yourself. Show her ladyships' maid around.'

Elsie looked nervously surprised.
'Thank you ma'am.'
'It won't be a regular occurrence.'
Elsie bobbed again.
'No ma'am, thank you ma'am.'

They watched as the girl left and there was another tense silence. Eventually Molly broke it.

'You want to get to know me. Well, I don't like being waited on and titles make me uncomfortable. I've managed on my own for most of my life and until recently I've had very little and been glad for it. I've seen and been through quite a lot in this last year and this is who I am and I won't be changing any time soon.' she smiled sweetly. 'Shall I pour?'

The older woman looked at her for a second but with Mollys blank eyes, the girl was impossible to read. Her features softened slightly.

'I thank you for your honesty. Please sit.'

Molly sat opposite the woman as she poured them both a cup of tea from a delicate china pot.

'Where did you meet my son?'

'A ball. Lady Samantha's. It was last year.'

She put the pot down as she spoke.

'We heard about that. Some hideous foreign woman killed a dozen men. Totally ruined the library apparently. Caused quite a stir.'

Molly bit her lip and thought carefully before she replied, the woman watching her intently.

'I think the hideous woman was Princess Vashti.' she paused and took a sip of tea. 'Princess Nareema Vashti, my adopted sister and best friend. It was only four men and to be honest, they were trying to kill her. I can't say much about the state of the library as I was kidnapped.'

'So, that was you, was it?'

Molly nodded and the older woman smiled.

'Marcus always likes to play the hero.'

'He saved my life.'

'He was to be engaged to Lady Samantha's daughter. It had been arranged. I'm still not sure what to tell Lady Samantha or Jane. Frankly, I'm surprised that they stayed last night. I know that Jane has feelings for my son. Is him saving your life a reason to think that he should be yours? What can you offer him that Jane can't? She would be a perfect…'

'No.' said Molly flatly, interrupting the older woman. 'The reason he is mine is that I love him. We've been through a lot together.'

'So I understand. How did he lose his hand? Is that something to do with you too? He's been very evasive about it. Jane is very upset.'

'She's upset! She didn't have to watch while it happened!' snapped Molly.

'What did happen?'

Molly looked at her.

'You'll have to ask him. It's not my place to say.' she replied defensively.

'Really? And yet you say you care for him.'

Molly stood and turned towards the door. She was going to leave before she got too angry.

'What happened to your eyes?'

Molly sighed and tuned back.

'You wouldn't believe me if I told you.'

There was a knock at the door and in came the housekeeper. She was a short, dour woman with a seemingly permanent scowl on her thin face.

'You wanted to see me ma'am?'

Marcus' mother held Mollys gaze for a second before looking at the housekeeper.

'Mrs Baddock. I have allowed the girl to be excused her duties today to keep her ladyships maid company. She will be back at work tomorrow and I'm sure she will work all the harder for her day of rest. In the meantime, we will be taking lunch in here.'

Mrs Baddocks' face went flat, her lips in a tight line and Molly could feel her glaring at her. Eventually she nodded.

'Very good ma'am.'

She shut the door and Marcus mother sat back in her chair.

'So, Princess. Tell me your story.'

Molly sat back down.

'You won't believe it and my name is Molly. I'm not a Princess.'

'I'll be the judge of who or what you are while you're in my house and you might find I'm more open minded than you think.'

Molly told her everything. How she had met Marcus, Portugal, Iceland, India, all of it. Throughout, the older woman was stony faced. At the end Molly sat back.

'That's quite a story.' said Marcus' mother after a long

silence.
  'It's what happened.' replied Molly with a shrug.
  'It all seems very fanciful.'
  'Are you saying I'm lying?'
  The older woman didn't say anything. In a fit of anger Molly jumped up, grabbed her teacup and threw it across the room. Before the older woman could protest, Mollys eyes flashed brilliant blue and the teacup stopped in mid-air, suspended in a swirling column of wind. The older woman looked on open-mouthed.
  'I don't have the power I did and if I use it too much then I get tired but I can still call it.'
  Concentrating hard, Molly slowly brought the cup back to her hand and carefully put it back on the table. She sat down heavily as her eyes began to return to normal.
  'How did you do that?' stammered the older woman.
  Molly held up her arm to show an exquisite silver bracelet with a finely cut sapphire in it. The gem was glowing brightly and almost pulsing in time with a brilliant spot of light in Molly's eyes.
  'This. This is what was given to me at the end. A thank you I suppose.'
  There was a stunned silence for a minute. Marcus mother regarded Molly critically and she was reminded of Jamail, the old seer of the Daughters of Kali. She had the same inscrutable gaze. Eventually she sat forward.
  'You really are telling the truth, aren't you?'
  'As much as I remember. Yes.' said Molly defensively.
  Another silence descended.
  'Do you love him?'
  'With all my heart.'
  'Well, you're not the sort of girl I would want my son to be associated with.'
  'Here we go,' thought Molly. 'Here it comes.'
  'But you love each other?'
  'Yes. We do.'

The woman paused.

'Well I certainly don't know what I'm going to tell Lady Samantha or Jane.' she shook her head and sighed. 'There will have to be a proper wedding of course. I can't have my son married by a ship's Captain. It isn't the done thing.'

'What?' exclaimed Molly.

'You seem to be the sort of girl that won't take no for an answer and I dread to think of the trouble you're going to cause him but as long as he's happy then I suppose I am too. And, of course, having a Princess in the family...'

Molly looked at her in disbelief.

'Do close your mouth dear, it isn't ladylike.'

'But... I'm not a lady. Or a Princess.'

'Well you certainly don't act like either, and I don't think you'll stand for being taught. Marcus has got his work cut out with you.'

The older woman stood up and Molly followed suit.

'You will to take separate rooms until you are properly married.' the woman smiled. 'And in the meantime, my name is Victoria.'.

She offered her hand and Molly shook it before pulling her in for a hug.

'Thank you!'

They broke apart, Victoria seemingly quite flustered but she rallied magnificently before her face took on a stern and hard expression.

'If you hurt him, then you will have me to answer to. Is that clear.'

'I understand. Thank you.'

Victoria sat down.

'We will organise the wedding as soon as possible. I will make the appropriate preparations but for now, welcome to the family.'

'What about, um...'

Molly realised she didn't know his father's name.

'James? Leave him to me. and now, I would like to see the sword you have.'

Marcus returned to the house with a certain trepidation. It had been an anxious morning that wasn't helped by having two giggling girls in tow or bumping into Jane and her mother.

Gwen had been delighted when her new friend Elsie had been allowed to come to the village and Marcus had given them some money to spend and then had followed them round for two hours while they shopped. Matters had got worse when he was stood on the village green when Jane and her mother had come past in their carriage. They had stopped and Lady Samantha had given him a piece of her mind while he could see Jane sobbing in the back of the carriage. It hadn't been his intention to hurt Jane but Molly had come along and she had just sort of slipped his mind. Feeling wretched and tired, he was quite glad to get back but nervous about how Molly and his mother were getting on.

He entered the house to find Mr Tanning, the butler, standing in the hallway along with the housekeeper Mrs Baddock. They gave the girls a hard look before turning to Marcus.

'What's the matter?'

'We don't know sir. They had an early lunch in the drawing room then asked for a large basket of apples. Then they locked the door.'

'Apples?'

Marcus frowned and went to the drawing room door and pressed his ear to the wood. There was a muffled thump as something bounced off it and then laughter.

'Your father is out sir.' said the butler.

'Thank you Mr Tanning. Leave this to me. Could you find Gwen and um...' he struggled to remember her name, 'her friend, some lunch please.'

'Very good sir. Would like something?'

'What? Oh, yes. Thank you.' he said distractedly.

The butler and housekeeper left, with Gwen and Elsie following on behind.

Marcus knocked smartly on the door.

'Molly? Mother?'

There was some more laughter before the door was unlocked and opened. Marcus looked on in surprise. His mother was stood in the middle of the room with Molly's sword in her hand and bits of apple all over the floor. His wife was stood in the doorway.

'What are you doing?'

'Nothing much.' said Molly with a smile. She looked tired and Marcus frowned.

'One more.' said his mother and Molly moved to an almost empty basket by the fireplace.

She plucked an apple from the basket and threw it into the air. Her eyes flashed blue as she used the power of the bracelet to catch it and make it hover in front of his mother who swung the sword with a surprising deftness to slice it neatly on half.

'Mother! Molly! What are you doing?'

His mother turned to him, a smile on her face and in her eyes and lowered the sword.

'Getting to know each other.'

'Have you been drinking?' enquired Marcus.

'No. Why should we have been?' said Molly.

Marcus shook his head.

'I think that's probably quite enough, don't you? Molly, you look worn out.'

She sat down on the chair.

'Actually I do feel a bit tired.'

His mother handed the sword back to Molly before she turned to her son.

'You have my blessing to marry. Although I do think she's going to be trouble and you're going to have your work cut out with her. She's stubborn and wilful and ordinarily not the sort of girl I'd approve of but she loves you. That's enough for me.'

Marcus was stunned. This was the most open he thought he'd ever heard his mother.

'While you are here you will take separate rooms. Until your wedding that is, which I will begin to arrange shortly. I know you won't want to wait so we will have a small affair with the banquet at the ball. You, Molly and I will meet with Mr Glossop the vicar tomorrow, I will write to him shortly and you can deliver it. Any questions?'

Marcus looked at his wife who had lent back in the chair and closed her eyes with the blade across her lap. No help there.

'What about father?'

'I will discuss it with him later.'

She also turned to look at Molly.

'I think maybe you should help her to bed then you can head to the vicarage.'

Marcus nodded, feeling slightly shell shocked.

'Right. Yes. Of course.' he mumbled.

Carefully he took the sword from her and put it away in its box before helping Molly up. She leant against him sleepily.

'Where're we going?'

'You're going to bed.'

'Alright. I could do with a lie down.'

He guided her up to their room and safely into bed before returning.

'What did she do to you?' he asked as he sat down opposite his mother.

She reached over and patted his knee.

'She told me the truth.' she replied flatly. 'Not what she thought I wanted to hear. She's a live one and I like her. Even though I shouldn't. She has no education, no proper upbringing, no social status, no family to speak of, she's rude, her manners are terrible, her eyes are wrong and she has a tattoo! Of all the women you could have chosen, why her?'

Marcus looked at his mother blankly.

'She's different.' continued his mother. 'She's got a certain something that I like. She will never be a lady, not in the proper sense, but I don't think you care, do you?'

'No. I love her because she's different. She has a strength that...' he tapered off, trying to find the right words.

'She is different. I'll give you that.'

Marcus nodded

'She is. She doesn't fit and I don't think she ever will. She knows it too and doesn't care. Although she was very nervous about meeting you and father.'

'I can understand why. She's not our type at all.'

'Do you really like her?'

'Yes.'

Marcus smiled.

'I'm glad to hear that.'

She patted his knee again.

'It's incredible what she can do with that bracelet of hers.'

'Yes. But you really shouldn't encourage her. It tires her out quickly.'

'She doesn't need any encouraging.'

'No. She never does.'

'Will she be alright?'

'Yes. She'll sleep for the rest of the afternoon I expect. I'll wake her for dinner.'

'Very good.'

Chapter Five

Dark Feelings

'Where are you taking me?'
'Shut up.'
Rebecca stumbled along in the dark with the big man behind her. He'd bound her hands tightly and shoved her along, prodding her in the back with a thick wooden club when she slowed down.

The night was dark and heavy rain earlier in the day had left the ground soft and muddy. She was scared beyond belief.

They crested a small hill and she realised where she was. In front of them was the old abbey. To the left was the chapel, its ruined shell roofless but it still had all four walls and most of the tower. Gathered in a circle outside the chapel were a dozen or so people, all dressed in black and each holding a flaming torch.

With her heart hammering in her chest and her eyes on the circle, she slipped, going down heavily only to be hauled up and pushed along again.

'Please.' she sobbed.
'Shut up.' snapped the big man angrily. 'If I hear one more noise from you, you'll regret it.'

As if to emphasise the point, he cracked the wooden club across the back of her legs. She fell forward with a cry but he unceremoniously dragged her to her feet once more, heedless of the marks his thick fingers were leaving on her arms.

He pushed her into the centre of the circle where she sprawled on the wet grass. One of the figures in the circle carried a large book, rather than a torch. He stepped forward.

'Tonight, we will summon a Hound. One to begin to sow the seeds of fear which will ease the way for Carnothal.'

He looked around the hooded figures.
'Prepare her!'

Molly woke suddenly with a scream on her lips. She didn't know where she was. The room was dark and she could still hear his laughter. The awful sound rang in her ears and she tried to run but the sweat soaked sheets tangled around her and she fell heavily on the floor.

Rising to her hands and knees and screwing her eyes shut, she forced the memories away and tried to compose herself, repeating over and over.

She was safe.

He wasn't here.

She was safe.

When she was sure her legs would hold her up she stood and padded to the window. A large moon hung heavily in the sky and cast shadows across the perfectly manicured and maintained grounds below her.

She rested her head on the cool glass. It was getting worse. She'd have to do something.

Her thoughts turned to the small glass vial she had stored in the top drawer of the dresser. The bitter tasting liquid it contained helped her sleep. Sometimes. She didn't like to use it. It left her with a headache that lasted all day but sometimes there was no option.

As she turned to leave the window, she thought she saw a flash of purple light in the distance. It was there for less than a second and gone before she turned her head back.

Had it been there at all?

She rubbed her eyes and peered into the moonlit night. There was nothing there. It must have been her imagination. She was tired. That was all.

Hardly making a sound, she walked to the dresser and took out the glass vial. It was about the length of her finger and half full and Molly looked at it for a long time before she put it back in the drawer.

She was safe.
He wasn't here.
It had been a bad dream.
Hadn't it?

She went back to bed and reached under her pillow, pulling out a long knife. She slipped it out of the scabbard and watched the moonlight reflect off the blade as she tilted it one way and another.

The pain would show her she wasn't dreaming. It always did.

She let out a slow, long breath, gritted her teeth and stabbed the blade into her forearm, cutting it deeply. Unable to supress a low moan of pain, she let the bloody knife fall on the floor from her shaking hands.

It appeared in the dark. Around it old stones lay in tumbled heaps. The afterglow of its arrival clung to them like a purple moss and beneath it was a torn corpse. It may have once worn a white dress but now it was difficult to tell. The body was ripped and shattered from its coming.

It had forced its way into the world through the offering to act as a guide for the Master. It had been summoned before its brethren. It would find those that called it and show them the way. It turned around, raising a dog like head to sniff the air.

Catching a scent, bloody drool fell from a mouth that held rows of razor sharp teeth while powerful muscles glistened wetly as it twisted its skinless body around and bounded away across the grass.

The next day Marcus, Molly, Victoria and Gwen travelled down to the village in the carriage. They'd arranged an appointment to see Mr Glossop the local vicar to discuss the wedding.

'You look tired.'

Molly looked up at her husband and smiled. It didn't reach her eyes.

'I'm fine. Didn't sleep very well.'

He lent across to take her hand and she couldn't supress a wince as he moved her arm.

'Are you alright?' asked Marcus.

'Yes. Just a knock. It's a bit sore but it'll be fine.'

'Let me see.'

'It's fine…'

Her protests were hardly out of her mouth when he rolled up her sleeve. Under the fine cloth was a deep purpling bruise.

'How did you do that?'

She yanked her arm back and pulled down the sleeve.

'When I was training the other day. I must have bashed it or something.'

Marcus frowned.

'Honestly. I'm fine.'

She squeezed his hand.

'Honestly.'

He held her hand for a second longer before sitting back, not saying anything else but worry on his face. Next to him, his mother was watching them both intently. Molly looked away to stare out of the window.

'What's that?' she asked, changing the subject and pointing to a mass of ruined buildings up on a nearby hill.

Marcus looked out.

'That's the old abbey. Has been a pile of ruins since I can remember.'

'Can we go and have a look?'

'Not now.' said Victoria sternly. 'We have an appointment to keep.'

Molly frowned and folded her arms across her chest like a petulant child.

'How about tomorrow?' said Marcus.

Molly nodded.

'That would be nice.'

The coach rumbled to a stop outside of the prettiest church Molly had ever seen. It was in a perfectly kept churchyard with a pale stone tower and weathered walls. They dismounted, Marcus helping the women out of the carriage.
'Ah, Lady Kane!'
Both Molly and Victoria turned to see a fat man wobbling down the path towards them. He was balding with what little hair he had combed over the top in a vain attempt to cover the spot while his multiple chins moved in a disconcertingly fluid manner.
Molly felt herself immediately disliking him as he mopped his brow with a silk handkerchief, dabbing at the sweat even though it was still chilly in the morning air.
He stopped under the little ivy-covered archway that led into the church yard.
'Lady Kane. It's so delightful to see you and Master Marcus! My it has been a few years since you were here last.'
He turned his attention to Molly and Gwen.
'And who do we have here?'
Molly smiled tightly as Marcus introduced her.
'This is Her Royal Highness Lady Molly Carter and her maid, Gwen.'
The fat vicar grabbed Molly's hand and mashed his lips against her knuckles. It was all she could do not to shudder.
'A pleasure to meet you.'
Molly nodded and tried not to look disgusted, instead turning to her maid.
'I think you'd better wait here Gwen.'
The girl nodded.
'Very good Your Ladyship.' replied the girl.
'Mr Glossop. Did you get my note yesterday?' asked Victoria.

'Yes. I did and I was quite taken aback. This is very unorthodox. It is very short notice to arrange a wedding.'

He lent away from Molly and covered his mouth with one of his hands, as if this would stop his half whisper being heard.

'Is she, you know, with child? Out of wedlock?'

'Certainly not!' said Marcus, taking Molly's hand.

The vicar rallied.

'I have to ask you know. The church takes a very dim view of such things. It is still short notice. There are the banns to be read and other, um, financial, considerations.'

Marcus frowned.

'I'm sure we can come to some mutually beneficial arrangement.' said his mother.

'Of course, of course.' he blustered the vicar. 'Now let me show you and your dear fiancé the church and then we can retire to the vicarage for tea and to discuss matters further.'

Victoria nodded and the vicar turned away, leading them towards the church.

'It was built in fifteen eighty-four by monks after the abbey just up the road at Brillington was burnt down.'

He turned to Molly with a conspiratorial look.

'Some say, it was destroyed by the monks themselves after they found the devil in the catacombs beneath the hill.'

He smiled at the look on Molly's face.

'Don't worry dear. There's no truth to that. There aren't any catacombs up there. Plenty of people have looked.'

He grinned again before turning back to the church and began talking again.

'Now, the tower itself…'

Molly tuned out his prattling as they approached the building and tried to admire it but something was wrong. There was a burning itch on her back. She stopped suddenly and Marcus turned.

'What's the matter?'

She shook her head.
'Something. I don't know.'
'Are you feeling alright?'
She smiled tightly and nodded.
'Yes. Don't fuss.'
Marcus looked at her. When she told him not to fuss, something was usually up.
'Are you sure?'
'Yes. Let's get this over with.' she tried to change the subject but her light tone was forced. 'Hopefully this won't be like the last church we were in.'

Marcus smiled as he remembered Portugal. That church had a secret passage under the floor which led to some caverns housing one of the Stones of Gunjai. It had then been burnt down by the vicious Tong Li after they had escaped him.

'It's nothing like that. I've been coming here all my life.'

'Like what?' asked the vicar as they caught up with them in the doorway.

'We don't have much luck with churches,' said Molly. 'The last one we were in burnt down.'

The vicar looked at them disbelievingly before he decided it was a joke and laughed nervously. Molly smiled tightly, the itch on her back was getting worse.

The vicar led them inside. It was a pretty church. Two rows of heavy oak pews lined the sides with a deep red carpet running up the middle to the altar at the far end behind which stood two lines of stalls for a choir. Beautiful stained glass adorned the windows and a high vaulted ceiling was decorated with a painted fresco. To the left and right of the choir stalls were deep stone sarcophagi with carved figures on the heavy looking lids.

'I'm afraid I have to apologise for the smell.' said Mr Glossop.

'What?' asked Molly, snapping back to reality.

'The smell.' he repeated. 'There's something a bit musty in the air. The local ladies think a rabbit or something has burrowed under the foundations and died.'

Molly sniffed and caught the scent he was talking about. It was a bitter, sour smell and she wrinkled her nose. Mr Glossop smiled and his chins wobbled.

'Don't worry good lady. We'll have it sorted for your big day.'

He moved on and began to explain who the intricately carved statues laid on the top of the sarcophagi represented. Molly ignored him as she had other things to think about.

The further she moved in, the worse the pain in her back got and she clung on to Marcus tightly. He glanced at her, seeing the grim lines in her face before speaking.

'Excuse us. My fiancé would like some air.'

He quickly turned them around and almost dragged her out, as her legs were like lead and didn't want to work. Once outside the pain began to lessen but he took her straight to the carriage and sat her down.

'What's the matter and don't tell me not to fuss.'

Molly took a deep breath which she let out slowly.

'My mark. It hurt. I've not felt anything like it since...'

'Since when.'

'Since I was chained to the altar in the market and thought I was going to die.'

The colour drained from Marcus face.

'He spoke the words and I felt the fear and pain of the previous sacrifices. My mark hurt and burnt. Just like now.'

'He's... He's not here is he?' asked Marcus hesitantly.

Molly shook her head.

'No. It's not him. He was destroyed. It's... I don't know.'

She looked down, hoping she sounded more convincing than she felt.

'Is everything alright?'

Marcus turned to see his mother and the vicar coming

back down the path from the church.

'Yes. It's...'

'I was feeling a little faint. It must be the excitement.'

Victoria narrowed her eyes but the vicar was completely oblivious.

'Happens quite often my dear don't fret. Now who's for some tea? We can discuss the details.'

Marcus looked at Molly who nodded with a tight smile.

Holding on to him tightly, they were led across the churchyard to the small vicarage on the far side. This time however there was no pain from her mark, even when they walked close to the church. Molly thought she should write to Nareema about it.

Chapter Six

A Meeting on the Road

Two hours later Molly and the rest left as quickly as they dared without looking impolite. The vicar waved them off.

'That's settled then. Two weeks on Saturday. I'll see you in church on Sunday of course.'

They made polite noises and hurried back to the carriage. The sun was high and Molly couldn't help but feel relieved about being in the open air.

The vicarage was small and stuffy, full of papers and books and clutter that seemed to accentuate the size and well, obesity, of the vicar.

He had an aging housekeeper who had bumbled around, serving tea and cake and more tea and it had all Molly could do to keep her revulsion in check. There was something about the man she didn't like. Something slimy. She shuddered as she sat down.

They were silent for a few minutes as the coach rumbled home. Eventually Victoria spoke.

'So are you going to tell me what happened in the church? I don't believe for one second that it was nerves or excitement.'

Molly sighed.

'My mark hurt.'

'Mark?'

'My tattoo. Something made it hurt.'

'What?'

'I don't know. It passed and I'm fine now.'

Neither Marcus or his mother looked convinced by the explanation but it was the best Molly could do. She didn't know why it had hurt either.

Molly shuddered again.

'Actually, can you stop the coach please?'

'Why?'

'I want to stretch my legs. I'll walk from here.'

'Why on earth...'

'Please. We've been cooped up in the vicarage all morning and I would like some fresh air.'

Victoria frowned but signalled the driver to stop. Molly clambered out.

'I'll come with you.' said Marcus.

'No. It's fine. You go on ahead. I can manage.'

He went to say something else but she shut the carriage door. He pulled down the window.

'Are you sure?'

'Yes. Don't fuss. I'm sure I can manage to walk a couple of miles.'

'Then at least take Gwen with you.'

'I can manage.'

'It's alright Your Ladyship. I don't mind a walk.'

Gwen had gotten out of the opposite side and come around the back. Molly looked at Marcus and sighed.

'Alright. Happy?'

'No. But you're going to do it anyway.'

She smiled and stretched up to give him a kiss before slipping on her glasses.

'Of course I am. We'll be back in time for lunch. Go on.'

Before he could say anything else, the carriage began to roll away.

'Lunch is at two!' Marcus called out. 'Don't be late.'

'I won't.' she said, waving goodbye.

They both watched the carriage disappear into the distance before they started walking. Molly picked up a stick and began idly swatting at the verge.

'Why did you want to be a maid?' Molly asked.

Gwen looked at her.

'Don't know. It's a good job. You and the master are kind. There's nothing much else I can do.'

'Why not? And please don't call him 'master'.'

'But he's the head of the house. It's the done thing. I know my place.'

Molly sighed.

'Technically, it's my house.'

'Oh.'

They walked in silence for a moment.

'What do you want to do in the future?' asked Molly. 'You can't be a maid all your life.'

Gwen considered this.

'I want to get married. Have a family. Be happy. I know we won't have much but we'll have enough. It'll be perfect.'

Molly smiled.

'That sounds nice.'

'What about you Your Ladyship?' asked Gwen before adding hurriedly, 'Not that I'm prying or anything.'

'I don't know. Get married. Again. Then I suppose I'd better learn how to be a lady although I don't know if I want to.'

'You aren't like any lady I've ever heard of.'

'You're not the first person to tell me that.'

They walked along in listening to the birds in the trees and the swish of the grass in the fields.

'Are you excited? About getting married I mean?' asked Gwen.'

'Not really. Marcus and I are already married. This is just a show for his parents and the world. I mean, I don't have a dress, bridesmaids or anyone to give me away. Not that I need giving away.'

'Oh.'

'No one I know other than Marcus will be there. I think it's going to be a lonely day.'

'That's sad. It should be the happiest day of your life.'

'It was the first time.' said Molly sadly, remembering the day aboard the Endurance. She had been among friends. People who had cared what she thought, not... She shook the thoughts away and changed the subject.

'I hope you didn't mind me asking Elsie to drop in on you the other day.'

'Oh no. Thank you, Your Ladyship. It was nice to have a bit of company.'

'That's good. I know what it's like to be alone and away from home.'

'Elsie is nice. Although you should hear the stories she tells. She's been working up at the house for a year or so. They're very strict up there. Mr Tanning once beat her and locked her in the cellar for a day and a night when she broke some of the best china.'

Molly's eyes narrowed and she frowned.

'Did he?'

'She said so. She said that I've got it easy working for you.'

'And have you?'

Gwen backtracked hurriedly.

'You're nice and kind Your Ladyship. You and the master...'

Molly stopped suddenly in the road.

'Right.' she snapped. 'I've had enough. My name is Molly and his is Marcus. He is not the 'master'. Not of you and certainly not of me. I am not a lady. Until last year I had nothing. These titles and names make me uncomfortable and I don't like them.'

Gwen looked at her, horrified.

'But Your Ladyship...'

'Stop. Say that once more and I'll...'

She sighed. I'll what? Beat her? Then that would make me like them.

'Just please don't. I have a name. If it troubles you that much then call me Molly in private. Any other times to you can call me whatever you like.'

Gwen stood still open-mouthed. Molly looked at her hard before she tutted angrily and stalked off up the road. Gwen hurried after her.

'I'm sorry your Ladys... Um, Molly. It doesn't seem right, that's all. You're a lady despite what you think. You've got money and a house and servants and...'

'And they're all things I don't need.' snapped Molly.

She stormed up the road for a few more feet before sitting down heavily on the verge. Gwen sat next to her.

'I'm sorry.' said Molly. 'I'm a bit of a mess. My head is all over the place. This trip isn't going as I hoped it might. I so badly want to cry right now but I can't.'

The girl reached out and very tentatively put her hand on her arm.

'It doesn't hurt to have a cry every now and then. Even for a lady.'

Molly smiled sadly and squeezed Gwen's hand.

'I can't. The power that took my eyes even took my tears. I can't. I haven't been able to cry since India and God knows I've wanted to.'

Gwen didn't know what to say. Molly let out a slow breath and composed herself.

'I'm sorry. I...'

She tailed off as she thought she saw movement in the trees opposite. The woodland on the other side of the road was thick and choked with briars and brambles.

'What?' asked Gwen.

Molly waved her to silence and stood up. Around them the birds had gone quiet. A slow breeze carried a smell with it. A sickly, rancid tang, like the smell in the church but much more pronounced. Molly walked slowly across the road, not taking her eyes off the trees.

'Molly!'

She turned as Gwen shouted to see a horse and rider hammering down the road towards her. It was almost on top of her when she was shoved from behind and fell headfirst into a muddy puddle at the side of the road. She splashed around in time to see the Gwen take a glancing blow from the animal and spin to the ground.

'Hey, watch where you're bloody going!' she shouted after the rider as she picked herself up and rushed over to Gwen.

The girl was sat in the road looking dazed with a small cut on her forehead.

'Are you alright?'

The girl nodded and Molly helped her up as the man on the horse came back.

'Why don't you bloody well watch where you're going!' demanded Molly.

The man on the horse looked at her. He was in his mid-twenties and handsome, with a strong face and clear blue eyes. His cream trousers and blue velvet jacket were expensive. He looked at Molly, covered in mud and mucky water.

'How dare you speak to me like that. Don't you have any respect for your betters, you stupid girl?' he snapped angrily.

'What?'

'What're you doing messing about in the road anyway? Don't you have work to be doing?'

Molly glared at him.

'I don't have time to stand here talking with the likes of you. I have business to attend.'

He didn't even attempt to hide the disgust in his voice. Without another word and leaving Molly speechless, he wheeled his horse around and rode off. Molly picked up her stick and threw it after him with a curse.

'Bastard!'

She turned back to Gwen. The girl was ashen faced.

'Are you sure you're alright?'

'I think so. Just a bit shook up. That's all.'

She looked at Molly oddly.

'What?'

'I didn't know ladies knew language like that.'

Molly smiled.

'You'd be surprised at the language I know.'
She looked around.
'I think if we cut across those fields then we'll get home quicker. You need to clean that cut.'
Gwen nodded and they headed into the fields without a backwards glance at the trees.

Marcus was in the drawing room with his mother when there was a polite cough from the butler.
'Excuse me sir, ma'am, Mr Crawford is here to see you.'
'Who? Richard? Show him in!' said Marcus.
The butler nodded and left, returning a moment later with Richard Crawford. He was a little older than Marcus, dressed in cream trousers and a blue velvet coat.
'Marcus!'
The men embraced.
'It's good to see you again.'
Richard turned and acknowledged the seated woman.
'Aunt Victoria. My mother and sisters send their warmest congratulations and will be delighted to attend the wedding. They will be coming up in a few days.'
'Thank you Richard. Although…'
Richard had stopped listening and turned to Marcus, bombarding him with questions
'What happened to your hand? So where is the filly that's captured your heart? Is it that sweet little Jane? If not, do I know her? Have we met?'
'I think that's a possibility.'
Everyone turned to see Molly standing in the doorway with Gwen hovering behind.
Marcus was straight to her side.
'What happened? You're a mess.'
She shrugged.
'Some idiot on a horse ran us off the road.'
'What? Who?'
She smiled and took off her glasses, fixing an open-

mouthed Richard with a penetrating glare.

'We have a visitor, Molly, please let me introduce you to my cousin. Richard Crawford.'

Marcus carefully guided Molly into the room.

'Richard, this is my fiancé. Her Royal Highness, Lady Molly Carter, sister of Princess Nareema Kareen Vashti, daughter of the Maharajah of Sunjian.'

Molly knew Marcus was showing her off and didn't even mind him using all of her titles just this once. It was worth it to see the smug look and colour drain from the man's face.

'Highness...' mumbled Richard weakly.

'Nice to meet you.' she said, 'Now, if you will please excuse me, I need to change. Come Gwen.'

She turned and swept out of the room with as much royal dignity as she could muster, with Gwen following on behind. Marcus could see that she was trying not to laugh and he frowned.

'Well, she's um... Well... You can meet her properly later.'

By the time they'd gotten to the top of the stairs, they were both struggling to keep the laughter in. The practically ran to Molly's room and as soon as the door was shut, it burst out, leaving them breathless.

'Did you see his face? I thought he was going to be sick!' Gwen wiped her eyes.

'I'll run you a bath Your Ladys...' she saw the look Molly gave her. '... Um. I'll run you a bath.'

'It'll wait. Let's have a look at that cut first.'

'It's nothing.'

'Do as you're told. Sit on the bed.'

Gwen thought about arguing but decided it wasn't worth it and did as instructed. Molly took a towel and brought the wash basin over before carefully cleaning the wound.

'It's not deep.' she turned away and rummaged through a bag, coming back with a small clay pot. Taking the lid off, she scooped a small amount of a foul smelling brown ointment onto her finger. Gwen wrinkled her nose at the pungent aroma.

'Yes. I know it stinks but it will help the cut get better faster. Trust me.' said Molly.

'Alright.'

'Now this is going to sting.'

Molly applied the salve to the wound and Gwen flinched.

'Ow!'

She sat back, wiping her hands on the towel before handing the pot to the girl.

'All done. Keep it clean and use the ointment again tonight and then for a couple of days.'

'Thank you Your... Um, Molly.'

The girl looked down embarrassedly.

'It don't feel right.'

'Well you'd better get use to it. That's what I want so that's how it's going to be.'

There was an awkward silence before Molly smiled.

'Thank you.'

'For what?'

'For pushing me out of the way.'

Gwen smiled back but was unable to meet Mollys white stare.

'It wasn't nothin'.'

'It was.'

Molly went to the dresser and came back with a small wooden box about eight inches to a side and two deep. It was made of a dark hardwood, inlaid with pearl coloured lines.

'Here. I want you to have this.'

'I can't...'

'Take it. I'm not taking no for an answer.'

She pushed the box into Gwen's hands who nervously looked up at Molly and then down at the box. Carefully she opened it.

Inside on a bed of deep blue velvet was a pendant and chain made of finely worked silver surrounding a pale green gemstone. Alongside sat a pair of matching earrings. Gwen looked up at Molly in surprise.

'I can't take this Your Ladyship!'

'Why not?'

'It's not right. I'm only your maid, this is...'

'You probably saved my life and I thank you for that. I also would like it if you would be my bridesmaid.'

'What?'

'I don't have any friends or family here. I need a bridesmaid and I can't think of anyone else I'd like or trust. So, you can consider the jewels a gift. I'll make sure you have a dress that matches. What do you say?'

'I'd, um... I'd love to.'

'Good.'

Molly stood up as there was a knock at the door. Gwen dashed over to open it.

'I'll run you a bath Your Ladyship.' she said as Marcus came in.

'Thank you.'

Gwen left and Marcus closed the door.

'Are you allowed to be without a chaperone in a ladies chamber?' asked Molly playfully.

He smiled back and came across to her.

'I thought you weren't a lady.'

Molly grinned and wrapped her arms around his neck, pulling him close.

'I'm not.'

Marcus kissed her lightly and the gently pushed her away.

'You certainly don't smell like one. What have you been rolling in?'

She looked down at herself.

'I don't know. Gwen shoved me out of the way and I fell over. Your cousin nearly ran me down.'

'He swears he didn't see you until the last minute.'

'He would.' she replied sarcastically.
'Molly. Please.'
'Gwen was hurt.'
'But she's alright?'
'Yes, but...'
'Then there's no harm done then.' interrupted Marcus.
'That's not the point.' said Molly sharply.
He took her hand.
'I know. I'm sorry. Please? Richard is one of my oldest friends. We grew up together. He's a good man once you get to know him.'
She sighed.
'Alright. I'll try. But my first impression is that he's a complete tit.'
Marcus laughed out loud.
'Thank you.'
'I've asked Gwen to be my bridesmaid.'
Marcus frowned, his laughter falling away quickly.
'But she's...'
Molly interrupted him angrily.
'Don't you dare say "she's just a servant".'
'But she is! And besides, mother was going to suggest that Richards sisters did that for you. They're very nice.'
'No.'
'Molly...'
'No Marcus. I'm the one getting married. I don't know who they are and they probably won't like me. I want Gwen. I trust her.'
'Now you're just being silly.'
'Silly? Marcus, Gwen just saved me from getting run down by a horse! She is going to be my bridesmaid and that's the end of it.'
'Mother won't be pleased.'
'I don't care. I'll tell her myself.'
She stormed towards the door and Marcus grabbed her wrist and pulled her back.

'Stop. Please.'
She glared at him angrily until he let go.
'Please.'
She sighed once more and sat on the bed.
'I don't see why we need to get married again. We had a perfect wedding on the Endurance. I had a dress and everything and we surrounded by friends. I haven't even got anyone to give me away.'
Marcus sat next to her.
'We'll work something out.'
'I suppose.'
They were silent for a second.
'What happened to my wedding dress anyway?' asked Molly. 'I know I left it aboard the ship when I, well, when I left but I haven't seen it since.'
Marcus looked down guiltily.
'Ah, um... I know what happened to it.'
She looked at him.
'I sort of tore it up.'
'Tore it up? Why? It was my wedding dress!'
'Well I took it when we got back to England and then met Rami. She was hurt and I had to find a dressing after I'd stitched her shoulder up. It was the longest, cleanest thing I had to hand.'
'You tore it up to make bandages?' her tone suggested that she could hardly believe what she was saying.
'Yes.' Marcus looked down again. 'Sorry.'
They went silent again.
'It was probably what I would have done anyway.' she said with a resigned sigh. 'I didn't think I'd be needing it again.'
'No.'
'So now I have no dress either.'
'Sorry. Mother is arranging for a dressmaker to come next week. We can get you something better.'
'It won't be better!' said Molly angrily. 'That one was

perfect. It was brought with care and friendship and if anyone is going to fit me for a dress, then it's going to be Mrs Hopkins.'

'Molly...'

'No Marcus. Gwen and I are going back to London tomorrow. Mrs Hopkins will fit us for our dresses and that will be that.'

'Molly!' said Marcus sternly. 'No. Please. We're here to relax and enjoy ourselves. We've had nothing but adventure since... Well pretty much since we met. The last year has been hard on both of us. Just relax. Let mother handle it. She likes this sort of thing.'

'But then it won't be my wedding.' she protested.

'*Our* wedding.' he corrected before sighing heavily. 'Both you and I know we don't need this. Captain Brody married us and I truly believe that it is enough. Mother has other ideas and this is for the look of the thing. Just let her have it. We'll turn up, smile and have an enjoyable day. Please.'

Molly looked at her hands in silence, picking some of the dried mud from her fingers.

'Alright.' she said eventually. 'But Gwen is still going to be my bridesmaid. And I don't want a massive dress. Just something simple.'

'Then that's what you shall have.'

She smiled at him sadly.

'I'm sorry. I'm just having a bit of trouble adjusting.'

'I know. But you'll get there. We'll get there.'

He squeezed her hand.

'Now go and clean up and we can have lunch.'

Half an hour later Molly came downstairs to a delightful smell wafting from the dining room and her stomach rumbled. Marcus and Richard were waiting for her in the hall. Richard bowed low as she reached the bottom.

'Your Highness. I'm dreadfully sorry about this morning. I didn't see you until the last...'

'Mr Crawford.' said Molly, interrupting him. 'I am not a filly or any other form of animal and if you're rude to me or my maid again, I'll knock you on your back. Is that clear?'

Richard gave Marcus a sideways glance with an amused half smile. Molly frowned.

'Don't mock me Mr Crawford.' she said icily.

He nodded, the smile falling away, but only just.

'I'm sorry Your Highness, please allow me to escort you to lunch.'

He offered her his arm, and with a look at Marcus, who shrugged, Molly took it and allowed him to lead her into the dining room.

After the meal, Molly and Victoria had retired to the library to discuss the wedding whilst he and Richard had moved to the drawing room. Marcus father had grumpily gone elsewhere. He didn't like Molly and made that perfectly clear which had made the meal uncomfortably tense. Marcus walked to the sideboard.

'Drink?'

'Yes please.' replied Richard, taking a long cigar from his jacket pocket and lighting it from a spill from the fire.

Marcus poured them both a brandy and sat in a chair near the fireplace. Richard sat opposite him and puffed his cigar for a moment.

'Well, she's a feisty one and that's a fact.'

Marcus swirled his drink around the glass.

'Please don't talk about her like that.'

Richard grinned.

'Sorry old chap but you've got to admit, she's going to be a handful. Where did you two meet?'

'Lady Samantha's ball last year.'

'Oh I heard about that one. Sounded quite the party. Some foreign woman went mad and killed two dozen people.'

'It wasn't two dozen people. She did kill four but they

were trying to kill her. I was there, remember.'

'Was she mad?'

'Well,' said Marcus after some consideration, 'She was very, very angry but as sane as you or I. Of that I can assure you.'

'Well you can't trust these foreign types.' said Richard after a moment, blowing out a long stream of smoke.

'I trust her. And I would be careful if I were you. The "foreign woman" is Molly's adopted sister. If she hears you saying anything like that about her she really will knock you down.'

'Oh come on,' said Richard. 'She's just a girl and a slip of a one at that. I'm not afraid of her.'

'I'm not saying you should be afraid, I'm just saying that I'd be more cautious.'

'She's already got you wrapped around her finger then?' Marcus smiled.

'I supposed she has.'

'What happened to her eyes? They're very... Very strange.'

'She hurt them while we were in India.'

'How? Is that where you lost your hand?'

Marcus sipped his brandy. How was he going to explain this? He sighed.

'She contracted a rare fever and barely survived. It hurt her eyes and it was weeks before she could see again. As for my hand? Well, it was a boating accident.'

Richard eyed him suspiciously but with a smile on his lips. Eventually he spoke.

'Well I know that's a load of rubbish but if you don't want to tell me then that's fine. I'll ask your betrothed, I bet she'll tell me.'

'Richard!'

His friend grinned widely blowing a smoke ring which sailed lazily upwards.

'Calm down, I won't ask her. But of course, if it happens

to come up in conversation...'
  Marcus smiled back.
  'You sir, are incorrigible.'
  'And that is why we're still friends.'

Chapter Seven

Ancient History
1584 AD

'What in God's name is going on?' shouted the abbot as he ran out to the courtyard and looked around. The cloisters were ablaze as was the refectory. Monks were scurrying backwards and forwards from the well in a vain attempt to control the blazes. The abbot grabbed a monk as he ran past.
'What's going on?'
'I don't know. We're on fire!'
'I can see that Sebastian. How did it start? When? Get the fire in the refectory under control.'
The monk nodded and hurried off to begin organising the rest of the abbey.
Subconsciously, the abbot had taken his cross out from underneath his robe and was clutching it tightly. He looked at the fire once more before striding purposefully towards the chapel.

The last brick fell away, revealing the solid oak door behind it. The dry atmosphere down here had preserved it and the age blackened wood was as solid now as it had been all those years ago.
Carefully, the boy knocked the wooded bar from its position and heaved the door open. The room beyond was lit by a strange purple glow which seemed to emanate from a stone table in the centre of the room. Next to the table was a body, now no more than a dried-out husk. He licked his lips nervously and entered.
As he moved, the glow from the table got brighter and he fancied there was a voice, just on the edge of hearing. A voice which promised him power and glory. The same

voice that had been haunting his dreams in the three years he had been a novice at the abbey.

Approaching the stone table, he saw a thick book with the strange light pouring out of the pages.

'Open me. Release me.'

He jumped at the sudden voice and looked around. Apart from the corpse, he was alone.

'Release me.'

On the thick leather cover was a cross, carefully drawn in still wet blood, while across the top and bottom was more blood in two wavy lines that crossed over each other, giving the effect of a chain link.

'Release me!'

The voice was a roaring noise in his head and he almost stumbled, such was the violence and anger it contained. With a shaky hand, he began to rub off the blood from the cover.

'Stop Peter. You don't know what you're doing!'

The boy looked up to see the abbot standing in the doorway. The purple light gave his features a sickly pallor and he took a step back.

The abbot moved towards the boy, every step sending shocks of pain through his body. He'd gone to the chapel to make sure that the fire hadn't spread and found the entrance to the catacombs wide open.

Fearing the worst, he'd hurried down and his fears had been confirmed. Now the wards set over three hundred years ago were weakening. He could feel the malevolent presence of Carnothal in every fibre of his being as he sought to escape.

He should have kept a closer eye on the boy. There had been warnings from his fellow monks but he'd brushed them aside. He should have been more vigilant. Now the abbey was paying the price.

'Did you start the fires?'

Peter nodded dumbly. Inside his head, the voice was screaming at him and it was all he could do not to run away.

'Why?' asked the abbot, taking another painful step closer. The book could sense he was here and was trying to stop it being released.

'The voice. The voice said I could rule the world.'

'And do you believe that?'

Again, the boy nodded.

'It's all lies. The book and the voice are the same thing. They are a demon, Peter. A demon from the darkest pits of Hell. We have kept this thing imprisoned here for three centuries. It cannot be allowed to escape.'

'You're lying.' shouted the boy.

'No. Peter. You have to listen…'

A wave of noise hammered around the room, sending both of them to their knees. The abbot felt blood running from his nose and ears as he tried to get up, his head ringing. Across the room, Peter used the altar and dragged himself up.

'No. Don't…'

With a sweep of his hands, Peter wiped the rest of the blood from the cover. With a violent snap, the book flew open, purple light flooding the room. It was so bright that the boy was blinded in an instant. He stumbled backwards, crying out as he hit the wall.

The abbot took his cross from his robes and hauled himself to his feet.

'You will not escape demon.' he shouted. 'The Knights Templar entrusted us to contain you and with our faith and purity we have done so. We will do so again!'

He forced himself to walk forwards, each step pure agony, until he reached the stone table.

'Peter. Help me.'

The boy was cowering against the wall, a horrible white goo leaking from where his eyes use to be.

'Peter!'

The boy dragged himself over on his hands and knees and reached the stone table at the same time as the abbot. The old man helped him up and together they forced the book shut. With shaky hands, the abbot snapped the cross from the chain around his neck.

'With the blood of the faithful and power of God, we bind you.'

He drove the end of the crucifix into his hand and drew a cross in the centre with his own blood before he began to trace a chain like pattern on the cover.

There was an inhuman roar and from the edges of the book flashed purple fire. It lashed out in all directions at once, catching both the abbot and the boy and incinerating them instantly. The inferno rolled out across the room and down the corridors, searing everything in its path until it exploded out of the entrance in the chapel.

Sebastian ran back to the abbots' chambers but the old man wasn't anywhere to be found. He hurried back outside and as he watched, purple tinged fire erupted from the chapel, sending shards of the ornate stained-glass windows in all directions and blowing the roof off in a crash of burning timbers. A hurrying group was caught in the edge of the explosion and were cut down by the razor-sharp storm of glass.

The abbey was lost. The refectory, cloisters and now the dormitories were raging beyond their ability to control while ahead of him a fierce fire burnt in the chapel. He shook his head. If the abbot wasn't about then there was nothing for it. He'd have to take charge and evacuate.

Quickly he began shouting orders at the remaining monks and gathering the injured.

Such was the ferocity of the fire, it was days later before the abbey was cool enough to go near. They had lost more than half of their number, including the abbot and brother Sebastian thought and prayed on this as he walked around the ruins of the abbey. Smoke and heat still hung heavy in the air and fires still smouldered. Nearly the entire abbey had been devastated but as soon as he could, Sebastian had gone in to the chapel and was horrified to discover that the entrance to the catacombs was wide open.

Upon seeing this, he knew deep down what had happened and where the abbot had gone. The old man had left orders about what should happen if it came to the worst.

Sebastian had muttered a quick prayer before sealing the entrance once more and filling in the hole that held the lock.

If the wards had been broken and Carnothal was loose, then he would rot for eternity, sealed beneath the ground.

Chapter Eight

Brillington Abbey

The sun was high as Marcus and Molly wandered down the road. Gwen had been persuaded to stay at the house, mostly by Molly agreeing to let Gwen do her job and look after her when they got back. She shook her head. Honestly. She wasn't an invalid.

'I don't see why we couldn't have brought the carriage.' said Marcus, mopping his brow.

'I wanted to walk in the sunshine.'

'But it's quite hot.'

Molly looked him up and down. She'd chosen to wear an Indian style dress of fine silk, given to her by Nareema. Marcus on the other hand...

'If you're warm, take your jacket off and loosen your collar!'

He sighed dramatically.

'Now you sound like my mother.'

'And do you take as much notice of her as you do of me?' asked Molly with a laugh.

Marcus pulled a face and she stuck her tongue out at him.

They had almost reached the worn looking path that led up to the abbey when they heard a horse coming down the road. Molly's light mood evaporated when it turned out to be Richard. He reigned in the animal in as he reached them.

'Hope you don't mind me joining you.' he asked as he dismounted. 'Haven't been up to the old abbey for years. Marcus and I used to go up there all the time when we were lads.'

'Well...' began Molly but Marcus spoke quickly, interrupting her.

'Of course we don't mind. Come on.'

Richard handed the reigns of his horse to Marcus and offered his arm to Molly.

'Your Ladyship.'

Molly frowned but took his offered arm and together they all headed up to the ruins.

'Local rumour has it that this place was once used for devil worship.' said Richard. 'They used to sacrifice innocent girls to the dark powers.'

'Really? And is that supposed to frighten me?' asked Molly.

'No. Of course not.' he replied, catching the look on her face. 'I was only saying…'

'Mr Crawford, I'll have you know that I've seen and done things that you wouldn't believe. A few tall stories will have to go a lot further than that to scare me.'

Behind them, Marcus laughed.

'You didn't laugh at that when you were ten.' called Richard over his shoulder. 'You nearly wet yourself when we were up here after dark.'

'I did not!'

Richard winked at Molly.

'He did.'

She shook her head but couldn't suppress a smile.

'We use to come up here looking for the catacombs and the treasure.'

'Treasure?'

'Uncle James has an old book that tells of miles of tunnels under the abbey where the monks stored their gold. We never found it of course.' he shrugged. 'But you know. Boys and their adventures… Marcus tells me that you were in India?'

'Yes.'

'Is that where you, you know, hurt your eyes?'

'I think that's quite enough Richard. Thank you very much.' said Marcus quickly.

His friend grinned slyly but said nothing else. They reached the outskirts of the ruins and Molly caught a scent in the air. Like spoiled meat.

'Can you smell that?' she asked.

Richard pulled a face and sniffed.

'Smell what?'

Molly glanced at her husband and then pulled away from Richard to head quickly towards the ruins.

'Molly?'

She stopped as she reached the first fallen wall. To the left was a large building that had most of a tower and its walls intact while around that were some other smaller ruins. Around the whole thing was an enclosing wall, tumbled down in places with grass and moss growing freely. A couple of large trees were dotted throughout, their branches peeking above the walls.

Molly stepped into the abbey proper, looking around cautiously. The smell was stronger here. Marcus joined her.

'What is it?'

'Something's wrong.'

'What?'

She shook her head and walked towards the building with the tower. Remnants of flagstones were visible beneath the grass, cracked with age.

'Marcus. What's going on?' called Richard from behind them.

Neither of them answered.

As they reached the tower, Marcus caught the smell too. It was one he'd become familiar with in his time in the army. The stench of death.

'Wait here.' he told his wife firmly.

She looked like she was going to protest for a second but in the end, she just nodded.

Taking a breath, Marcus went to the doorway, returning a second later, his face pale.

'Richard. Go and get some help from the village.'
The man looked confused.
'Now damn it!'
Richard mounted his horse and quickly rode away.
'Marcus? What is it?'
He didn't answer straight away so she walked to the doorway herself. As soon as she saw what lay on the flagstones she ran away from the building to be sick.

An hour later a small crowd had gathered. Molly had regained her composure a little and was stood slightly away from the building with the tower. The old chapel, as she was told later.

Mr Glossop the vicar had waddled up the hill, puffing madly, along with Richard and the village blacksmith and his son. The boy must've been no more than ten and Molly reckoned he'd be having nightmares about what he saw for years.

On the stone floor of the chapel was a body. It had once been a young girl of no more than thirteen or fourteen. She'd been torn to pieces. Her broken bones and entrails were scattered all around the old building, painting the stone with dark stains and it looked like she'd been dead for a couple of days.

The blacksmith identified her as Rebecca Miller, daughter of a farmer from up the vale a little way. She'd not come home a couple of days ago and the family had been worried sick. He quickly despatched his boy to go fetch them.

Marcus, Richard and the blacksmith, a huge and powerfully built man by the name of Sampson, stood around what was left of her body. Mr Glossop was to be heard heaving theatrically behind a nearby wall.

'What happened to her?' asked Richard.
'Wild dog maybe?' replied Sampson.
Marcus surveyed the carnage.
'Maybe…'

There were running feet and Sampson turned as the girls' father came hammering up the hill with his wife in tow.

Molly intercepted the woman and steered her away from the chapel. She didn't need to see her daughter like that. Sampson stood next to the farmer as he took in the horror, holding on to him so he didn't collapse as his legs gave way beneath him.

Richard and Marcus left quietly. Molly nodded as they passed, tightly holding the sobbing woman to her. The men went and sat a little way away.

'My God.' said Richard after a few minutes.

'Yes.'

They lapsed into silence again. Molly came over and sat down on the grass. Behind her, the farmer was comforting his wife.

'Did you see it?' asked Molly.

'See what? replied Richard.

'The floor.'

His brow furrowed.

'What?'

'I saw it. I scrubbed most of it away before the blacksmith got here.' answered Marcus.

Molly nodded.

'What?' asked Richard again.

'There were marks on the floor. Sand sprinkled in a pattern. Two circles, one inside the other with symbols between the two.' said Molly. 'Marcus, the night before last, I thought I saw a purple flash. I wasn't sure at the time but I am now. It might be related.'

'Purple flash?'

'My room faces this way, doesn't it?'

Marcus nodded.

'Something *is* going on. I don't like it. Maybe that's why my mark hurt yesterday.'

'Mark?' asked Richard. 'What are you talking about?'

'Don't worry about it.' replied Marcus.

Richard looked at them and bemused.

'Is this some secret code? What do you two think happened? It's probably like the blacksmith said. It was a wild dog or something. She just got lost and…'

'There's a girl dead up there.' snapped Molly, pointing towards the chapel.

'And what can I do about it. What did happen then? Devil worshipers? Magic?' he huffed 'I don't think for one second that…'

Molly stood up angrily.

'Mr Crawford. You can think whatever you like. Just don't do it around me.'

She stormed away and down the hill towards the road.

Richard looked at Marcus.

'What did I say?'

Marcus looked at him with a sigh.

'Just don't. Please. If she trusts you enough to tell you what she's been through in her life and what happened in India then you'll understand.'

'Why wouldn't she trust me?'

'Just leave it.'

Marcus stood and followed Molly, leaving Richard sat on the hill.

Chapter Nine

Plans

The room was heavily in shadow and thick with incense. Arranged in a circle were the twelve cloaked figures and in the centre stood the scarred man, his hood thrown back. He turned to look at the others with a disturbing smile.

'Brethren, we are close.'

'Did it work?' asked one of the circle.

'I believe so.'

'What's that supposed to mean?'

This was from the largest in the circle. He stood head and shoulders above the others and was almost as wide. The scarred man rounded on him.

'It means what I said.'

'How do we know it was one of them hound things? I saw the body. I...'

'You need to have faith.'

'Faith? We're risking everything and ...'

The scarred man stepped close and struck the figure in the chest with his open palm. Instantly the big man went down. From the depths of the hood came strangled noises as he struggled to breathe.

'I have enough faith for us all brother. Trust in me and we will prevail. But if your trust were to falter...'

Slowly he rolled his hand into a fist, squeezing it tightly and on the floor the man began to clutch at his chest with one hand while the other clawed the dirty floor. He watched him writhe in pain for a second before opening his hand and turning to address the others.

'We have a just over a week until the equinox of the lines. Our ritual yesterday will have brought us help and will begin to sow the seeds of fear around us. That fear will begin to weaken the barriers between the worlds. Be vigilant. We are too close to fail.'

'How many more must we bring?'

This question was nervous as they all glanced at the big man on the floor. He was sprawled awkwardly, making pathetic noises. The air around him had the acrid stink of urine.

'The book demands six more. Two of those will be the final sacrifices. Their pure blood will allow Carnothal into this world.'

'Why the others then? Can't we just…'

The speaker went silent as the scarred man rounded on him.

'The others are for the book.' he snapped. 'Without them, we will not be able to bind him to our wills. If he, or his heralds were to be loose then our plans would have been for naught. He would destroy us.' he roared, before smiling and lowering his voice to something resembling friendly. 'That is why we need the others. Is that clear?'

The hooded figures nodded.

'Good. Now go.

The next few days were a bit of a blur. Molly had been fitted for a dress, which despite her misgivings, was one of the most beautiful things she had ever worn. It was pale cream silk covered with shimmering pearls and lace.

Likewise, Gwen also had a fitting. Her dress, would also be cream, offset by wide pale green ribbons around her waist.

Victoria hadn't been happy about it but Molly had put her foot down. In the end, they'd comprised. Gwen would be her maid of honour whilst Marcus cousins, Tilly and Hannah would be bridesmaids, on the strict understanding that they do as Gwen asked. It also transpired that Victoria had already arranged for the cousins to have similar dresses to Gwen, much to Molly's annoyance. She hadn't even been asked!

Marcus and Richard had gone to London to be fitted for suits as Richard was obviously going to be Marcus' best man. Molly had decided that whatever happened whilst they were in London, she didn't want to know about. It wasn't that she didn't trust Marcus. She did with all her heart, it was that she didn't trust Richard.

There was something about him that she couldn't get on with. He was polite and nice enough but there was always a sense of superiority about him. He knew he had money and expected lower classes to do exactly as he wished.

Unfortunately, the lower classes included women as well as the servants. It was something that didn't sit well, but he was Marcus' cousin and close friend so she'd have to put up with it. At least until they were married and went back to London.

Molly spent some of her time in the library, reading up on the abbey. The only book she could find was a battered old volume bound in red leather by a man called "Augustus Black" that had been tucked on a high shelf.

She'd leafed through it slowly, doing her best to understand the contents.

The book was written in an odd style. Like a diary rather than an historical account, but the writer kept going off on a tangent as if he were distracted or struck with fever. He'd in turn be lucid and describe the daily goings on at the abbey before raving like a madman about a book they'd found in the unholy catacombs beneath the abbey and the "Hounds", "Heralds" and someone called "Carnothal".

Molly couldn't place it, but that name nagged at her. As if she'd heard it before, but didn't know where from and that left her with an unsettled feeling inside.

The last pages described a fire which seems to have started in the chapel. What caused it, the author didn't know but the abbey was destroyed and then abandoned.

Many monks perished in the fire and it was said to have burned out of control for three days. Those that survived the blaze moved to the village and worked themselves to death building the church. None of them spoke a word after the fire, taking a vow of silence, as if to talk about what had happened would bring ruination onto them.

As the monks died, the bodies disappeared. None were buried in the graveyard. It was as if they just vanished into thin air. Secrets, catacombs, monsters. All things that would fire a young boy's imagination she supposed. That was probably why Marcus and Richard has liked it.

Marcus' mother and father had wandered into the library on the second afternoon. James had plucked the book up from the table while Molly was trying to read, ignoring the angry look that Molly flashed at him. He flicked through the pages and gave a huff of disparagement.

'Fiction. The lot of it. All stuff and nonsense. Why're you reading such things? Filling your head with fanciful stories. Shouldn't you be out picking flowers or something? I'd say doing things that a lady ought to be doing but…'

He left the rest of the words hanging, unspoken, in the air and stalked away. Molly flushed red with a mixture of embarrassment, shame and anger but she bit her tongue, in case she were to say something untoward.

Victoria on the other hand, excused herself and left. Molly heard the argument from two rooms away and decided that she better stop and find something else to do. Something away from the house.

Saturday morning came. Marcus was due back and the village fair was in the afternoon. Gwen was quite looking forward to it, as was Molly. She'd never been to a fair before and was excited to see what was going on.

Early in the morning she'd slipped away and walked down to the village. On the green, opposite the church, some men were erecting a large tent while women bustled around, carrying baskets of this and that.

Molly smiled and sat up on the churchyard wall, watching the activity and enjoying the sun on her face.

'Ah! Lady Carter!'

Molly's feelings of relaxation and simple enjoyment slipped away as the vicar came across to her.

'Hello Mr Glossop.' she replied wearily, getting down from the wall.

'What brings you to town so early?'

'Nothing really. I wanted a walk and this is where my feet brought me.'

'Splendid! It's good to get out and see the wonder of God's creation if you can. May I interest you in some tea?'

'No.' she said hurriedly. 'No thank you. I must be going.'

'Very good. Very good. I expect I'll see you this afternoon?'

'I expect so.' said Molly, forcing a smile.

He smiled back, his chins wobbling disconcertingly.

'There will be competitions and I will be one of the judges. Would you care to join me?'

'I couldn't...'

'Nonsense! I'll let Mrs Bagshaw know we have our final judge. I'll see you at two.'

Before she could protest any further, the man turned and headed to the church.

'Great.' thought Molly. 'An afternoon in his company.'

She sighed and lent back against the wall and closed her eyes, once more beginning to enjoy the feel of the sun on her skin.

After a moment, she snapped her eyes open and looked around, suddenly alert. It sounded like someone was crying. It was soft and almost in the edge of hearing, but it was there.

Slowly she turned around and tried to work out where it was coming from. Somewhere in the churchyard.

As quietly as she could she stepped through the ivy covered arch. The sound was coming from the left, away from the church itself and towards the far edge of the graveyard. Feeling tense, she walked between the silent graves.

She turned around. Even the birds had stopped singing. The far side of the graveyard was bordered by a heavy wood and Molly was sure she was being watched.

Forcing down a growing fear, she bent and picked up a stout branch, holding out in front of her like a sword, before slowly advancing on the trees. There was something there. She was sure of it. There was a thin, acrid smell to the air as she neared the trees. A little like spoiled meat.

She stopped walking and hefted the branch as from the wood came a low growl. It was almost too soft to hear but she felt it. It pulled directly at her deep primeval senses and fuelled the fear that coursed through her body.

Gritting her teeth, she took a step forward. From the trees came a louder growl and a sudden rustle of branches as whatever was there moved quickly away.

Molly shivered nervously and decided she should be getting back, not wanting to stay in the suddenly chilly churchyard a second longer.

Chapter Ten

A Fight at the Fair

The carriage rumbled towards the village. Molly was sat next to Gwen and opposite was Victoria with a stern look on her face. This was probably due to the fact the maid, Elsie, was sat next to her.

Molly had told the girls that they could both come to the fair. This had caused much outrage and muttering from the housekeeper but the other junior staff member, the male ones at least, had been given permission to go so Molly didn't see why Elsie should miss out, so she had given the girl the afternoon off herself.

Victoria wasn't best pleased especially when she found they were all riding in the coach. Molly didn't mind, the older woman would get over it, after all she had been young once and to be honest, Molly wanted the company.

The carriage slowed to a stop and the door was opened by the vicar. He helped Victoria and Molly down, leaving the two servants inside as if they hadn't even been there.

'Your Ladyship! Your Highness! Thank you for coming to our humble fete!'

Molly deliberately ignored him for a second, turning back to the girls in the coach.

'Here.' she handed Gwen a small pouch of coins. 'Don't be late back and take care.'

'Thank you Your Ladyship.' replied Gwen, echoed a second later by a nervous looking Elsie.

Both girls dismounted and were on their way before Molly turned back. The vicar looked confused and Victoria was frowning.

'Ah, yes. As I was saying... Um... If you will please follow me I would like to introduce you to our committee...'

He turned and led them towards a gaggle of people stood

near the tent. Victoria fell in beside Molly.

'You really shouldn't encourage the servants. It gives them ideas above their station.'

'If they're not encouraged, then how do they grow?' aske Molly.

Victoria looked at her as if she were mad.

'Grow? They don't need to grow! They need to learn their place! It's bad enough that you insist on having your servant as your maid of honour but I would appreciate it if you didn't interfere in the running of my household any further.'

'I pay the girl to work. Not be taken out on jolly trips and then given money to spend on who knows what. Your maid might see this as normal but I do not and I will not tolerate it any longer. Is that clear?'

Molly looked at Victoria. The older woman was annoyed and it showed. Not wanting to antagonise her any more, even though she had a few things to say about "learning their place", Molly just apologised and left it at that.

Ahead of them the vicar had gathered the group together. All were women of varying ages, each was dressed to their finest. Molly was introduced to them one by one and each gave her a curtsey as if she were better than them.

She considered telling them to stop it but knew it wouldn't do any good. She was a Princess and they couldn't see past that. In the end, Molly just smiled.

'It's very nice to meet you all.'

The next hour was, in Molly's eyes, one of the most boring of her life. There were only so many flowers she could look at or nervous people she could speak to. It was a huge relief when she felt an arm around her waist and turned to see her husband. He was smiling widely.

'Marcus!'

He nodded to the vicar and the assembled women.

'If you would please excuse me I would like to borrow my

fiancé for a moment.'

He turned and steered her out of the judging tent and into the sunshine.

'Thank you for rescuing me. I don't know how much longer I'd have lasted. I've missed you.' she told him.

'It's my positive duty to save a damsel in distress. I've bought you a present. Close your eyes.'

Molly frowned.

'I don't like surprises.'

'Trust me. Please.'

'Alright.' she said resignedly and did as he asked.

He took her hand and led her through the fair to come to a stop near the village inn.

'Open your eyes.'

Molly looked up, straight into the face of a horse. She stepped back in surprise.

'Do you like it?'

'It's a horse.' replied Molly.

Marcus smile dropped slightly.

'Well... Yes, it is.'

She turned to look at him.

'We live in London. Where am I going to put a horse?'

'I told you, you should have bought some jewellery.' piped up Richard who was stood nearby.

'Don't you like it?'

Molly regarded the animal for a moment. What she knew about horses you could fit on the head of a pin. Of course, she could ride and feed them but that was about it. She was no judge of pedigree or breeding. This one was a fawn colour with a white band running down its nose and white patches on its body and upper legs.

'It's a pretty colour.' she said eventually.

'Pretty colour?'

Behind them, Richard burst out laughing.

'I'll leave you to it. I'm going to get a drink.'

He wandered off, still chuckling to himself. Molly turned

to Marcus and smiled warmly.

'I love it. Thank you.'

Some of Marcus' enthusiasm returned.

'You don't have to walk everywhere now. I can show you around the rest of the estate.'

Molly decided not to tell him that she liked walking everywhere, instead giving him a gentle kiss on the cheek.

'Thank you.'

He smiled in return.

'Hey Marcus, come and have a look at this.'

They looked up to see Richard standing by the inn. He waved them over.

'Here. Look after this please.'

He passed the reigns and a coin into the palm of a nearby boy who tugged his forelock dutifully and led the horse away.

'I wish you wouldn't do that.' muttered Molly.

'Do what?'

'Assume people are there to do as you tell them.'

'I did say please. And I paid him!'

Molly frowned again but didn't say anything else. Instead she followed Marcus and Richard around the back of the inn.

Set up in the yard at the back was a square made of rope, held up in each corner by a stout wooden pole. Inside was the giant that was the blacksmith and surrounding the square on all sides were laughing and drinking men. A smaller man in a brown suit and hat came forward waving a battered walking stick in the air.

'Step right up. Think you can last three minutes in the ring with the Sampson, the undefeated champion? Not beaten in a dozen fairs running. Penny a go. If you last there's a sovereign as a prize.'

He flourished a shiny gold coin that disappeared into his pocket as fast as it had emerged.

'How about you sir? Or you?'

He began pointing at people with his stick until a young man stepped forward and took off his jacket and cap, handing them to his cheering friends.

The man was in his early twenties with bushy brown hair. He clambered over the rope and faced the giant. Molly watched intently as they began circling each other.

The younger man dived forward and threw a punch but the bigger man sidestepped neatly. He had a quickness that was unexpected. The crowd cheered and Molly saw money changing hands.

'One minute.' shouted the ringmaster glancing the pocket watch in his hand. The challenger threw a quick punch which contacted solidly against his opponent's chin but the blacksmith was unfazed, he darted forward to grab the young man, bodily picking him up and throwing him over the ropes and into the crowd to cheers and playful booing.

The ringmaster climbed over the rope and raised the hand of his giant.

'Still undefeated! Anyone else care to try?'

He pointed at Marcus with his stick.

'How about you sir? A fine gentleman like yourself?'

Marcus smiled and held up his right arm, showing his obviously missing hand.

'I'm afraid not.'

The ringmaster turned to Richard.

'You sir?'

'Not likely!' he grinned and grabbed Mollys hand, raising it in the air. 'What about her? My friend says she's a bit of a slugger!'

The crowd erupted into laughter as Molly snatched her hand away and glared at him and then at Marcus.

'I said no such thing.' Marcus said quickly as he saw the look on her face.

'What about it?' continued Richard, enjoying the growing laughter and Molly's embarrassment. She stepped forward and raised her voice above the crowd.

'I won't fight. Not him anyway.' she said, pointing to the blacksmith before turning to Richard. 'I'll fight you instead.'

The crowd gave a roar, sensing the sport to come. Richard looked at her, his grin was wide.

'I was only joking. I wouldn't want to hurt you.'

'You won't. I warned you not to make fun of me.' she raised her voice again. 'So, are you man enough to fight a girl or are you all mouth and no trousers?'

Richards smile slipped slightly as he sensed the crowd shifting against him. He glanced past her to Marcus who was fuming with anger and then around at the crowd.

'I really don't...'

Molly grinned.

'You don't have a choice.'

She turned to the ringmaster and had a whispered word. He shrugged, raised his stick high and shouted.

'Ten minutes!'

Without another look at either Marcus or Richard, Molly stalked away.

Marcus caught up with her just past the inn.

'Molly where are you going?'

'To get my bag from the carriage. You don't expect me to fight in a dress do you?'

He put his hand on her arm to stop her walking away.

'Don't. Please.'

She rounded on him.

'He thinks I'm a joke. Apart from your mother, and sometimes I'm not sure about her either, your whole family and staff think I'm a joke. I dread to think what everyone else that I don't know is going to think. Well it stops now. If they want to think ill of me then fine. I don't care but I'm not having him...' she jabbed a finger back towards the inn '...him, make fun of me. I'm not standing for being humiliated in public. There was no need for that.'

'I'll get him to apologise...'
'No. It'll be as fake as the last one.'
She pulled out of his grasp and stormed away.

The ringmaster looked at his watch with a smile.
'It's been fifteen minutes. I don't think she's coming back.'
Marcus looked at his friend.
'I don't think you'll be that lucky.'
Richard laughed.
'Come on old boy. She's just a girl. I...'
A silence fell on the crowd as Molly strode into the yard. She was dressed in a tight fitting black leather jumpsuit with sturdy knee length boots. She plucked a half full tankard of ale from the unresisting hands of a man as she neared a gawping Richard. Slowly she finished the drink before passing it back.
'So, are we fighting or what?'
Behind Richard, Marcus closed his eyes. At least she hadn't brought her sword. He lent forward and whispered in his friends' ear.
'Don't say I didn't warn you.'
The crowd went wild as Molly climbed under the rope and a few seconds later a stunned looking Richard was pushed forward by the eager onlookers. Once inside the barrier, he seemed to regain his composure and began to remove his jacket and shirt, playing up to the crowd. The ringmaster came over to Molly.
'Are you sure about this lass?' he whispered.
She smiled and removed her glasses, fixing him with her penetrating white stare.
'Of course.'
He shook his head, a look of concern and fear on his face.
'Molly, please don't.'
She looked down at Marcus.
'I won't hurt him. Much.'
He frowned.

'That's not what I meant and you know it!'
'Don't fuss. It'll be fine.'
Around the ring, money was swiftly changing hands as wagers were placed. Richard bounced into the centre. Prancing about and playing up to the crowd.

'Well you're a game girl, I'll give you that. And that getup? No wonder he fell for you! Always did like a bit of leather did Marcus.' he grinned. 'Tell you what, I'll give you a free shot. Give me your best.'

He stuck his chin out, goading her to hit him. She tensed and Richard jumped back with a smile, bouncing about on the balls of his feet.

Molly glanced around and her eye caught Gwen and Elsie who were stood in the far side. The girls were staring in a mixture of shock and awe and just past them were Victoria and Mr Glossop the vicar. Their expressions were a sight to be seen. Not so much awe as the girls, but most definitely more shock.

'Come on.' said Richard. 'Give me your best shot.'
'Molly. Stop messing around.'
She glanced at Marcus who shook his head. She smiled at him sweetly before rolling her shoulders and stepping towards Richard.

Twenty minutes later Marcus was sat in a small back room off the main bar of the inn with Richard laid out on a rough table.

Marcus sighed and emptied a pint pot of ale over his friends' face. The man spluttered and sat up suddenly, groaning loudly as his senses caught up with him.

'Dear god. What hit me?' he asked groggily, holding his head in his hands.

'Molly.' replied Marcus, trying to keep the satisfaction out of his voice.

'What with? A tree?'
Marcus smiled and sat down.

'Let me see... You said "You're only a girl why don't you give in now? How hard can you hit anyway." I think that annoyed her even more and she punched you...' Marcus counted off on his fingers '...three times, then she kicked you in the head.'

Richard groaned again.

'It's not sporting to kick a man while he's down.'

'Oh you weren't down. Not at that point. You didn't go down until she kicked you in the stomach and the got you with a beautiful uppercut. You almost left the ground!' Marcus patted him on the shoulder. 'I think you'll have a hell of a black eye in the morning.'

Richard swung his legs off the table, wincing at the movement.

'And you're going to marry her?'

'Yes. Again.'

'Then you're a better man than me! She's a devil!'

He lurched to his feet and began pulling his shirt on.

'I need a drink.'

Marcus smiled.

'Ah, about that. Do you remember saying "If she can knock me on my back then I'll buy everyone a drink"?'

Richard groaned again and headed for the door. The main taproom was hushed, with men, women and children gathered around Molly. She was sat on a table, a mug of ale to her left as she told them of their adventures with the Stones of Gunjai. All eyes turned to the two men as they came in. Molly smiled widely and addressed the audience.

'See, I told you I hadn't killed him!'

There was some giggling and muted laughter. The whole bar seemed to be hanging on her every word. She took a sip of her beer and stood up as Marcus and Richard reached her. Richard cleared his throat and looked around at the sea of interested faces before turning back to Molly.

'Your Highness. I apologise for my behaviour. On my honour, it won't happen again.'

Molly regarded him coolly for a second.

'I hope it won't.'

He bowed, trying to stifle a grunt as his battered muscles protested.

'I assure you. It won't happen again.'

'He don't want to take another beating!' piped up someone from the back. Richard straightened and smiled.

'Too bloody right I don't.'

There was laughter around the room.

'Well that's the matter settled then. Friends?'

She held out her hand and Richard shook it.

'Of course.'

'Good.'

Marcus offered her his arm.

'I think we should be going. Don't you? We'll see you at home Richard after you've paid your bill.'

Molly went to go but a small child stepped in front of her.

'Are you going to finish the story?'

She smiled at him.

'Maybe later.'

'But I want to know what happened.'

There was a chorus of agreement.

Molly crouched down and smiled at him.

'Tomorrow. I'll come back tomorrow afternoon.'

'Really?'

'Yes. I promise.'

This seemed to please him and he went back to his mother who was stood nearby. The woman dipped a small curtsey with a tight smile. Molly could tell that the woman was suspicious of her and to be honest, she didn't blame her, what with the rumour mill at full pelt after the Miller girl had been found dead. She straightened and addressed the crowded inn.

'I'll see you tomorrow.'

The crowd began to disperse and Marcus whispered.

'Richard sisters and mother are coming tomorrow

afternoon. Mother would expect you to be there.'

Molly looked at him.

'Expect?'

'Molly, please.'

'If they want to see me then they'll have to come and find me.'

She headed towards the door only to be stopped by a nervous cluster of girls, Gwen and Elsie included. Nearby stood a group of men who also looked uncomfortable.

One of the women stepped forward. She was probably about the same age as Molly but with long brown hair. She looked down for a second.

'Um, Your Highness...'

There was some muttering from the assembled group and Molly smiled.

'Yes?'

'Um... There's a dance this evening. We know a lady like yourself is probably busy and it wouldn't be the thing to be seen at but...'

She tapered off as Molly looked at her, her eyes quite bright in the dimness of the room.

'It sounds like fun and I've had precious little of that recently. What time is it?'

'Eight o'clock. In the barn at Mr Gaskins farm. Just down the lane.'

'I'll see you there.'

She swept out past the girls who erupted into a loud and excited conversation. Marcus followed her, looking annoyed and with Gwen in tow.

'What's that look for?' asked Molly without turning around.

'You can't go to that dance. It's not the sort thing a lady should be seen at, mother will have a fit...'

'Why?' asked Molly simply, with an innocent smile on her face.

'Well, it's not right, they're...'

'They're what? Common? Not our sort? Peasants?'
'No, I mean...'

Molly reached the church wall and sat down, waiting for him to continue. He looked at her in silence.

'I don't care what people think Marcus.' she said eventually. 'You should know that. Less than a year ago, the people up at the house wouldn't have even looked at me. I was beneath them. I still am.'

She pointed back towards the inn.

'Those people in the bar. I've not felt as comfortable with anyone since we got back from India. My life has turned into a show. You're always telling me what I'm supposed to do.'

'But you don't listen.'

'No. I don't. Not always. But that's the way I am. If that's not good enough then don't marry me. I'm not changing. I've told your mother that and that's how it is.'

'That's not fair! You can't... protested Marcus.

'No. It isn't.' she snapped back.

There was an awkward silence. Molly saw Gwen hovering nervously a few feet away.

'Yes Gwen?' said Molly.

The girl stepped forward with a glance at the angry looking Marcus.

'Beggin' your pardon Your Ladyship, but the vicar and lady Victoria are looking for you. They want you to present some prizes.'

Molly looked at Marcus.

'See! All they can see is a title. Last year they wouldn't have given me the scraps from their table.'

'Not that you'd have asked.'

Molly jumped off the wall and followed Gwen.

'No. I wouldn't. I did try to beg for food at a big house once. When I was eleven. The housekeeper and butler gave me a sound thrashing for even daring to ask before throwing me in the gutter with a warning never to come around again. I never did.'

She stalked away, leaving a stunned Marcus in her wake.

Chapter Eleven

Barn Dance

After another tense evening meal at the house, Molly was happy to get back to her room. Marcus had obviously told his mother that she wouldn't be around to meet Richards family and that she was going to the village dance. It also seemed that someone had mentioned the fight between her and Richard to Marcus' father.

Well, she wasn't going to apologise for it. The arrogant bugger had deserved it. She sighed and shook her head as Gwen came over with an armful of dresses. Molly wasn't quite sure where she'd got so many from. The girl put them on the bed.

'How about this one?' she asked, holding up a deep red dress with wide skirts and a plunging neckline.

'Too formal. I want something plain.'

Gwen picked out a simple mustard coloured dress with long sleeves and fine lace around the neck and hem.

'Almost perfect.'

'Almost?'

Molly smiled and took the dress before pulling the lace off the neck. Gwen looked on horrified.

'Oh don't look like that. Now shouldn't you be going to get changed?'

'Changed?'

'Well, aren't you coming with me? Marcus isn't.'

From the tone of Mollys voice, Gwen decided it wasn't prudent to ask why.

'Can I really come with you?'

'Of course. Why not? What about Elsie?'

Gwen looked down in an embarrassed silence. Molly raised her eyebrows.

'Well? What about her?'

'I don't want to get her into trouble.'
Molly sighed.
'Gwen, I'm not likely to tell anyone.'
'She didn't come back after the fair. She stayed in the village. With a boy.'

The way Gwen said it, it was like this was the most scandalous thing in the world.

'I told her she'd get into trouble but she wouldn't listen.'
Molly shook her head.

'Well, she will get into trouble, I've no doubt about that and I'll try and see to it that they're not too hard on her but I have had to promise Victoria that I'll not interfere with the running of the house.'

'As long as they don't lock her in the cellar again. That really scared her.'

'That is *not* going to happen.' said Molly with an edge to her voice that almost made Gwen flinch.

'Do you want me to help you dress?' asked the girl after a tense moment.

'No. I can manage. Go and get ready. We'll be leaving soon.'

Gwen nodded and hurried away. Molly watched her go before sitting down heavily on the bed. She was beginning to hate this house and the stupid people in it.

Surprisingly, she realised that Marcus had fallen into that category as well. He was different here. More pompous. More fixated on title and station.

Maybe he wasn't the man she had fallen in love with.

That thought left her with a heavy heart and a burning need to cry. Taking a deep breath, she pushed the thought away and began to get changed.

Marcus had made a point of ignoring them as the left and headed towards the village. Molly had felt her anger rising as she had stormed from the house and down the drive, dragging Gwen along in her wake.

They had walked along in a stony silence for the best part of a mile before Molly announced that on Monday they were going home.

'Home?'

'Back to London. I can't stand it here anymore.'

'What about the wedding?'

'I don't care about the wedding. It's not important.'

Gwen didn't say anything, instinctively knowing that Molly didn't mean it.

They arrived at the farm and joined the throng of people heading towards the barn, with both of them getting curious and nervous glances. Molly knew that the hushed conversation that was flitting around was about her.

The barn had been cleared and swept, with a few barrels of ale off to the left. Some food was on a rickety table near that and at the far end a group of musicians with a rag tag selection of instruments were playing a jaunty tune. One of the girls that had invited Molly rushed over to greet her, dipping in a curtsey.

'Your Highness.'

Molly smiled tightly, already seeing the evening disappearing into a tide of politeness and fawning over her title.

'Hello.'

'Thank you for coming.'

'I was hoping it would be fun.' replied Molly tersely.

The girl looked confused.

'Won't it be?'

'It will if I have anything to do with it.' said Molly before heading off towards the band.

She clambered up onto their makeshift stage, stuck her fingers in her mouth and whistled loudly. The music stopped and a hundred confused looking pairs of eyes swung her way. Molly waited until she had got their full attention.

'Right.' she shouted. 'My name is Molly. Molly Carter.'

She scanned the audience for a second, letting that sink in.

'It's true that I have an adopted sister who *is* an actual Princess and apparently that makes me one too, but not tonight. Tonight, I'm just Molly. I don't want to feel different or be treated differently because of some stupid title that I don't like, don't deserve and didn't earn.'

She sighed.

'What I'd like is to have fun and maybe a drink and a dance. Please?' her last words were almost pleading.

The villagers looked from one to another for a second before someone shouted from the back.

'Well then get off the bloody stage so we can get dancing!'

Molly laughed and jumped down, stumbling as she landed and falling headlong into the arms of a nearby man. He was around the same age as her but with brown eyes and dark brown hair. With his weather-tanned skin he was quite handsome and there was a mischievous twinkle in his eye.

He held her for a couple of seconds longer than necessary before he set her on her feet.

'Alright?'

'Yes.' replied Molly, feeling the blush begin to creep up her face. 'Yes. Thank you.'

He offered her his hand.

'Michael Barnet.'

'I'm...'

'Molly. Yes, we heard.' he said, cutting her off with a disarming smile.

Molly blushed further.

'So what do Princesses drink?'

'What have you got?' she replied.

Marcus paced up and down the library while Richard sat in a deep leather armchair, brandy in one hand and a huge cigar in the other. His eye was turning a yellowy purple colour.

'Sit down, have drink. She'll be alright. I pity anyone who tries to stop her.'

'I still don't see why she had to go. I asked her not to.'

'You should have told her not to. She needs to learn her place!'

Both men looked up as Marcus father entered the room.

'Father...'

'If, god forbid, she's going to be in this family then she's going to have to damn well learn to do as she's told.'

Marcus looked at his friend and then at his father.

'Well? What're you waiting for? Go and get her and drag her back. She must do as you tell her. Women should honour and obey their husbands!'

Richard shrugged and finished off his brandy before standing and taking the tense Marcus by the arm.

'We'll go and find her directly uncle James.'

The man made a harrumph noise.

'See that you do.'

Richard guided Marcus out of the room.

'You'd better go and get her old chap. Although I wish you luck. She won't stand for being dragged anywhere if I'm any judge.'

He patted Marcus on the shoulder and headed towards the stairs leaving his friend standing in the hallway.

Molly sat down to catch her breath. She'd danced and twirled and laughed with Michael and had more fun than she'd had in ages.

'Here.'

Gwen came over and handed her a pint pot full of a cloudy amber liquid.

'What is it?'

'Cider apparently.' said the girl as she sat down next to Molly, her own pot in her hands.

'Having fun?' Molly asked.

'Sort of.'

'Why only sort of?' asked Molly, taking a sip of the cider. It was bitter and sharp and she pulled a face.

Gwen looked at her.

'I can't find Elsie.'

'Maybe she's still with her boy?'

The girl shook her head and pointed across the room.

'No. He's over there. He said she left just after we did this afternoon. She'd decided that it wasn't worth all the trouble she would get into.'

'Then maybe she's back at the house?'

'I didn't see her. You don't think they've locked her in the cellar again, do you?' asked Gwen nervously.

Molly shook her head.

'I don't expect so. We'll find out when we go back. I promise.'

On the stage the musicians were getting ready to start again.

'May I have this dance?'

Molly looked up to see Michael, his hand outstretched and a smile on his lips.

'Of course sir.' replied Molly with a beaming smile of her own.

She took his hand and allowed him to help her stand. She turned and called back to Gwen as Michael dragged her towards the dance floor.

'I promise we'll find Elsie, but for now, enjoy yourself, go and find someone to dance with.'

Marcus rode slowly down the lane, the sounds from the dance loud in the still evening. He reigned his horse in as he reached the entrance to the field. A bonfire was burning bright and lanterns were strung up around and about.

He dismounted and walked towards the barn, music playing loudly from within. As he approached, he saw

Gwen, walking alongside a young man. He called her over.

'Where's Molly?'

The girl glanced nervously at the barn.

'She's in the barn sir. Least, that where she was last I saw her. She was dancing.'

Marcus set his mouth in a grim line.

'Get yourself back to the house please.'

She looked at him.

'Now!' he snapped angrily.

She bobbed a curtsey.

'Very good sir.'

He didn't wait to see what she did, expecting her to do as she was told, and strode straight for the barn.

The inside was loud and full of people. He wandered around the edge of the room, looking for Molly but couldn't find her. In the end, he asked a young couple.

'Have you seen Molly?'

'Who sir?'

'The Princess damn it. Lady Carter?' he snapped back.

The girl looked at him for a moment before pointing outside.

'She was dancing, I think she went to get some air.'

Marcus grumbled a thank you and headed outside. He went around the side of the barn and stopped dead. There she was, alongside a young man. They were walking away from him but he knew it was her.

Their body language spoke volumes, the way she laughed at some unheard joke, the way he moved closer to her. Inwardly Marcus cursed himself, why had he let her come? He struggled to keep his anger in check as he saw them stop.

Molly leant forward and whispered in the young man's ear before giving him a kiss on the cheek. Marcus was about to storm over and make his presence known when Molly gripped the young man's arms tightly.

As he watched, his anger turning into concern, she doubled up as if in pain before dropping to her knees. Her lips were curled back and teeth grinding together as she fell on all fours.

Marcus ran towards her as the man began to shout for help.

Molly and Michael headed out of the barn. It was warm and she needed to get some air. They walked along in silence for a moment, Molly acutely aware of the handsome man next to her.

'So are you really a Princess?'

'Apparently so.' said Molly with a shrug.

'I thought all Princesses could dance.'

Molly laughed but her good mood fell as she was reminded of Marcus. He'd said the same thing at Lady Samantha's ball the year before. She stopped and smiled sadly at him before leaning forward and speaking softly.

'I've had a lovely time. Thank you for treating me like a normal person.'

She gave him a kiss on the cheek and he flushed red.

'Wait till I tell everyone I got kissed by a Princess!'

Molly smiled but it quickly turned into a grimace as her mark flared painfully.

'Are you alright?' Michael asked as she grabbed him for support, her fingers digging deeply into his shoulders. Beneath her, her legs turned to jelly as her tattoo blazed.

On her back, the eagle felt like it was on fire, every intricately rendered feather was a fiercely burning inferno. Gritting her teeth and trying not to scream, she fell onto her hands and knees as she dimly heard Michael begin to shout for help.

Marcus reached her as she slumped sideways onto the floor. He put his hand on her side as he knelt down.

'Molly, it's Marcus. What's the matter?'

She has her eyes screwed shut and was tense throughout every muscle in her body.

'My mark.' she managed to hiss between gritted teeth.

Marcus touched her back and could feel an incredible heat pouring off it. Molly cried out as his hand made contact. Around him a crowd was beginning to form. He looked up at nervous faces.

'I need to get her inside.'

A nearby woman nodded.

'You can use the farmhouse. This way.'

Marcus lent back down.

'We're going to take you inside.'

She didn't answer.

'You.' he said to Michael, 'Get her other arm. Don't touch her back.'

Together, the two men took an arm each and pulled Molly to her feet. She sagged heavily between them as they hurried across to the farmhouse.

Marcus was sat in the kitchen with Michael. Gwen had gone upstairs with Molly and the farmer's wife. There was a tense silence in the room, both men regarding each other critically.

Marcus opened his mouth to give the younger man a dressing down when Gwen came in, followed by the farmer's wife. Both men stood up.

'She's sleeping. I think it best if she stays here tonight.'

Marcus nodded to the farmer's wife.

'Thank you.'

'You'd better be getting along Michael.' she said, 'I'll see you out.'

She escorted him from the room leaving Marcus and Gwen alone.

After a moment, Marcus spoke.

'I'm sorry about earlier. I shouldn't have spoken to you so harshly.'

'It's alright sir. I shouldn't have left her. I'm sorry. I got carried away what with the dance and that. I'm her maid. I should have done my job.'

The girl looked down, unable to look at him and that made Marcus feel worse.

'It's not your fault. She doesn't give people much choice. I *am* sorry about the way I spoke to you. You may be in our employ but you are a person, not a thing.'

Gwen smiled weakly.

'What happened?'

Marcus shook his head and sat down.

'I don't know. Something about her mark. It was so hot...'

'May I speak freely sir?' asked Gwen after a small silence.

'Of course.'

'She, that is, her ladyship...'

'She's called Molly. Don't think I don't know that's what she asked you to call her in private.'

Gwen blushed.

'Well... Molly... she said she was going back to London. She said she didn't like the people up at the house and had had enough of their stares and unfriendly ways. They don't like her sir. Not the master at the house or the staff. I've heard them talking about her behind her back. But I think she knows it too.'

Marcus was stunned.

'But... But what about the wedding?' he stammered.

'She said she didn't care about that. But... But I know she's lying about that bit. I can tell.'

Marcus didn't know what to say.

'She's also not sleeping sir. She's been having nightmares and is taking something to help her try to sleep. She puts a few drops of it in some wine before she goes to bed. It comes from a little glass bottle in the top drawer. She thinks that I don't know. I don't like telling tales sir, but I just thought you'd better know.'

The girl turned to leave.

'Where are you going?'
'Back to the house. To pack my things.'
Marcus stood up.
'What? Why?'
'I've broken her confidence. I don't think she'd want me to tell you what I know but I'm worried.' she looked at her feet before adding, 'I thought you'd fire me sir.'
Marcus smiled sadly.
'Of course you're not fired. She doesn't talk to me anymore. I thank you for telling me.'
'Thank you.'
'My name is Marcus.' he replied with a sigh. 'If it's good enough for Molly then it's good enough for me.'
'I couldn't possibly do that.'
'Nonsense.'
Gwen didn't reply.
'She doesn't make it easy for anyone. She's very independent.' said Marcus.
'I'm supposed to be her maid sir. If she won't let me do things for her then I could at least keep her secrets.' she said eventually.
Marcus sighed.
'Look. You're not fired. Despite what she thinks or says, she does need our help.'
Gwen nodded and looked at her feet.
'Is there anything else?'
The silence from the girl told him there was.
'Come on. What is it?' he asked kindly.
'It isn't my place to say sir.'
'Tell me.'
She glanced up and then straight back down again.
'She's lonely. I mean there's people in the house but she don't speak to them. They honestly try and avoid her and you sir, beggin' your pardon, you've been different.'
Marcus mouth formed a tight line.
'In what way?'

Gwen plunged on, she'd gone this far and it was too late to back out.

'You've been distant sir. You don't spend any time together. Neither of you. She misses you. She wanted some company tonight, wanted to be among people who didn't treat her too differently. That's why she came to the dance.'

She looked up at Marcus. There was an oddly resigned look on his face.

'I'll go back to the house sir and get her ladyship some clean clothes.'

Quickly, she left before Marcus could say anything else, almost bumping into the farmer's wife as she came back in.

'Your lady is up in the spare room if you want to see her sir.'

'Thank you.'

'I'll show you where it is.'

He followed the woman up a narrow flight of stairs to a small room over the kitchen. Molly was laid on a narrow bed, sleeping peacefully. He turned to the farmer's wife.

'Thank you.'

She nodded.

'I'll be downstairs if you need me. I'll put the kettle on. Oh, and don't mind Michael. He didn't mean nothing by it. They were just dancing. She wanted to dance and he was the first to offer.'

Marcus nodded and she left, closing the door behind her. He pulled up a rickety looking chair and sat by the bed before taking her hand. How many times had he seen her like this? Too many.

He thought back to Gwen's words. Why hadn't he seen it? Why had it taken the maid to tell him? Had they moved so far apart?

Gwen walked sadly out of the farmhouse and back across the yard. In the barn, the music was still playing but quite a lot of people were milling around outside. Several of them asked her how Molly was but she didn't have an answer for them.

She walked down the lane and back towards the road to the house and hadn't made it as far as the farm gate before there were running feet behind. She turned to see the Albert, the young man she had been dancing with. He was out of breath.

'Where're you going?'

'Back to the house. My mistress is sick. I need to…'

'Let me walk with you.' he said quickly.

Gwen shook her head, feeling a blush begin to warm her cheeks.

'No. Its fine. Go back to the dance.'

'But there's no one there that I want to dance with.'

'I'm sure that's not true.'

He looked down with a smile.

'Well maybe. But you're not there so it's kind of true.'

Gwen blushed further but she smiled.

'I've got to go. I really need to…'

She tailed off as a heavy, foetid, sticky scent appeared on the breeze. It left an awful aftertaste at the back of her throat. Like a bitter medicine or meat that's gone over.

Around them the insects in the grass stopped and a heavy cloud obscured the moon, casting dark and forbidding shadows.

Without realising, they took a step towards each other. Both could feel the change in the air and it unnerved them.

'Do you smell that?' asked Albert, his words hardly more than a whisper.

Gwen nodded and took his hand for reassurance.

'Yes.'

'Thank God. I thought…'

They both looked towards the barn as the screaming started.

Back at the farmhouse, Marcus sat holding Molly's hand tightly. It hurt to see her like this. He kissed her knuckles.
'I love you.'
On the bed Molly twitched, snatching her hand out of his. She moaned fitfully and began to toss and turn, the movements getting more violent until she sat bolt upright with a stifled scream.
Marcus had jumped up when she had started thrashing and despite himself, he took a step back. Her eyes were full of swirling blackness and thin, bloody tears painted her cheeks. She looked at him for a second, as if she didn't know who he was.
'Molly?'
She put her hand to her mouth to try and stifle a sob and he came to her. Holding her and telling her that everything would be alright, hoping that he sounded more convincing than he felt.
'It's going to be alright.'
'Marcus. It's close.'
His brow furrowed.
'Close? What is?'
'We've got to stop it.'
'What?'
They both looked towards the door as from outside someone began to scream.

Gwen pounded back up the lane towards the barn with Albert in tow. They were still holding hands, Gwen almost dragging him along. People were flooding out of the barn in a panic. She grabbed a girl as she fled the other way.
'What's going on?'
'A monster!'
The girl pulled away and ran for her life, as if Hell itself were chasing her. Gwen let go of Albert and ran towards the barn as out of the building came a "thing".

It was about the size of a large dog and ran on all fours but it had no skin or eyes. Wet muscle glistened in the lamplight as it prowled across the yard, turning its head left and right and sniffing the air before opening its mouth to show row upon row of blood stained teeth.

Something grabbed Gwen's hand and she almost screamed out loud.

'What the hell are you doing?' asked Albert.

The creature turned towards them, its head snapping around quickly. Gwen couldn't see any eyes but she knew it was looking directly at her.

'I think we should run.' she whispered.

'I think so too.' he whispered back.

They turned and ran for their lives as behind them the thing broke into a loping run. Albert dragged Gwen behind a cart as the thing thundered past. It turned quickly, long sharp talons gouging deep furrows in the ground. They ducked down underneath the wagon and out the other side, running once more towards the barn.

It leapt, landing on the cart for a second before jumping high and crashing down in front of them. They skidded to a halt.

'Oh...' began Albert, taking Gwen's hand once more and pushing her behind him.

With a deep growl, the creature tensed and leapt once more, talons and teeth bared. Both Gwen and Albert closed their eyes, expecting to be torn apart by the monster but instead, there was strangled grunt of pain.

Gingerly opening their eyes, they found that the thing was suspended in mid-air, a few feet from them, surrounded by a swirling vortex of wind. In front of it was Marcus holding on to a pitchfork which he had driven into the creatures' stomach. Molly was on her knees in the dirt, halfway from the farmhouse. Her eyes were glowing with a sickly blue light and she had her hands stretched out in front of her. Her face was tense and body quivering.

'Get the hell out of here.' shouted Marcus. 'I don't know how long she can hold it.'

Gwen and Albert scrambled to the side as Marcus twisted the pitchfork and yanked it out, drawing a howl from the bloody maw. Blood splattered onto the ground where it began to smoke.

He rammed the pitchfork back in but this time aiming for the snapping jaws. One of the tines of the fork glanced off its teeth and drove straight upwards into its head while the other punctured the side of its face. It let out an unearthly screech and thrashed wildly, snapping the haft of the fork clean in two and sending Marcus sprawling.

Another pitchfork rammed home and Marcus glanced up to see Michael and several other men begin to attack the beast.

'Marcus!'

Molly dropped onto her hands and knees and the power she was using to hold the monster aloft and immobile vanished.

The creature fell heavily, impaling itself further on the embedded forks. It rolled onto its side as a heavy pickaxe was driven into its head, crushing its skull. The men pulled back slightly.

'What is it?' asked one of them in a hushed tone.

Marcus pushed himself to his feet.

'It's...'

The body twitched once and then exploded in a plume of brilliant purple fire. The heat was ferocious and drove the men away as the body was consumed in flames.

'Marcus.' Mollys voice was hoarse.

He turned from the rapidly dying fire and ran to his wife. She was slumped on her side, eyes still a disturbing black tinged with blue. He picked her up and for the second time that night, carried her away.

The farmer and his wife had taken her and once he was sure she was sleeping, he went back outside. A crowd had gathered around a blackened patch of earth where the thing had fallen.

There was no sign of a body and the dirt beneath had been fused almost like glass from the intense heat. The people parted as Marcus came closer. Some of the younger women were crying, being comforted their elders. One of the men stepped up to Marcus.

'What was it?'

Marcus shook his head.

'I don't know.'

'How'd she do that? Hold it in the air like that? Was it magic?'

He ignored him as he saw Gwen and the young man stood at the front of the crowd.

'Gwen.'

She looked up, her face still holding a vestige of fear. Letting go of Alberts hand she came over.

'Yes sir?'

'Are you alright?'

She nodded.

'Is Molly alright?'

'Yes. I think so. She's sleeping.'

'She saved my life.'

'She won't see it like that.'

Gwen glanced over her shoulder at the young man who was stood looking on.

'She saved his too.'

Marcus looked at him and beckoned him over.

'Yes sir?'

'You were very brave tonight. I thank you for looking after Gwen. My wife thanks you too.'

He nodded but looked confused.

'Gwen. Please go back to the house. I'll remain here with Molly.'

'Very good sir.'
She curtseyed and headed off.
'What's your name?' Marcus asked the boy.
'Albert, sir.'
'Would you please go with Gwen. See she gets home safely.'
'Of course sir.'
Marcus nodded and handed him a gold coin.
'Thank you again.'

The next day, Richard came back down with the coach for Marcus and Molly. He rode back on his horse with Gwen, leaving Marcus and Molly alone. Rumour was that a wild dog had attacked the dance. The same one that had killed the Miller girl. Even those that had seen it were saying the same. They couldn't think of anything else that it could have been.

Molly had gone further up in their estimations. Now she could fly and spit fire from her eyes, although the more superstitious amongst them muttered fearfully about witches and demons but the majority were holding her as a hero. Her eyes had returned to their normal white overnight. Marcus hadn't mentioned it. She seemed to have enough on her plate as it was. The carriage rumbled back towards the house, with its occupants sat quietly, Molly feeling exhausted and Marcus worried. Eventually he spoke.

'What do you think that thing was? How did you know it was coming?'

Molly shook her head.

'I don't know. My mark hurt more than I've ever felt it. Then I had a dream. It wasn't real. Half glimpsed shadows. Blood. Fire.' she tailed off and looked at her hands. 'I don't know.'

'Why didn't you tell me you weren't sleeping? Having bad dreams?'

'You'd have only fussed.'
'I'm your husband. It's my job to fuss.'
'It doesn't seem like it sometimes.'
'What is that supposed to mean?' he asked angrily.
'Since we've been here, more since Richard arrived, I don't see you. You're always out doing whatever it is you do. Your mother is busy with the wedding and everyone else hates me. I spend so much time alone in my room I don't know what to do with myself.'
'You could come with us when we're out.'
'I don't want to come with both of you. I want my husband back. I want the man who isn't only interested in flaunting his prize Princess wife off to everyone. I want the kind and gentle man I fell in love with.'
'I don't flaunt you!' he protested.
'As soon as Richard arrived you couldn't wait to wave me in front of him, titles and all. I bet it will be the same this afternoon, which is why I didn't want to be there. I'm not just a title you can use to impress your friends and family.'
The both lapsed into a sullen, angry silence. Eventually Molly broke it.
'I'm sorry. I'm tired and fed up of everything and everyone.'
'You don't need to apologise. I'm sorry I haven't been there for you.'
Molly smiled and it lit up the carriage.
'What a pair we are.'
Marcus laughed.
'Yes. We are.'
'I suppose Gwen told you about my sleeping?'
'Yes. She even thought I'd sack her for telling me. She's worried. I'm worried.'
'Why would you sack her?'
'For betraying your confidence and trust.'
Molly shook her head dismissively before closing her eyes and leaning her head back against the seat.

'I dream of him.' she said softly.

Marcus didn't say anything so she continued.

'Malor. He haunts my dreams. It's got worse since I came here.'

'But he's gone. You destroyed him.'

'I know, but that doesn't stop the memories. The pain.'

'Talk to me.'

'I can't. Not about that. Not yet.'

Marcus looked down. He knew Molly had been taken prisoner by Malor, an evil spirit who had possessed Prince Ramesh, Nareema's brother. But what had happened between that point and when they had rescued her, he didn't know. Molly wouldn't speak of it, despite his best efforts. He moved next to her and took her hand.

'I'm here for you. You don't know that, don't you?'

She squeezed his hand back and smiled tiredly.

'I know.'

Chapter Twelve

Family History

They arrived back at the house to find another carriage already there. The staff were unloading luggage and taking it inside. Holding Mollys hand, they went in. Gwen was waiting in the hallway with Mr Tanning, the butler, and Richard. His friend came forward.

'Marcus, mother has arrived early. She's in the drawing room.

Marcus nodded.

'Thank you.'

They went into the drawing room. Seated in her leather armchair was Victoria and opposite sat a hard-faced woman with grey hair tied in a severe bun. Next to her were stood two girls, both in their late teens and looking almost the same, dressed in immaculate pale floral print dresses with pale blue ribbons tied in their long brown hair. They all stopped talking suddenly. Marcus stepped forward.

'Mother. Aunt Sarah. Please may I introduce her Royal...' He stopped talking and turned to Molly, taking her hand with a smile.

'Please may I introduce Molly.'

Molly smiled nervously and took off her glasses. There was an audible gasp from both girls which was instantly silenced with a rebuke from their mother. She stood and came over to Molly, inspecting her with the same inscrutable gaze that Victoria possessed.

'I apologise for my daughters' behaviour.'

'Its fine.' replied Molly. 'I get it a lot.'

The woman turned to look at the twins.

'Still, that is no reason to have poor manners.' she glanced over Mollys shoulder to the doorway. 'I hear it was you that gave my son his black eye?'

Molly flushed red and hurriedly began to explain and apologise but the older woman cut her off with a sly smile.

'He probably had it coming. Isn't that right Richard?'

There was a mumbled agreement.

'I also hear that you fought off a wild dog last night. Even after being taken ill?'

Molly shrugged uncomfortably and the women regarded her coolly. Eventually Sarah spoke again.

'Victoria has been telling me all about you.'

'Has she?' Molly asked timidly.

'Yes. I must say that I find you remarkable.'

'Why?'

The woman smiled warmly.

'You've met my sister and you still want to marry my nephew.' she stepped closer and offered her a hand. 'You may call me aunt Sarah.'

Molly shook the offered hand.

'Thank you.'

Aunt Sarah turned away and sat back down.

'I was beginning to think that Victoria wouldn't find anyone that she approves of to wed her son, well, anyone worthwhile that is, but you seem to have done that.'

'Thank you. I think.'

'These are my daughters, Tilly and Hannah.'

The girls smiled nervously and one of them bobbed a curtsey.

'They are to be your bridesmaids I hear.'

Molly glanced at Marcus and then at Victoria, both were watching her carefully.

'Yes. I mean, if they would like to.'

Aunt Sarah burst out laughing and Molly jumped.

'If they would like to? My dear, they've talked of nothing else since we received Victoria's letter! Although I was expecting my nephew to be marrying lady Samantha's daughter, Jane.'

'She thought so too.' said Molly.

Aunt Sarah smiled.

'Still. A wedding is a wedding and it may surprise you to know but they are quite excited at the prospect of being bridesmaids, especially now they've found out it's to a princess. Isn't that right girls?'

They chorused a 'Yes mother'.

'I also hear your servant is going to be your maid of honour?'

Molly nodded slowly.

'Yes.' she replied suspiciously.

'Why choose a servant may I ask?'

'I trust her.'

'Well that's a good enough reason I suppose. Where is she?'

'I'm here, um...'

Gwen stepped forward, blushing furiously as all eyes turned to her. Sarah looked at her critically.

'What is your name girl?'

'It's Gwen, aunt Sarah.' piped in Marcus.

His aunt glared at him with an amused smile.

'I expect she can speak for herself. Can't you dear?'

'Yes ma'am.' replied Gwen quietly, looking at the floor.

Sarah looked at Molly.

'Tilly, Hannah, go with Gwen and show her your dresses. Make sure she approves. Be nice to her or I have no doubt you will feel the back of Her Highnesses hand. Richard, take Marcus and find something to do, you're making the place look untidy.'

The girls left, gathering a nervous looking Gwen and ushering her out. Marcus and Richard followed leaving the women alone.

'Please sit.'

Molly moved a high-backed chair in front of the sisters and sat down. There was a silence for a moment.

'Victoria, have you seen Elsie today?' asked Molly.

The older woman's brow furrowed for a second.

'The scullery maid? No I haven't. Neither have any of the staff. The girl didn't come home after the fair yesterday. Mrs Baddock is quite put out.'

'She seems to have disappeared.' replied Molly.

'Run away more like. She was seen with a boy at the fair.'

'That's probably it,' added aunt Sarah. 'Easier to run away with the boy.'

Molly made a mumbled agreement but something deep inside her was telling her something was wrong.

'Now dear, Victoria tells me you have quite a tale to tell.'

Molly smiled weakly.

'I do. And if you'd like to come with me this afternoon, you can hear it?'

'Why? Where are you going?'

'To the village. I promised yesterday that I would finish telling them the story.'

Aunt Sarah glanced at Victoria.

'Don't look like that. I made a promise.'

Victoria's face said everything. Molly stood.

'If you'll both excuse me, I'm quite tired.'

'Wait.' said aunt Sarah hurriedly. 'We'll come with you this afternoon, the girls and I, if you show me the bracelet I've heard about.'

Molly took a breath and nodded before rolling up her sleeve to show the finely worked silver with its inset sapphire.

Her white eyes flashed blue as in front of her a small vortex of wind formed around the chair, lifting it a foot from the floor. Aunt Sarah gasped in shock as Molly gently placed it back down. She closed her eyes and massaged her temples.

'If you'll excuse me.'

She turned on her heel and walked away, leaving aunt Sarah speechless.

Molly retired early for the night. She had a headache. The afternoon had been nice enough. She'd gone to the village as promised with Gwen, aunt Sarah and the girls in tow.

Tilly and Hannah were scandalised, excited, horrified and a little bit curious when they found the story was being told in the pub. They'd obviously had a very sheltered upbringing but aunt Sarah, well Molly decided that it probably wasn't the first pub she'd been in and from the way the ale went down, it probably wouldn't be the last.

The story has been told and much to the girls' excitement, beer drunk. Lots of people had asked if she was feeling better and Molly was thankful for their concern.

Afterwards they'd made their way back to the house and Molly had gone to bed. She lay back and closed her eyes. The throbbing in her head subsided a little but it was still there. Was she ill? No, she didn't think so. It was something else.

There was a gentle knock at the door. Molly sighed and waited for a moment, hoping whoever it was would go away. The knock came again and she sighed once more before speaking.

'Come.'

Gwen opened the door and came in carrying a tray. On it was a bowl of soup and a thick round of sandwiches alongside a large glass of wine. She placed it on a small table near the bed.

'You've not eaten all day your lady... Um. You're going to be poorly if you don't eat.'

'Gwen...'

The girl gave her a look that Molly hadn't seen before and it brought a smile to her lips. It was the look that said, "Don't mess with me right now, just do as you're told or you'll never hear the end of it.".

Molly shook her head.

'Thank you.'

She went to swing herself out of bed but Gwen wasn't having any of it. The girl fluffed the pillows and placed the tray on Mollys lap.

'How're getting on with Hannah and Tilly?' asked Molly between spoonful's. '…And for God's sake sit down and stop hovering around. I'm not an invalid.'

Gwen did as she was told, self-consciously perching on the end of the bed.

'Sorry Your Ladyship...'

Molly sighed.

'No. I'm sorry. I didn't mean to snap. I just can't be having everyone fussing all the time. Now, please tell me what you think of the girls.'

Gwen looked at her hands.

'You can tell me what you think you know. I wouldn't have asked if I didn't want to know.'

'They're... They're nice.'

'Is that it?

The girl shrugged, still staring at her hands.

'Come on. Tell me. You'll have to stop thinking you're going to get into trouble all the time. This is me you're talking to. I am trouble!'

Gwen smiled sadly, but still wouldn't look up.

'They're nice enough. Polite, but they're looking down their noses at me. They've not said anything but there's just something in the air. They stop talking when I go into a room and there's always a little giggling when they look at me. Like I'm not supposed to be there or something. Like I don't belong. I'm not on their level. Just a servant with ideas above her station.'

Mollys lips hardened into a thin line and anger clouded her face.

'I'll sort it out.' blurted Gwen, 'This is why I didn't want to tell you. I know how you feel about that sort of thing.'

'Let me...'

The girl stood up.

'No. You rest. I'll deal with it. I'm supposed to be in charge of the bridesmaids, remember?'

'Are you sure?'

'Yes. Now finish your soup.'

Molly smiled, despite her anger.

'Do you need anything else?' inquired Gwen.

Molly shook her head.

'No. Thank you.'

'Very good Your Ladyship. The master said he'd be along in a little while.'

She bobbed a curtsey and headed off, pausing at the door as Molly called out.

'I asked about Elsie. I'm sorry but no one's heard anything from her. She didn't come back here. Maybe she went with someone else?'

Even to her own ears, the words sounded hollow.

Gwen nodded, undisguised worry written into her face.

'Thank you for asking.'

Molly watched her go. She'd have to keep an eye on her and the twins. She'd also have to keep an eye out for Elsie. Something didn't feel right.

Molly was in the ornamental garden on the southern side of the house the next day. The sun was shining brightly against a cloudless sky. Marcus walked next to her, pointing out various features of the garden. She glanced across at him as he spoke. He was smiling and for the first time in a few weeks, she could see the man she had fallen in love with.

They stopped at a call from behind and turned to see aunt Sarah walking towards them.

'Aunt Sarah.' acknowledged Marcus as she approached. Molly just smiled.

The older woman patted Marcus' arm in a friendly manner.

'Go and get Richard and find something to do, there's a

good chap.'

Before he could reply, she'd stepped between them and taken Mollys arm, steering her away across the garden.

'I'll see you later then.' he called after them with a confused wave.

'Where are we going?' asked Molly.

'Officially? I'm going to show you the lake house. Unofficially, I'm going to show you lake house and we're going to have a drink. Victoria doesn't approve of drinking really. Says it tarnishes the soul but between you and me, my soul is pretty well tarnished so a little more won't hurt.'

Molly smiled as they walked along. She liked aunt Sarah. She was so much more down to earth than the rest of the family. The older woman spoke as they ambled down towards the lake.

'So how're you finding it so far?'

'Finding what?'

'Being a lady?'

Molly laughed.

'Difficult. I'm not lady material.'

Sarah smiled.

'Well I think you'd better start getting use to it.'

'I don't know if I want to.'

'Why ever not?'

'It just doesn't sit well with me. That's all. I'd probably better face up the fact that I'm never going to be a lady. Not the sort that Marcus deserves.'

'Now you're talking nonsense. Here…'

Aunt Sarah slipped a hipflask from a pocket in her dress and passed it Molly with a wink.

'A little tarnishing won't hurt.'

Molly smiled and took a sip. The liquid inside was fiery and burnt on the way down.

'God, what's in that?' she asked, wiping her mouth with the back of her hand.

The older woman smiled.

'Nothing cheap.'

Molly handed the flask back with a sigh.

'You're the most normal person I've met since I got here. Victoria has given me her blessing but I still think, deep down, that she doesn't really like me. James hates me and has made it perfectly clear that I'm "the wrong sort" and shouldn't be anywhere near his house, let alone his son. The staff at the house go well out of their way to avoid me. I mean, they won't even talk to me. Not properly anyway and in a few days' time, I'm going to be marrying into that.'

They'd reached the lake house. It was a wooden building with a balcony on the front that jutted out across the water. Underneath were two large pontoons that stuck out into the lake.

Aunt Sarah opened the door and went inside with Molly following. They went up a rickety set of steps to the second floor and out onto the balcony.

The older woman took a swig from her hip flask and handed it back to Molly. Neither said anything for a moment, both deep in thought as they stared out across the lake. Aunt Sarah spoke quietly.

'Victoria has had the best in life. She loves James dearly and Marcus even more. It has been hard on her find that he's grown up. He's become a man and found a love of his own, and not the one that she carefully arranged.'

'Lady Samantha's daughter Jane?'

'Yes. Between you and me, that family is on the slide. The marriage between Marcus and Jane would have given stability to them and a nice set of titles and land for Victoria.'

'And then I turned up.'

'So it would seem. You're not at all like the sort of girl I imagined my nephew to fall for.'

'You're not the first person to tell me that.'

'You are however, honest about who and what you are.'

'I suppose.'

The flask was handed back to aunt Sarah.

'Don't fret girl. Secretly, Victoria is over the moon about having a Princess in the family. Even if it's you. With your white eyes, tattoos and uncouth attitude.'

Molly laughed sadly and aunt Sarah turned away from the water, leaning back against the railing and raising the flask to her lips.

'Now take me. I was always the wild one. Got into more scrapes and kissed more boys than was proper. I was always in trouble and my father and mother fretted all the time. I wasn't interested in the "proper sort", even though mother wanted me to marry as best as I could manage.'

'My mother worked hard to secure a marriage between Victoria and James, and thus securing her future at least. Victoria married well and I… Well, I had a good time and when I thought it was right, I married too. My late husband, rest his soul, wasn't rich. Not like James. Not that we wanted for anything mind you. We me at a ball and went from there. The twins were born and a few years after, he died.'

'I'm sorry to hear that.'

Sarah shook her head.

'I've looked after the girls since then. We have enough money to keep us happy and I've tried to keep them away from all of the stuff that I did when I was younger.'

'Why?'

'Respectable ladies don't go drinking till two in the morning or get into fights.'

'So I'm not respectable?'

Aunt Sarah laughed at the look on Mollys face.

'No. You're not. Neither am I. But I want them to be. They'll find good husbands and be happy. That's all I want.'

Molly looked at her, confused.

'I'm sorry, but what has this got to do with me and Marcus?'

'Nothing in particular. But you might want to give Victoria and James a little space and time to get use to the idea that Marcus is marrying someone like you. It's a little close to home for Victoria.'

'Has married.' said Molly.

'What?' asked aunt Sarah.

'Has married. Technically we were married aboard the Endurance. By Captain Brody.'

Aunt Sarah grinned widely.

'I heard about that. I wish I could have been there to see the look on Victoria's face when you told her that. A ship!'

'It was special. I felt I belonged there. With friends and people who cared.'

Aunt Sarah looked at the floor.

'I've only been across to France a couple of times.' she said, changing the subject. 'I've not been halfway around the world.'

'Well it's not all that grand.' said Molly. 'I get terribly sick.'

The older woman laughed and handed the flask back to Molly and then gestured out across the lake and grounds.

'Marcus will inherit all of this when James passes on. Not that that'll be for a few years yet mind.'

Molly lent on the railing and took a pull from the flask.

'About this time last year, I was running for my life and being chased by three men. I was homeless and starving. Now look at me. Apparently, a Princess with servants and a house and a husband.'

'And which would you rather have?' asked aunt Sarah, taking the flask and knocking it back.

'This.'

'Then stop moping about. Use the titles. I bet they can get you into some cracking parties. I expect you've already got a reputation? If not, you will have by the time you get home. Use it. Have some fun. Live a little.'

'But what about Marcus? He expects me...'

'He expects nothing. You'll be the best wife you can in the way you know how. That's all that he wants. Sod the others. They don't matter. So what if the servants don't like you? Who cares? They'll do as you tell them because that's what they're being paid to do!' Aunt Sarah sighed and patted Molly on the shoulder.

'Look. Don't let them get you down. Have fun and enjoy yourself while you can.'

They stared at the water for a little while before aunt Sarah finished the contents of the flask.

'Come on,' she said, 'let's get back and see what's for lunch.'

They wandered back to the house, Molly feeling a little light headed as whatever was in the flask coursed through her system. Aunt Sarah on the other hand, well she looked like she could drink another flask of it and then some.

As they entered the hall, they heard raised voices from the library. They looked at each other and quietly walked to the door. Gwen was stood in the middle with Tilly on one side and Hannah on the other.

The older girls had a small wooden box which they were throwing to each other, just keeping it out of Gwen's reach.

'Give it back!' snapped Gwen.

'Why?' asked Tilly with a smirk.

'Because it's mine. Her Ladyship gave it to me.'

Tilly threw the box back to Hannah who opened it, twisting away from Gwen.

'Well these are nice,' she said, taking a pair of earrings out and holding them up. Gwen made to grab them but she danced to the side and snapped the box shut before throwing it back to her sister. Tilly caught it and took out a matching necklace.

'Give them back.'

'Why would a servant have such expensive things?' asked Hannah snidely.

'I don't think she should.' replied Tilly.

'Maybe we should keep them then.' said her sister.

'But you can't. They're mine.' protested Gwen.

'Not anymore...'

'Is there a problem here?' asked Molly, stepping into the room with a face like thunder. Behind her they could see their mother who looked just as angry.

Hurriedly the girls put their hands behind their backs, hiding the jewellery and box. Gwen looked down at the floor.

'The Princess asked a question.' snapped aunt Sarah.

'No mother.' said Tilly.

'Gwen was just showing us her jewellery.' added Hannah.

'I think you should give it back now, don't you?' said their mother.

The girls nodded and handed the earrings and necklace back. Tilly smirked again as she passed the box back, making sure she let go before Gwen had hold of it properly and it clattered to the floor. Molly went over and picked it up. Gwen couldn't look at her and she could tell the girl was on the verge of tears.

'I would like to have a private word with my maid of honour.' said Molly, emphasising the title.

'Of course, Your Ladyship.' said aunt Sarah. 'Girls. Come with me.'

They filed dutifully out but Molly didn't miss the look that Hannah gave her. The one that said, "Tell on us and you'll regret it.". She also didn't miss the look on aunt Sarah's face and would put money on the twins getting a ferocious earful in a few minutes.

'Sit down.' said Molly as the door closed.

Gwen did as she was told, staring into her lap.

'Do you want to tell me what that was all about?'

'It was nothing.'

'It was.'

The girl shook her head and stood up.

'I'll sort it. Now if there's nothing else you need me for, I'll…'

'Gwen. Please.'

The girl looked at her for a second before she burst into tears.

'They don't like me. I'm a servant. I'm trying but…'

Molly held her for a moment until she'd composed herself.

'I'm sorry.' she said, wiping her eyes with the back of her hand.

'I don't think it's you that needs to be sorry.' replied Molly. 'Shall I speak to them?'

'No. It's fine.'

Molly raised her eyebrows.

'Honestly. They're just…'

'Taking the piss?' said Molly bluntly.

Gwen looked at her, horrified at the language but unable to hide a smile.

'A bit. Yes.'

Molly stood up and went to her.

'Tell me if they ever do anything like that again. I'll make sure I have words.'

The girl smiled tightly.

'Very good Your Ladyship.'

Molly watched her go and shook her head. She really would have to keep an eye on those two.

Chapter Thirteen

Missing

Molly had been for a ride, enjoying the late summer sun as she rode around the estate. Her horse, which she had named Jess, was a fine tempered animal and was a joy to ride.

Molly had taken herself for a look around, it being pretty much the first chance she'd had to go on her own.

The estate was enormous. The lake was bordered by heavy woodland and expansive, but perfectly maintained, lawns. To the north there were more trees and pasture.

The ride gave her time to think.

She would be getting married tomorrow. Again. She smiled at the thought.

Marcus and Richard were staying in the village as Victoria considered it bad luck for the groom to see his bride before the wedding, so reluctantly, on Marcus' part at least, they had gone to the inn.

After a pleasant afternoon, heavy clouds began forming on the horizon and moving quickly towards her, so Molly had returned to the house before it rained.

A servant met her outside and took her horse to the stables. He almost choked when she told him she could do it herself but in the end, she had given in and let him take it. It wasn't worth the trouble arguing which was something she was finding more and more often.

She wandered into the house and up to her room where she changed before heading downstairs. There didn't seem to be anyone around apart from a couple of the smartly dressed servants. She called one over.

'Have you seen Gwen?'

He shook his head nervously and cast a glance towards the maid he was with.

'What?' asked Molly.

There was another sideways glance between the servants.

'Where is she?'

The girl stepped forward, trying not to look at her.

'We, um, you'd better ask the master.'

'Why?'

Both of them clammed up and stood there looking at their feet. Molly sighed angrily and turned away, heading to the study where she found Marcus' father sat behind a large desk.

'Have you seen Gwen?'

He looked up, irritated at being disturbed, more so when he saw who it was.

'Who's Gwen?' he snapped.

'My maid.'

'The thief.'

Molly took a step back.

'What? Gwen wouldn't...'

James reached into a drawer and took out a wooden box, about eight inches to a side which he dropped onto the desk.

'Mr Tanning found her with this. Now I know you have a very lax view of discipline with your household staff but there is no way that I can see that a servant...' he put a spin on the word that made it sound like it was little higher than the dirt beneath his feet. '... A servant could have something like this.'

Molly picked up the box, recognising it immediately. It was the box containing the necklace and earrings that she had given her.

'I gave this to her.'

James looked at her angrily.

'What did you do that for, you stupid girl?'

Mollys face darkened as James continued.

'I can see no reason at all to give a servant something like this, furthermore...'

'She is my maid of honour. You knew that.' said Molly harshly, pointing a finger at him.
'How dare you speak to me like that my girl.'
Molly put her hands on the desk and lent in towards him.
'I am not your girl.'
Her voice was hard with a steely edge.
'Where is she?'
James jumped up.
'You impetuous little...'
Molly banged the desk.
'Where is she?' she shouted.
'Mr Tanning handles staff discipline but I told him to give her a damn good thrashing and to send her on her way.'
'If he's hurt a single hair on her head...'
Molly left that hanging in the air and turned and stormed out.
'How dare you threaten me! Come back here this instant!'
She ignored the rest of tirade directed at her retreating back and headed to the kitchen.

Most of the servants were there, eating their evening meal around the large table and all jumped as Molly crashed through the door. Mr Tanning stood, looking slightly guilty and nervous.
'Can I help you Your Ladyship?' he asked.
The words were barely out of his mouth before Molly grabbed him by his jacket and bodily slammed him down onto the table, sending food and servants scattering.
'Where is she? What have you done with her?' she growled.
The terrified man mumbled incoherently and Molly grabbed a long kitchen knife that had been on the table.
'Where is she?'
He didn't answer but his eyes flicked across to the cellar door. Molly drove the knife into the table an inch from his

ear and let him go. Without another word she strode across, threw the door open and stepped inside.

She had hardly gone down three steps when the door was slammed shut and locked and she was pitched into darkness.

'Gwen?'

Victoria and Sarah arrived quickly with Hannah and Tilly in tow. A terrified maid had come bursting into the sitting room, babbling about how the Princess has gone mad and attacked Mr Tanning and how they'd locked her in the cellar.

The women came quickly to find the kitchen in uproar. Food and plates were scattered all over the place and Mr Tanning was sat on a chair, his hand being held gently by the housekeeper. There was a large kitchen knife driven deep into the table top. He jumped up again.

'What is going on?' demanded Victoria.

'She's gone mad ma'am.' said the housekeeper. 'Burst in here demanding to know where her maid was. Then she attacked Mr Tanning and we locked her in the cellar.'

'Is she still there?' asked aunt Sarah.

There were some nervous glances between the staff.

'Yes ma'am.' replied the housekeeper. 'I haven't seen the like! She was like a wild animal! She...'

'Shut up.' snapped aunt Sarah and the woman went silent in surprise. Her mouth opened and closed a few times before she decided that she'd better not say anything else.

'Where is her maid?' Victoria asked pointedly.

'She's gone your Ladyship. Just as the master ordered.' said Mr Tanning.

Victoria narrowed her eyes at him.

'Just what did he order?'

'I caught her thieving your Ladyship. A necklace and earrings from the Princess. I told the master and he told me to give her a sound thrashing and to send her on her way.

So that's what I did.' his tone was defensive.
 The sisters exchanged glances.
 'You stupid man...'
 Victoria's words were cut off as the door to the cellar exploded outwards, sending wood in all directions. A piece a foot long embedded itself in the wall opposite, missing the housekeeper by inches. She looked at it and then fainted.
 As the dust settled, Molly strode out. Her face was furious and eyes were blacker than the pits of Hell.
 She headed straight to Mr Tanning and grabbed him. Without seeming to try, she hauled him up and slammed him against the wall, holding him in one hand with his feet off the floor. He gibbered in terror.
 'Molly!'
 She felt a hand on her shoulder and saw aunt Sarah standing there.
 'Please let him go.'
 Molly turned back to the man and after a second, she dropped him on the floor and, ignoring everyone else in the kitchen, headed out into the hall. Aunt Sarah recovered first and dragged a young servant to his feet.
 'Go to the village and get master Marcus.'
 The man gawped at her.
 'Hurry.' she snapped.
 'Yes ma'am.'
 He stumbled out of the back door and with another glance at each other, the sisters followed Molly.

 They hurried through the house as ahead of them came a huge splintering crash. They arrived in the hallway to find James standing looking slightly stunned, amidst the wreckage of a large solid oak dresser that had been against the wall. It had taken three men to move it but now it was little more than smouldering matchwood.
 'James?'

He looked at the women.

'What is she doing? How did she do that?'

He gestured to the carnage around him.

'Which way did she go?' asked aunt Sarah.

'What?'

'Where did she go?'

'Upstairs.'

The women picked their way through the mess and onto the stairs. Victoria turned and fixed her husband with a withering state.

'You and I will have words later.'

He opened and closed his mouth a few times but didn't reply and the women quickly headed up the stairs.

Mollys door was wide open and they drew up short just outside. The girl was pulling up a leather jumpsuit and both got a good look at the huge eagle that was tattooed on her back.

They'd known it was there but the sheer size and detail of it was astounding. It covered almost all her back, with its wings running up over her shoulders and upper arms.

'Molly?' said aunt Sarah hesitantly.

Tilly and Hannah joined them on the landing.

'What's she doing?' whispered one of the but was shushed into silence by Victoria. Aunt Sarah looked at them and then stepped into the room.

'Molly. I think that's quite enough. Don't you?'

The girl turned. Her face was deathly pale and drawn with her eyes nothing but black orbs.

'Don't tell me what to do.'

Her voice was wrong. As if there were several people speaking at once.

She finished buckling up the front of her suit and picked up her sword from the bed which she strapped to her back.

'What're you going to do?'

'Find Gwen.'

'But you can't go now. It's dark and raining. You'll never

find her.'

Molly pinched the bridge of her nose and frowned as if she were in pain. Aunt Sarah took another step towards her.

'Are you alright?'

Molly looked up.

'Get out.'

The older woman made no move.

'I don't think...'

'Get out!' Molly shouted at her. 'Get out and leave us alone! Get out now!'

Aunt Sarah stumbled backwards and out of the door as around her the temperature dropped and a deep sense of fear fell across the room.

She was barely across the threshold before the door slammed shut. The sense of fear intensified and she could see it in the eyes of the others on the landing. Tilly burst into tears and Victoria was shaking visibly.

There was a crash of breaking glass and then a moment later the terror began to subside leaving all of them shaken. None of them said anything for several minutes until Victoria managed to stammer.

'What was that?'

Aunt Sarah let out a breath she didn't know she was holding and shook her head.

'I don't know.'

With a trembling hand, she reached out and touched the door handle. It was icy cold. With another look at the women on the landing, Sarah turned the handle and the door fell open. The room was deserted. The large window to the left was broken and the rain was beginning to lash in from the driving wind outside.

They all stepped inside, subconsciously keeping in a tight group for protection. Their breath misted in front of their faces and aunt Sarah could see ice on the water in the wash basin.

'Where's she gone?' whispered Hannah, her voice still laden with fear.

Aunt Sarah straightened.

'I don't know.'

Gwen stumbled down the muddy track. She was lost, cold and hurting. Tears stung her eyes almost as much as the wind driven rain and her back, bottom and legs were raw from the beating she'd been given at the house.

She tried to remember how it had happened but it was all a bit of a blur. She'd been looking at the necklace and earrings that Molly had given her when the Mr Tanning had come to her room for something.

He'd seen the jewellery and accused her of stealing it. Her protests earned her nothing but a clip round the ear and he'd dragged her off to see the master of the house. The old man was just as vocal, agreeing with his household staff and once more, her protests had earned her another slap, this one catching her in the side of the face and splitting her lip.

The master told his man to "teach the little thief a lesson" and she was promptly dragged to the kitchen where two of the younger lads held her down across the kitchen table while the butler took his belt to her.

She'd lost count of the number of times he struck her but by the time he'd finished, her back and bottom were a blur of pain and she couldn't see through the tears.

One of the lads hauled her up and half dragged, half led out of the door, his grip on her arm tight and painful. He marched her out of the house and down a muddy lane for about half a mile before he pushed her roughly against a tree, deciding that he could have a little fun of his own.

His groping hand touched her once before she kneed him hard in the groin and ran off. Now she was lost. The night had come in fast along with the wind and rain. What's more, the trees had run out and she found herself scrambling along a muddy path through a field.

She shivered uncontrollably. She was wet through, with no money and nothing to her name. She daren't go back to the house, even if she knew where it was.

A peal of thunder sounded, deafeningly loud in the night, and she almost screamed as a flash of lightning lit up the field. Clamping her hands over her ears, she ran as fast as she could through the growing storm until she could run no longer. The pain from her back, the cold, the fear and sheer exhaustion got the better of her and she fell headlong into the mud and lay still.

Chapter Fourteen

Ancient History
1729 AD

Father William Sashford ushered the last of his congregation out of the church and locked the door. He was a tall man with a wiry frame and blue eyes. His greying hair was thinning on top but at sixty, he thought he was doing well.

He had been performing the Lords work here at the church for nearly forty years and soon it would be time for him to choose a successor. He probably should have done it before now but there was always so much to do.

In the two-hundred or so years the church had been standing, the current priest would choose a lad to supplant him when it was time. There were many things that the new priest had to know. Secrets that had to be passed down, as they had been from the monks that built this place after their abbey had been destroyed. The evil that their faith had to keep in check and the dark stain it had left on the monks.

He recalled the time when Father Bartholomew had told him.

'Listen closely boy.' the old man had said. 'I have much to show you and little time left to do it.'

The father had been in his late fifties but cancer and failing eyesight were ravishing his body. The old mad had peered at him intently with his rheumy eyes before asking,

'Is your faith strong boy?'

William had nodded.

'Yes Father.'

'It had better be. Lock the door.'

He had done as he was told and walked back to the man in the centre of the church. He was staring up at the ornately carved ceiling. Not really seeing but there was a wistful look on his face. As William had neared, the old man looked down.

'Are you ready?'

'What for?'

The old priest had frowned and walked towards the back of the church to where the sarcophagus of St George lay.

'Come here.'

William had followed and stood next to him.

'What do you see?' the old man had asked.

Now it was William's turn to frown. He'd seen this sarcophagus hundreds of times. It was about waist high and made of stone. Deep inscriptions were carved around the edges although William had never managed to decipher them. He supposed they were a variation of Latin that he hadn't been taught. Laid flat on the top was a stylised carving of a knight with his sword clasped to his chest in both hands.

'Well?' the priest had demanded. 'What do you see?'

'Saint George?' he'd ventured, only to be rewarded by a clip round the ear.

'Look again.'

He'd stared at the stone knight for a good few minutes before the old priest spoke again.

'Look at what's hiding in plain sight.'

He reached up and twisted the pommel of the stone sword. There was a grinding noise and the whole top of the sarcophagus slid back, while a portion of the side dropped into the floor revealing a dark staircase that led down.

The old priest looked at him once more.

'Is your faith strong?'

William had swallowed as he looked down into the darkness. Eventually he'd just nodded.

'Good. Follow me.'

He'd been led down the stairs and into a musty room with alcoves cut in the stone. In each was a skeleton. The old man lit a torch and ignored the bodies completely.

'Where are we?'

'This is where the monks that built the church were laid to rest.' he said, as he pressed a hidden switch, closing the sarcophagus above them with a resounding thud.

'I heard they all disappeared.'

'No. They're here. Protecting us with their faith even unto death.'

'I don't understand.'

'You don't need to understand. Just come with me.'

He headed off down another flight of steps and then into another short corridor which ended in a heavy wooden door. Reaching into his vestments, the priest had produced an iron key. After unlocking the door, he had paused, turning back to William.

'What do you know of the monks?'

'Monks?'

'The ones who built the church?'

William had thought about it.

'They built the church after the abbey was burnt down. They lost quite a few of their number and moved here. I've read that not one of them said a word after the abbey was destroyed and they worked themselves to death. Although none of their bodies were ever found.'

'True enough.' The priest had replied. 'True but also wrong.'

He heaved the door open.

'The monks were protecting something. Something dark. It was brought back from the crusades. Back from Jerusalem. They looked after it until the fire. It caused the fire you see.'

'What was it?'

'A book.'

'How can a book start a fire?'

The old priest had frowned and turned away, heading into another small stone room and unlocking a door on the far side with William following on behind.

'The abbey was built above some old caves. There's miles of them. They crisscross the land, cut out of the stone by God knows who and for God knows what purpose. The monks built the church here because it was above an entrance to the tunnels. They needed to get back in. Even though they didn't want to, they had to make sure it wasn't free.'

'What wasn't?' William was more confused now that ever.

The door led into another corridor but this one was hand carved from the sandstone. It ran straight for around a mile before ending in a round room with three other corridors leading off it. Father Bartholomew headed off down one of them until they reached another heavy door. This one had a large lock but also a stout wooden beam across it, held in place by two iron brackets.

The priest removed the bar from the door and William saw that underneath there were symbols painted onto the wood. There was a large cross and above and below that, a representation of a chain. These were alongside some deeply carved crosses and other more occult looking symbols.

'You must never open this door. There is no key so I don't know what's beyond it. I do know that it's the book the monks were protecting.'

William swallowed nervously. An unsettling fear had wormed its way into his stomach.

'You can feel it, can't you?' said the priest.

He nodded.

'What was it?'

'Carnothal.'

'What's that?'

'Not what. Who. A demon. A thrice cursed monster from Hell, bound and sealed in a book. Our faith is what is stopping its spirit from escaping.'

'A demon?'

Now William was worried. The fear grew and he wanted to run away.

'You are going to take over from me as its keeper. We have to keep it imprisoned. If someone were to get hold of the book and to let it out…'

The old man shook his head.

'Well it doesn't bear thinking about. Give me your hand.'

William looked at him in surprise.

'What?'

The old man grabbed his arm and slapped his palm against the wood. It was oddly warm and instantly he was filled with anger and rage. He tried to pull away but the old man held him fast.

'Let go of me.' He'd shouted. 'Let me go. I'll kill you…'

Father Bartholomew had smiled before he drew a knife and drove the point of it through Williams hand, pinning it to the wood.

He'd screamed as the pain lanced through him and could only watch as the old man dipped his finger in the blood pouring from the wound and drew over the marks of the cross and chains on the door.

'You can feel the anger, can't you? Trust in the Lord and you will prevail. Fight the temptation of the demon. Your faith is stronger than he!'

William screamed again as the priest pulled the knife out, wrenching it from the wood and his hand in a spray of blood. The last thing he remembered was father Bartholomew smiling as he'd slipped to the floor.

William had awoken to find himself laid out flat on the floor of the church. His hand had been bandaged but ached like nothing else he'd ever felt. He sat up and looked around.

Night had fallen and the church was lit by hundreds of candles. Knelt in front of the altar was father Bartholomew. His hands were clasped and William could hear him praying softly. He stood and walked unsteadily over to the priest.

'Father?' he asked quietly.

It was a moment before the old man replied.

'Look to the cross.'

Williams brow furrowed but he did as he was told. On the altar stood a gold cross. It glinted in the candlelight and in that instant, William knew. The spots of flickering light dazzled him and he knew. God was with him. He would always be with him.

Father Bartholomew had smiled kindly.

'Your blood is bound to the church now. When I go, you will take over. We will keep the dark forces at bay.'

The priest smiled at the recollection of Father Bartholomew. The old man had finally died after another eight years. By the end, his body was bent and warped and his mind had started to fail. It was a blessing that he lasted so long but, William was ashamed to admit, it was also a blessing that he had now gone to a better place.

He sighed. Such thoughts were unbecoming of one such as he. His faith was as strong now as it had been. Now to put the faith to use.

Checking the church was empty and secure, he walked to the sarcophagus of Saint George as he had done twice a month for the last fifty years.

He twisted the pommel of the sword and the lid slid back. Checking the church was empty once more, he went down the steps into the dark.

From his vantage point in the entrance to the church tower, the shadowy cloaked figure watched the priest descend. He smiled to himself, the ritual scars on his face twisting and making his humour dark.

They had found it. After four hundred years of searching, the brotherhood had found its resting place. Quietly he slipped out of the tower and followed.

William lit the lantern that he picked up from the floor of the monks resting chamber. He offered a small prayer, as he always did, to those that were laid to rest in the alcoves before heading down further.

Unease settled across him as he reached the door in the sandstone. The heavy wood still marked with the cross and chains which William now knew were drawn in blood. His blood, Father Bartholomew's' blood and the blood of countless faithful before him.

Habitually, he gripped the silver cross he wore on a chain around his neck and said another small prayer before lifting the heavy wooden beam from the iron brackets and placed it on the floor.

As if sensing the movement, his senses were assaulted by the anger of what was imprisoned beyond the wooden portal.

'I cast thee aside, demon.' muttered William, reaching into his robes to produce a small vial containing a mix of thrice blessed holy water and his blood.

Taking a deep breath, he un-stoppered the bottle dipped his finger in the mixture. As he raised his hand to re-draw the symbols he was startled by a voice from close behind him.

'Don't.'

The vial fell from his grasp and shattered, splashing the contents across the stone floor. William turned around to see a man with a deep hooded cloak wrapped around him.

'What...' he began before the man hit him in the chest with his open palm. The blow knocked him back a step and he suddenly felt his heart and lungs gripped like a vice. He dropped to his knees as the man threw back his hood to reveal a face and shaved head covered in scars in the shape of circles and stars.

The man crouched down as William struggled to breath.

'Carnothal has been bound for a long time. We have searched for him for centuries. You will not bind him any longer.'

William gasped. He couldn't breathe. Feebly he clutched the hem of the intruders' robe as the man curled his hand into a fist. The pain intensified and William fell on his face.

'Carnothal will have to wait a little longer for release. It will be another eighty years until the powers are aligned and the historic wards are weak enough but the brotherhood is patient. I have found him but it will be another to have the honour of unleashing him.'

The scarred man watched, as on the floor William died, his heart and lungs crushed from inside, never having the chance to pass his knowledge onto the next priest of the parish.

His last thoughts were that he had failed. The secret was now held by another. One who would not keep the thing imprisoned...

Chapter Fifteen

Deep Trouble

Gwen awoke with a start. Her head was swimming and body ached and it took her a moment to realise she wasn't in the field. Underneath her was a solid stone floor and someone had covered her with a blanket. It was a coarse weave and was itchy but it was warm. Gingerly she sat up, her body protesting at the slightest movement.

She looked around. She was in a rough cut low stone room about six feet across and four or five deep. The far wall was made up of iron bars with a hinged portion to act as a door.

A couple of candles burnt in an alcove outside and she could see a similar prison across the way from her. Beginning to panic, she scrambled to the bars and found them solid.

'Hey. Help!' she shouted, rattling the bars.

There was movement from the cell across the corridor.

'Shhh. Don't shout. He'll hurt you if you shout.' came a whispered warning.

Gwen let go of the bars and sat on her heels.

'Elsie?'

'Gwen?'

'Oh my god Elsie. What happened to you?'

The girl in the cell across from her moved towards the bars and into the poor light of the candles. Her face was bruised and she had a black eye.

'Are you alright?' asked Gwen.

'Not really. I'm scared.'

'Where are we? What's going on?'

Elsie shook her head.

'I don't know. There were half a dozen other girls here when I was brought here. He comes and takes one every day. They don't come back.'

'Who does? Elise what happened?'

There was a heavy clunk and the sound of a door on squealing hinges. Elsie scurried back away from the bars into the shadows, her face a mask of fear.

In the narrow corridor beyond the bars came heavy footsteps which resolved to belong to a man wearing a heavy black robe with a deep hood which hid his features. He placed two plates, one outside each cell along with a couple of battered tin cups.

Gwen shifted back away from him until her back hit the wall. He turned and regarded her. The hood giving him an evil, unearthly look and even though Gwen couldn't see his face, she could feel his eyes boring in to her.

'Eat.'

His voice was thick and loud in the small space.

'Eat.'

She glanced at the plate, it held some bread and cheese and her stomach rumbled, she couldn't remember when she'd eaten last. With a glance at the other cell and seeing no sign of Elsie, Gwen cautiously moved to the bars, never taking her eyes off the man. He nudged the metal plate closer to the bars with his toe.

Gingerly Gwen reached through the bars and as her fingers touched the food, he bent and grabbed her wrist, yanking her forward and into the bars. She cried out as her head struck the metal and tried to pull back but he was too strong for her.

He reached through and grabbed her other arm, pulling it through ironwork. He held both her wrists tightly in one of his hands and dragged her back so her face was pressed against the metal.

'You do not shout. You do not make any noise at all. Do you understand?'

Gwen nodded as much as she could.

'I understand!'

He reached into his robe and produced a rough length of rope which he used to tie her wrists together, with an iron bar between them. He knotted it tightly before picking up her plate of food. The cup he left on the floor. Just out of her reach.

'Do you understand?'

'Yes.' Gwen sobbed quietly.

'Good.'

He turned and walked away, leaving Gwen with her wrists bound to one of the bars. The door squealed closed and was locked. A second later, Elsie hurried up to the bars of her cell.

'Gwen? Are you alright?'

She shook her head, struggling against the ropes around her wrists but they were fastened tightly. She heaved herself into a sitting position. Elsie watched her for a second.

'If you're quiet, he doesn't hurt you. I learned that.' she whispered, pointing to the bruises on her face.

Carefully, Elsie broke the bread and cheese on her plate in two and tossed a piece of each across to Gwen. Awkwardly, she stretched to pick them up.

'Thank you.'

They ate in silence, Gwen having trouble with the food until she found a way to get it in her mouth with her hands bound on the other side of the bars.

'Do you know where we are?' she asked, longingly looking at the cup of water that was just out of reach.

Elsie shook her head.

'No idea. I woke up here.'

'What about the cellar of the house?'

'No. We're not there. I should know.'

'What happened to you? Last time I saw you was at the fair. That was a week ago.'

Elsie shrugged.

'I left John at the fair a few minutes after you left. I thought it wasn't worth the trouble I'd get into, fun though it would have been.'

'I was walking along the road when a cart came up behind. I looked at it and moved over. Then someone grabbed me from behind. Next thing I knew I'd got a sack over my head and they trussed me up like a turkey. I tried to scream but they hit me on the head I think. After that...' she shrugged again. 'what about you?'

Gwen told her the events of the day, feeling detached from the words as if it hadn't happened to her.

'I always knew old Tanning was a bastard.'

'I think they did it in purpose. They don't want Molly in the family.'

'Is Molly Her Ladyship?'

Gwen nodded.

'She lets you call her that?' asked Elsie with disbelief in her voice.

'She insisted. But it is a bit weird. I mean, she's my employer. It seems impolite.'

'She's not normal for a toff.' replied Elsie, idly picking at the hem of her dirty dress.

'I wouldn't know.' said Gwen. 'She's the only one I've ever known. She's nice though. A bit distant sometimes and she doesn't like me doing things for her. Even though that's my job and that's what they pay me for.'

'Definitely not a normal toff. The lot up at the house are alright but nothing like that. Some of their guests though! They'd expect you to wipe their arse if they thought they'd get away with it. It's the women who are the worst. The men tend to ignore you, unless they've got wandering hands that is, but the women are usually mean and spiteful. You're there to do their bidding and they make sure you know it.'

'Molly isn't like that.' said Gwen quietly, resting her head against the bars.

'No.' agreed Elsie. 'Your mistress is alright. She showed me her tattoo!'

'She got that in India. Along with her bad dreams.'

'What happened?'

'Well you heard the story that she told.'

'About the magic stones?'

Gwen nodded.

'There were other things that happened. But she won't talk about them. Not even to the master. I only know by accident. She talks in her sleep sometimes. When he isn't there. That's when the dreams are the worst. I've sat with her at night, listening to her cry. Someone called... ' Gwen tried to remember the name. '...someone called Malnar I think. He did something to her. Hurt her. She's scared of him.'

They both lapsed into silence, lost in their own thoughts.

'Well she can't just have disappeared. She must have climbed out of the window or something.' exclaimed Richard.

He and Marcus had been rudely interrupted at the inn by a frantic and soaking young servant from the house. He looked like he'd run all the way to the village and there was real fear in his eyes as he burst through the door.

They'd given him a brandy and after he'd stopped coughing at the strong liquor and calmed down a bit, they managed to get the story out of him.

'She's gone mad sir! Lady Crawford sent me to get you. You'd better hurry, she almost killed Mr Tanning and then she exploded the cellar door. The kitchen is a right state sir. She's gone mad!'

They quickly had their horses saddled and rode as fast as they could through the growing storm to the house.

Aunt Sarah and his mother were stood in the hallway while a couple of servants were sweeping up a pile of broken wood. His father was scowling and stood off to one side, while the girls, Tilly and Hannah were sat on the stairs. Both looked scared and both had been crying.

'Mother! What's going on?'

The older women exchanged looks.

'Your fiancé has gone.' said his mother eventually.

'Gone? Gone where?'

They'd all retired to the drawing room where they could talk. Aunt Sarah had explained what had happened and then what the women had seen and felt. Marcus paced up and down.

'She didn't climb out of the window.'

'She must have done, otherwise...'

'Drop it Richard.' snapped Marcus testily. 'She didn't climb out.'

'Well what did she do? Fly?'

Marcus ignored him.

'I'm going to find her.'

He moved towards the door and his aunt laid a hand on his arm.

'You'll never find her. Not in this weather. Wait until the storm clears in the morning.'

'I can't,' replied Marcus with a shake of his head. 'I lost her in India and that was one of the hardest things I've ever done. I swore I'd never lose her again.'

Outside a huge peal of thunder sounded alongside a brilliant flash of lightening. Richard stepped up to his friend.

'Mother is right. We'll look in the morning. It's not good looking tonight.'

His words were surprisingly soft and kind and Marcus closed his eyes.

'I promised myself I'd never ever let her be alone again.'

'Well I say good riddance.'

Marcus turned quickly to look at his father. The old man was sat in an armchair by the fire and looked troubled.

Since Molly had destroyed the dresser in the hallway he hadn't said much but had downed three or four large brandies.

'Father. I know you don't like Molly but you've gone too far.'

'Marcus!'

He looked at his mother.

'I'm sorry but it's true. None of us, me included, has made her feel welcome here. Well that stops now. I'll find her and bring her back and then I'm marrying her. That's the end of it.'

His father rose, somewhat unsteadily, to his feet.

'Now look here...'

'No father. She gave her life to save me. I love her and am marrying her whether you like it or not. Hell, I have married her! This is just for show to impress your friends. As far as I'm concerned, she is my wife and I will not let her be belittled any longer. I don't care what you think and you can cut me out of your will and disown me for all the good it will do you. She is part of my family. She *is* my family and I'll not stand by while she is in trouble.'

He turned and stormed out, slamming the door behind him.

The silence that he left in his wake was tense and embarrassed.

Richard looked around and could sense that Victoria was about to give her husband a piece of her mind.

'I'll go after him. Tilly, Hannah you come too.'

The girls could also feel the oncoming tirade and hurried after their brother. They found Marcus in the hall, standing in the doorway and staring out into the driving rain. Richard glanced at his sisters before putting a hand on his friends' shoulder.

'Marcus. We'll find her in the morning. I promise.'

There was no answer forthcoming. Richard guiltily looked at the girls again.

'I'm sorry Marcus. You're right. I've been nothing but rude to her since I arrived. I...'

Marcus sighed.

'You're not the only one. I've neglected her. I knew how she was feeling before we came but I still did nothing to help. If anything has happened to her, I'll never forgive myself.'

Outside the thunder cracked again.

'Come back in. Have a drink or something. She'll be fine. She's seems a very capable woman.'

'No. I'm going to bed. I want to be out at first light.'

Gwen snapped awake at the squeal of hinges and the heavy footsteps. She had fallen asleep and her body and shoulders protested as she moved. Her bound arms had forced her to sleep at an uncomfortable angle and preventing her from even reaching her blanket.

She shivered uncontrollably. Across the way, Elsie was twitching fitfully in sleep until the man in the black robe kicked the bars. She jerked up and scampered to the back of the cell.

Gwen tried to pull back but her bound wrists stopped her. From the folds of his robe he pulled a knife before crouching down in front of her. He took her hands and hauled her forward until her face pressed against the bars.

'Are you going to be good?'

Gwen nodded, fearful eyes unable to leave the knife in his hand. The blade moved forward slowly until it's tip rested against her cheek.

'Are you going to make a single sound?'

She shook her head, the movement small as she tried not to cut herself on his blade. The hood regarded her intently and she could feel the tears rolling down her cheeks.

'This was your only warning. Understand? If I need to tell you again, you will regret it.'

He moved the blade and slit the ropes at her wrists and

Gwen pulled back quickly. The man straightened and pushed the cup of water close to the bars with his boot. With a final look at the girls, he turned and left.

Gwen didn't know what to do first. Massage some life back into her hands, drink the water or burst into tears. In the end, she did the latter. Elsie moved back to the bars.

'Are you alright?' she asked softly.

'No.'

Taking a deep breath, she tried to pull herself together. Still shivering, she grabbed the blanket and wrapped it around her shoulders before reaching through and taking the cup. It was too big to fit through the bars but she managed to get the water into her mouth. It was chilly and tasted stale, but oh so good.

The next day dawned bright and clear. Marcus and Richard rode out as the sun was coming up. Aunt Sarah rose early too. The previous evening had been tense and she had left Victoria and James in the drawing room.

Despite his bluster and pomposity, the poor man stood no chance against his wife. She almost felt sorry for him. Almost.

She hadn't slept well, the look on Mollys face had been something to behold as was the feeling of absolute dread that had settled over them. But there was something else. Something she had said. "Leave us alone." Who were "*us*"?

She decided she probably ought to talk to Marcus before he left but missed him by about five minutes. Deciding on a course of action, she woke Tilly and Hannah and after a small breakfast they headed out to see if they could find Molly or her maid.

The girls were understandably nervous, as was she, but nevertheless they left the house with a firm aim in mind. The grass around the estate was wet from the overnight rain but the day promised to be good.

'Where are we going to look mother?' Tilly enquired as they walked through the ornamental gardens.

Aunt Sarah stopped and looked around, deep in thought for a few moments.

'We'll try the lake house. Come on.'

They all trudged to the lake and skirted it until they arrived at the wooden structure. The building looked forbidding with its shadowed windows giving nothing away.

Aunt Sarah tried to push the thoughts of dark and evil forces from her mind and put her hand on the door but that just made it worse. A quick glance at the girls and she saw they were feeling something similar.

'Are you sure it's safe mother? I don't like this place.' said Hannah.

She was about to tell her to stop being silly when she realised she knew what she meant. There was something in the air. A bit like they had felt last night. Aunt Sarah licked her lips.

'Wait here.'

With a deep breath, she pushed the door open.

Inside the room was dark. She could hear the lapping of the water and smell the damp wood hung in the air.

'Molly? Are you here?'

Her voice was barely a whisper and croaked from her throat. All she wanted to do was leave and that was precisely why she didn't. Moving further into the gloom she cracked her shin on something and swore loudly.

Behind her the door creaked open and she jumped.

'Mother?'

It was Tilly. She sounded scared.

Aunt Sarah closed her eyes, fighting down the urge to run and hide. Taking a deep breath, she called out, hoping the building fear didn't sound in her voice.

'Molly! I know you're in here.'

Around her the shadows grew and the temperature

dropped.

'Mother?'

Both of the girls had moved inside and their hands found those of their mother. Bolstered by their presence, if not their courage, aunt Sarah called out again.

'We're not leaving.'

The echoes of her voice had hardly disappeared when the feeling of dread lifted slightly and the morning sun broke through the gloom. Aunt Sarah saw Molly straight away. She was in the corner of the building, sat on the floor with her knees pulled up to her chin and pressed into the corner as far as she could get.

'Go and find Marcus and Richard.'

Tilly and Hannah hesitated.

'Now!'

They hurried away. Aunt Sarah watched them go before slowly walking over to Molly. As she got closer she could see that the girl was cold and wet. Her hair hung in lank rivulets down to her shoulders and she was shivering. On the floor next to her was a knife, its long blade covered in blood. There was a tear in her leather suit in the thigh which was also covered in blood.

'Molly. It's me. Aunt Sarah.'

'Leave me alone.'

Aunt Sarah wasn't sure but she could have sworn Mollys words were shrouded by a black mist which formed in the air in front of her face. Looking around, she grabbed an old sack which she tore to make a makeshift blanket.

'We were worried about you.'

She glanced down at the knife again.

'Are you hurt?'

Molly shook her head. The older woman edged closer until she could wrap the sack around her shoulders before she reached into a pocket in her dress and produced her battered hip flask and took a swig.

'Here.'

Molly looked at it for a moment and then took it with trembling hands.

'You look frozen. Come back to the house and warm up.'

'I can't.'

'Why not?'

She didn't answer straight away but when she did, Sarah almost felt her heart break. She had never ever seen anyone look so lost or sad before.

'They all hate me and I need to find Gwen.'

'Marcus and Richard are out looking for your maid...'

'She's called Gwen.'

'Gwen. Marcus and Richard are looking for her.'

'They won't find her. She's gone. I've let her down.'

'Come back to the house...'

'They all hate me. I can see it in their faces.'

Aunt Sarah sat down next to Molly and took the flask back.

'They don't hate you. No one hates you. They're scared of you.'

She didn't add the final thought "I'm scared of you".

'They should be scared. I'm a monster. A freak.'

Aunt Sarah took a swig and pressed the flask back into Molly's hands.

'You're not either of those things.'

'I lost my temper yesterday.' said Molly quietly, staring at the water. 'It all came out. The house, the people, the attitudes. When I found out they'd hurt Gwen I lost it. I've never ever felt so angry in my life. Not even when...' she tailed off as an uncomfortable memory skirted across the surface. She took a long drink from the flask and looked at aunt Sarah.

'If you hadn't stopped me. I would have killed him.'

'No you wouldn't.'

'I would have.'

Sarah felt a shiver run down her spine at the girls' tone. She cleared her throat and tried to change the subject.

'Let's get you back and warmed up.'

She stood and Molly allowed her to help her up. Under her hands, Sarah could feel the girl shivering.

'Why are you being nice to me?'

The older woman looked at her in surprise.

'What sort of question is that? It's about time someone was. Come on. I promise that when we get back, you'll be left alone. None of the servants will come anywhere near you.'

Chapter Sixteen

Wedding Bells

About an hour later, Molly was sat on a bed in a new room with a blanket wrapped around her shoulders. Marcus had seen her and, apart from a small admonishment that was less than she deserved, he'd been happy she was alright.

He'd wanted to stay with her but she didn't feel like company. Once more, she wished she could talk to Nareema. She let out a deep sigh. Where was Gwen? There was a timid knock at the door.

'Come.' she said wearily.

There was a hushed argument outside before the door opened. It was Tilly and Hannah. They stood in the doorway like naughty children.

'Come in. I won't bite.'

They looked at each other before stepping into the room. They kept a respectful distance, which Molly could tell gave them enough space to run if she turned into a ravenous beast. She smiled slightly.

'What can I do for you?'

Once more they looked at each other before Tilly spoke.

'We, um... Your Highness... We...'

Molly sighed and rubbed her eyes.

'My name is Molly. That's it. Just Molly.'

Her words were angrier than she intended and the girls clammed up straight away. She sighed again.

'I'm sorry. Look, I've had a difficult night and I'm a bit tired. What can I do for you?'

There was some nudging and an unspoken argument consisting of pointed looks and raised eyebrows. Eventually Hannah spoke.

'We're sorry.'

'What for?'

'We... We weren't that kind to your maid... To Gwen.' she said, hurriedly correcting herself as she caught the look on Molly's face. 'We were rude and we're sorry.'

Molly looked at them and they wilted under her white gaze.

'I know how you were with her. She told me and I heard you, remember?'

The girls looked at the floor.

'We also told Mr Tanning that she'd stolen the necklace.'

'But you knew that I'd given it to her?'

They nodded.

'Do you know what they did to her?'

A shake of the heads?

'They took her to the kitchen and Mr Tanning beat her with his belt before they threw her out in the storm!'

They were shocked.

We didn't mean...' began Tilly.

'Yes you did.' snapped Molly. 'You knew exactly what you were doing.'

She stood and the girls took a fearful step back.

'It was mean and spiteful. Why did you do it?'

'We…'

'We don't know. She's not like us.' said Hannah.

'And I thank God for that! She's a good girl. Gentle and caring. You two on the other hand…' Molly turned away and looked out of the window.

'What're you going to do?' asked Tilly tentatively.

'Are you going to tell our mother?'

Molly sighed. There was nothing she could do about it now.

'No. I'm not. But I expect both of you to apologise to Gwen when she is found. You'll tell her exactly what you've done and ask for her forgiveness. Is that clear?'

The girls bobbed a curtsey and chorused "Yes, Your Highness".

'The quicker you learn that servants are people and not things, the better your lives will be. I will be watching you both carefully from now on. Do you understand?'

The girls looked at each other, shifting uncomfortably from foot to foot.

'Is there anything else?'

'Um... Your High... Um… Mother said that we should help you get ready. As your... as Gwen isn't here.'

'Get ready? Ready for what?'

'Your wedding.'

'Wedding? I can't get married!'

'Aunt Victoria was most insistent. Marcus and Richard have already left for the village and the guests will begin to arrive in a few hours.'

'I'm not getting married today. Gwen isn't here...'

'We'll stand in for her. You won't want for anything.' said Tilly hurriedly.

'That's not the point! I...'

'Well I hope I haven't come all this way for nothing lass.'

Molly shut her mouth at the new voice before breaking into a huge grin. Standing in the doorway was a large man with a bald head and a scar down one cheek. He was smiling widely.

'Captain Brody!'

Molly dashed over and gave him a hug, almost knocking him off his feet.

'Steady on lass! And you should know by now that my name is Owain. I've retired. I'm not a Captain any longer.'

Owain Brody had been the Captain of the Endurance, a merchant vessel originally chartered to take them all to Portugal on their quest for the Stones of Gunjai.

Since then, they'd been through a lot together and Molly owed him and his crew a lot. It was the Captain that had married her and Marcus the first time.

'What are you doing here?'

'Marcus dropped into Nancy's place a week back to see

me.'

'I hope that's all he saw!' replied Molly and Brody smiled. His fiancé Nancy ran a brothel in Gosport.

'Aye lass. That's all he saw. You have my word on it.' Brody didn't mention Richard. He'd seen plenty!

'Marcus said you needed someone to give you away. So, if you'll accept the arm of a worn-out old pirate then I'll be glad to oblige.' he bowed theatrically.

'I can't get married. Gwen...'

'I've heard about that too. Davis is in the village now, rustling up a few local lads we'll have her found in no time.'

'Mr Davis is here too?'

'Aye lass. You're like a daughter to him! He'd not miss his child get wed. Again.'

Molly smiled. The low feelings of the morning and previous night lifting slightly.

'Now. Don't you worry about a thing. I'm sure these charming ladies...' he turned to Tilly and Hannah, bowing low before kissing their hands. The girls giggled embarrassedly, flattered by the attention. '... These charming and beautiful ladies will be able to help you get ready.'

Molly bit her lip. It was all organised and there were guests arriving for a ball later whether she got married or not.

'I suppose it's all sorted out, isn't it?'

'It is.' chorused the girls.

Molly knew that she was only trying to convince herself, and Captain Brody had come all this way...

'Alright. As long as someone tells me as soon as Gwen is found.'

Brody grinned.

'Of course lass. Now, get yourself ready.'

He gave her a peck on the cheek and headed out of the room, calling loudly for a servant or someone to show him to a room. Molly smiled. She could see that he'd get on famously with aunt Sarah. James and Victoria? Maybe not so much. She turned to the girls.

'Right. Off and change, both of you.'

'Don't you need us to help you dress?' enquired Hannah.

'No. I can manage that myself I'm sure. I will probably need some assistance later.'

The girls hesitated for a second before bobbing a curtsey and hurrying away. Molly followed them and closed the door. Looks she was getting married after all.

Gwen was huddled in the corner of the cell, for that's what it was, when the cloaked man came back. He ran a large, heavy looking wooden stick along the bars and they rang ominously.

'Wake up!'

Gwen pushed herself back as far as she could go. The hood looked in her direction once before unlocking the door to Elsie's prison. He pushed inside and there was a brief scuffle followed by a ringing slap. The man emerged from the shadows, dragging a crying Elsie by the hair. Gwen rushed to the bars.

'Get off her!'

The man snarled and rapped the wooden stick hard against the metal, missing Gwen's fingers by less than an inch. She fell back.

'Shut up if you know what's good for you.'

Elsie fought him as he dragged her along but he brought the stick down hard against the backs of her legs and she dropped to her knees. He hauled her up again and off down the corridor.

The door squealed open and then shut with a resounding bang, blocking off Elsie's sobbing cries. Gwen looked out of the bars, tears flowing freely. What was he going to do? Where had he taken her?

She moved back into the corner and wrapped the itchy blanket around her. She sat in a disturbing silence, only broken by the sound of her own frightened crying. She was alone now. With Elsie there, she hadn't felt so afraid. But now? Now she was on her own and very scared.

Molly had dressed and then relented to the inevitable fussing as seemingly all of the women in the house insisted of helping her get ready. Hannah and Tilly had done her hair, plaiting in small red flowers in. Eventually she'd had enough.

'Right. That's about as ready as I'm going to get.'

She stood and went to her jewellery box. Opening it she took out one piece. A small silver brooch shaped like a bird in flight, which she pinned to her left breast.

'Is that it?' asked Hannah

'What do you mean?'

'We thought Princesses had armfuls of diamonds and rubies and...'

'I have. I just don't think I need to wear them.'

'Why ever not?' exclaimed Tilly.

'What makes you think I'm a normal Princess?'

The girls looked down.

'Sorry. We just thought...'

'Look. I'm not a Princess. I'm Molly. Just plain Molly. This is all the jewellery that I need. It was a present from my sister the first time I was married.'

There was a knock at the door. Tilly opened it and in came Marcus' father with Mr Tanning trailing behind. Both men looked uncomfortable but the butler more so. Molly narrowed her eyes.

'Leave us please girls. I believe that your aunt and mother require some help with the flowers.' said James.

With a final glance at Molly, they bobbed a curtsey and did as they were told, quietly closing the door behind them. There was a tense silence.

'How can I help you?' asked Molly eventually.

'Mr Tanning, wait outside for a moment.'

The butler did as he was told, obviously grateful to be out of the room, and the old man began pacing the floor.

'I don't like you.' he said bluntly. 'If I had my way, Marcus would be marrying Lady Samantha's daughter and that would be the end of it. But...'

'But what? You're stuck with me?' she said bitterly.

'But even I can see that my son is completely infatuated with you. He professes love and as much as I want to deny it, he does love you. Maybe even more than I love my wife. I saw as much yesterday. He wanted to go out into the jaws of the storm to find you. He even stood up to me for the first time in his life. That surprised me, I must admit, but I'm glad he did. He's become more of a man than I could have hoped.'

Molly frowned.

'And?'

James looked up at her, as if seeing her clearly for the first time.

'I don't like you, but I love my son. His heart and head are set on marrying you this afternoon.'

'Good.'

'Don't take that tone with me girl. This is my house and I expect a little respect.'

'Respect needs to be earned...'

'It does,' he snapped. 'And I'm not the only one who is failing in that.'

Molly sat on the bed and closed her eyes for a second. He was right. She'd been so caught up in the terror of the whole thing that she'd been acting like a spoiled brat. But the blame wasn't solely with her.

'I'm sorry.' she said eventually. 'I've behaved badly but I can't say I've felt that much acceptance from you either.'

'No. You haven't.'

The old man sighed.

'I think we should just agree to get along for the sake of Marcus and Victoria and to that end, you both have my blessing.'

Molly stood up and offered her hand. James looked at it for a second before shaking it. He sighed.

'Even though I have just said what I've said, and that still doesn't change my opinion of you, I have something important to give you.'

He called out and the butler came back in holding a deep wooden box. James took it from him and opened it. Inside was a silver and diamond tiara with matching necklace and earrings. He took out the tiara.

'This belonged to my great grandmother. She wore it when she was married, as did my grandmother, mother and then Victoria.'

'It's beautiful.' said Molly quietly as he handed it to her.
'It is.'

Molly turned it over in her hands. The workmanship was exquisite.

'I do to know what to say.'

James placed the box on the dresser.

'Promise me you won't disappoint him.'

'I'll try.'

'That'll have to do I suppose.'

He turned to go but looked back as he reached the door.

'I'm sorry about your maid. I overreacted. I thought you might leave but I can see that you're just as stubborn as Victoria. I'll apologise in person to her when she is found.'

With that, he left.

Gwen cringed when the door opened again, not twenty minutes later. The robed man was there once more with his wooden stick in his hands. He banged it on the bars.

'Are you going to be good and come quietly or do you need a lesson like your little friend?'

'I'll be good.' she replied, wiping away the tears with the back of her hand, her eyes not leaving the club in his hands.

He looked at her in silence for a second before taking out a heavy key and unlocking the door. It swung open and he moved towards her and despite her best efforts, she moved away from him.

Without a word, he grabbed her ankle. She cried out in panic as he hauled her towards him.

'Shut up!' he shouted.

Gwen risked a glance behind him and saw the cell door was open. This was her chance.

She lashed out with her free leg, catching him in the knee. He crumpled with a curse and she scrambled away from him on her hands and knees.

He moved quickly, grabbing her ankle but she kicked out once more her booted foot hitting him in the side of the head. He let go and she darted out, slamming the cell door behind her and taking the key.

'You're going to pay for that you little bitch.' he roared, throwing himself at the bars in a vain effort to reach her. His hood had fallen away and she got a look at his face for the first time.

He had a shaggy beard and unwashed hair, with a many times broken nose jutting out above angry brown eyes. Gwen recognised him instantly as the giant of the man at the fair. The one in the fighting ring. The blacksmith.

He shouted again as Gwen threw the key into the cell opposite and headed for the door at the far end. It squealed open on rusty hinges and she dashed through into a roughly circular room and straight into the arms of another robed man.

She darted to the left but he grabbed her dress, the dirty material tearing as he yanked her backwards hard enough to pull her from her feet. She landed heavily on her bottom and then he shoved her forward, pinning her face first on the rocky floor. Another pair of hands dragged her arms behind her and bound them tightly.

There was a tense silence, broken only by Gwen's sobbing. The man on top of her got up before dragging her upright. She got a look at his face and her heart sank. It was Michael. The man Molly had been dancing with. How many of the village were involved?
'Let me go!'
She tried to fight him but he slapped her across the face.
'Pack that in.'
Michael turned to another robed figure.
'Albert, go and find out where Sampson is.'
The man hesitated, staring at the shocked looking Gwen.
'Now!'
The door squealed once more as his companion did as ordered.
Gwen's mind was whirring. Not Albert too? He'd been nice. He...
Michael shoved Gwen backwards until she hit the wall. He raised his hand once more and she flinched.
'Don't ever try anything like that again.'
She nodded as behind him, the door burst open and the big man came crashing in. He had his wooden cudgel in his hand and murder in his eyes.
'Bitch!'
He dashed towards her but Michael put himself between them.
'Sampson! No.'
'She's going to learn a lesson.' he roared and Gwen cringed, terrified.
'No. Not now. She is to be unharmed. The Grand Master said so. Remember what happened the last time?'
The big man's anger flickered for a second to be replaced by something else. Fear?
'Calm down. Alright?'
Sampson took a few deep breaths and nodded, relaxing slightly.
'Good.'

Michael stepped back, his eyes never leaving Sampson. 'Alright?'

There was an incoherent, growled response.

He held Sampson's gaze for a second before turning back to Gwen. He roughly grabbed her and forced her out of a door on the opposite side of the room. Beyond lay a dimly lit corridor and he held her arm tightly as he dragged her down it.

'Where are you taking me?'

'Shut up.'

'But...'

He stopped and shoved her against the wall, raising his hand to her once more.

'One more word...'

Gwen nodded hurriedly and he hauled her away and down the corridor to another room. He unlocked the door and pushed her inside, following closely. The room was rough cut stone like the others, but this had a table and a narrow bench.

Sat on the bench was Elsie who was now wearing a plain white dress. She jumped up as soon as Gwen entered but didn't say anything. Her fear of the man behind her more than obvious. On the table was a wash basin and towel. Michael untied her arms and gave her a shove.

'Wash and change.'

'Into what?'

Michael took a simple white dress from a hook on the back of the door and threw it at her.

'You've got ten minutes and don't even consider doing anything stupid. Sampson already has a reason to hurt you and I won't stop him next time.'

He went out and slammed the door and they both heard the lock click. Gwen put the dress on the table, rubbed her wrists and looked around. Smokey torches burnt in sconces hammered into the stone walls and the only way in or out was the heavy wooden door through which she'd come.

'Are you alright?' Elsie asked tentatively.

Gwen nodded and they hugged.

'I thought I'd never see you again. What's going on?'

'I don't know. They brought me here and made me change into this.' Elsie gestured at the white dress she was wearing. It was the twin of the one on the table.

'What're we going to do now?'

Gwen shrugged and shook her head.

'I don't know but for now we'd better do as they say. I tried to run when they unlocked the door but didn't make it. The big one would have killed me I think if Michael hadn't stopped him. I don't want to give them an excuse to hurt us.'

Chapter Seventeen

The Heralds of Carnothal

'You look beautiful lass.'
Brody beamed as he saw Molly on the stairs. She blushed and looked down, trying to hide the smile on her face as she still felt guilty that she wasn't out looking for Gwen.

Behind her stood Tilly and Hannah. Both girls were grinning from ear to ear. Carefully Molly made her way down the stairs to the hall. Brody offered her his arm.

'You look fine. He's not going to know what hit him.'
From the library came Victoria, aunt Sarah and James. Victoria did a double take as she saw the jewellery Molly was wearing and then threw a disbelieving look at her husband. The old man shrugged slightly with a half-smile.

Victoria covered her mouth to hide her gasp as James stepped up to Molly and much to her surprise, dipped into a deep bow.

'Victoria, Sarah and I are going in the first carriage, the Captain, Tilly, Hannah and yourself are in the last if that is acceptable Your Highness.'

Molly opened her mouth to say something but couldn't find the right words. In end, she just said thank you. Behind Victoria, she could see aunt Sarah grinning widely. She gave her a wink as James escorted his wife outside. Brody turned to her.

'Come on lass.'
She let herself be led outside and was surprised again as she reached the steps. On the gravel drive were two open topped carriages. Gilt scrollwork carved beautifully into white painted wood and each pulled by pair of fine horses.

All of the servants of the house were lining the steps as an honour guard to see them off. Molly caught the eye of the butler and the housekeeper who were stood together on the top step. They both flushed white as she stopped and walked over to them.

'I'm sorry about yesterday. I lost my temper. It won't happen again.'

The butler opened and closed his mouth a few times before the housekeeper nudged him in the ribs with her elbow.

'Thank you, Your Highness.' he spluttered.

The housekeeper elbowed him again.

'From all of the staff, we... We wish you a pleasant day and...'

'And we hope that you and master Marcus are very happy together.' finished the housekeeper with a forced smile.

All the staff were still edgy around her and to be honest, she didn't blame them.

'Thank you both very much.' said Molly.

The butler bowed and the housekeeper dipped a curtsey as Brody led her down to the waiting carriage. He helped her and the girls in before he sat next to her.

'What was that all about?' he whispered loudly as they pulled away. 'He looked like he was going to shit himself!'

Molly grinned and both Tilly and Hannah covered their mouths to hide the giggling.

'I may have threatened him with a knife last night.'

'May have?'

'Alright, I did threaten him with a knife. I had him flat on his back on the table before I stabbed the knife into the wood next this head.'

Tilly lent forward conspiratorially.

'We heard that it took two of the boys to pull it out.'

Brody glanced at Molly who looked down, blushing embarrassedly.

'I don't think that's true. I was just a little angry, that's all.' she muttered.

The Captain shook his head.

'Looks like I got here just in time.'

He reached into his jacket and produced a hip flask and took a swig before offering it to Molly. She shook her head.

'Maybe later.'

'Aye lass. Girls?'

They looked scandalised.

'Sir!'

Brody grinned.

'A little tot won't do you no harm.'

Molly smiled.

'Oh what the hell.'

She took the flask from the Captain and took a hearty pull before passing it to the girls.

'It won't kill you. Probably.'

They looked at her, at the flask and then back at the Captain before Tilly took a dainty mouthful. She handed the flask to her sister as she spluttered and coughed.

'What is that?'

Brody took the flask back from Hannah who was covering her mouth to try and hide the grimace as the fiery liquid assaulted her senses.

'Best Jamaican rum. Treated myself to a barrel.'

He took another swig, grinned to Molly and patted her on the knee.

'They'll do you right lass.'

Molly smiled back.

Gwen was pulling the dress on when the door opened behind her.

'Someone give you a right beating girl, didn't they?'

She flushed red and quickly turned around, hiding the deep purpling welts from the thrashing the butler had given her. Elsie moved around and helped her button the back.

Standing in the doorway and flanked by Sampson and Albert was Michael. He stepped forward and the others moved in, closing the door behind them with a thud that made the girls jump.

'What're you going to do with us?' asked Gwen

There was no answer. Instead the men moved towards them, both Sampson and Albert holding lengths of rope.

Both girls backed away until they bumped into the wall. Albert grabbed Elsie's arm and she cried out, trying to pull away.

'Elsie, don't fight them.' said Gwen, never taking her eyes from Sampson.

The girl stopped struggling and Albert bound her wrists. Gwen was a scared as Elsie looked but didn't resist as Sampson tightly tied her hands. Once he was satisfied that the rope was secure he turned away.

'Elsie, it's going to be alright. We...'

Sampson span around and struck Gwen with the back of his hand, hard enough to send her crashing to the floor.

'Gwen!' screamed Elsie, vainly trying to get to her friend.

On the ground, Gwen could taste blood and the room was spinning. Sampson hauled her up and raised his hand once more.

'You're going to pay...'

'Brother!'

Everyone looked up at the shout. A newcomer was standing in the doorway. His robe was black but of a higher quality cloth than the other men. The deep hood completely hid his features and his arms were folded, hands disappearing into voluminous sleeves.

Slowly the big man lowered his hand. The newcomer was silent for a second.

'Apologise'

'What?' spluttered Sampson, outraged.

The man walked calmly toward him and stood in front of them. Sampson was a good foot taller and half as wide again as the other man but Gwen fancied that she could see the big man trembling.

'Apologise to the girl.'

'But Grand Master, she...'

The protests were barely off his lips when the man struck out. His right arm flashed from beneath his robe and he hit Sampson with the flat of his palm in the chest.

The blow wasn't hard and probably wouldn't have even knocked her over, but Gwen saw the effect it has on Sampson. His face went white and contorted in a grimace of pain. Beads of sweat popped out on his forehead and he gasped for breath. The man pulled his hand back slowly, his fingers curling into a fist. In front of him, Sampson dropped to his knees face going purple as he struggled to breath.

'Are you going to say you're sorry?'

Through clenched teeth, there was a grunt that may or may not have been an apology but it seemed to satisfy the Grand Master. He unclenched his fist and Sampson slumped to the ground.

As he pulled his arm back into his voluminous sleeves, Gwen caught sight of some ugly symbols that looked to have been burnt into his skin. She only saw them for a second but they made her flesh crawl. She shuddered involuntarily.

'Bring them. Carnothal is near. The equinox of the lines is upon us. We cannot waste any more time.'

'What're you going to do?' asked Gwen.

'The lines of power that cover the land converge on this place and the power they hold is at its peak. Your blood will be the final spilled to break the seal and Carnothal will rise.'

'What?'

He turned without another word and left and after a moment the girls were marched out. Sampson had struggled to his feet, face red and eyes wide.

He gripped Gwen's shoulder tightly as if daring her to try anything. They were led along a rough stone corridor past a T-junction and Gwen was sure she could smell fresh air wafting down from somewhere. She glanced at Albert. He was staring ahead. Deliberately not looking at her.

'Albert. What's going on?'

'Shut up.'

'Albert, please.'

He finally looked at her. He looked sick to the stomach.

'Please. Don't make this any harder than it already is.'

'Enough.' snapped Sampson from behind her, increasing his grip on her shoulder and she gasped in pain.

They moved further along until they reached a heavy wooden door that was reinforced by iron bands. There were deeply carved crosses and symbols in the wood but these had been scratched out and defaced. Next to the door, a large wooden bar was leant against the wall, obviously designed to drop into the two iron brackets on either side and stop it being opened from the inside. Why did they need that?

They stopped and Sampson increased his grip, his meaty fingers digging deeply into Gwen's arm. She could feel the tension radiating from him. Whatever the Grand Master had done had hurt and scared him.

The door was swung open and the girls exchanged nervous glances. Beyond the portal lay a circular stone room. Around the edge were eight robed and hooded figures, all chanting. The words were incomprehensible but filled the girls with dread.

Ahead of them stood the Grand Master. He was in front of a wide stone table upon which rested a thick leather-bound book and a wicked looking curved knife.

With a shove, the girls were propelled forwards. Elsie and Albert in front, with Gwen and Sampson close behind. Another man stepped out of the circle and took Elsie's free arm. She began to cry as they dragged her towards the stone table.

'Gwen!'

One of the men cut the ropes at her wrists and forced her

to bend over the stone table, the other fixing heavy iron manacles around her wrists, pinning her in position.

'Gwen! Help.'

Sampson clamped a hand across her mouth and held her back as she tried to get to her friend. Gwen bit down hard and tasted blood but the big man didn't flinch.

The Grand Master spoke, his voice a whisper but carrying easily over the mournful chanting.

'Brothers. Today we free Carnothal. With the pure blood of these offerings, his book will be complete and his assent from the world below will begin.'

With that, the droning chant began to grow and he picked up the knife. Roughly grabbing Elsie by the hair, he hauled her head back. Gwen tried to call out but with Sampson's hand clamped firmly across her mouth nothing but a murmur escaped. At the altar, Elsie was desperately trying to get away.

'Let go of me!'

Her fear filled eyes widened as he brought the blade up in front of her.

'Be still child. Your gift to Carnothal will not be forgotten.'

Without another word he slashed the knife across the girl's throat. The blade bit deeply and he let her head drop. The gushing blood flooded from the severed arteries to pour onto the pages of the book beneath her and the worn parchment soaked it up. Not a single drop was spilled. It was almost as if the book were drinking it.

On its pages, horrible images and words began to appear. Gwen watched Elsie die and sagged in shock. It was only the iron grip of Sampson that stopped her collapsing to the floor.

As Elsie's body went limp, two men moved forward and unfastened the chains that held her down before unceremoniously shoving her to the side. She fell in an uncoordinated heap on the floor with dead eyes staring at the roof. They returned to their places around the edge as the Grand Master looked up at Gwen.

'Do not fear child. It will be quick. I promise.'

He turned the pages of the book to some empty ones and nodded to Sampson.

With a shove, he propelled Gwen forward. She stopped immediately, trying to push back and away from her friend's body and the stone altar but he was relentless. Slowly but surely, Gwen was inched forwards.

'You murderer! You can't do this!'

She looked at Albert.

'Please. Don't let them do this.'

He looked at her and then at the floor, the hurt obvious in his eyes.

No one else said anything, there was just the low and terrible sound of the chant. Gwen had to escape. She couldn't let them get away with this.

They were almost at the altar when Albert surged forwards. He grabbed Gwen's arm and pulled her to the side.

'Get out of here.'

Sampson and the Grand Master shouted.

'Hey…'

'What do you think you're doing? The ritual must be completed…'

Albert put himself between Gwen and Sampson.

'This has gone too far. We can't do this.'

'It's a little late for that, isn't it brother?' said the Grand Master. 'Sampson. Get her.'

The big man darted forward but Albert crashed into him, sending both men to the floor.

'No. You can't.'

Sampson pushed the boy off and tried to grab Gwen but he tackled him once more, tangling his legs. The big man pitched forward, cracking his head on the edge of the stone table.

Gwen darted to the left as Sampson went down. He struggled to his feet, dazed and blood flowing freely from the long cut on his forehead, using the altar to pull himself up.

Before the Grand Master could do anything, drops of blood fell from Sampson's brow and splashed onto the empty pages of the book.

'No!' shouted the Grand Master, trying to wrench the book away, but it was too late.

On the page, the images and words began to form. This time they were black and they hissed as they formed. Dark, acrid smoke rose up, filling the air with a scent like burning flesh.

'No. The blood must be pure!'

Everyone in the room watched as Sampson went rigid. His knuckles turned white as he gripped the edge of the altar. Every muscle in his body locked tight as from his head the blood began to flow.

It dripped quickly for a moment but then poured out and on to the pages. It was almost as if it was being sucked out of his body and into the book.

Gwen scuttled back towards the door as the big man tensed further until his bones snapped under the strain. The cracking was one of the most horrible noises she had ever heard.

'Stop her.' the Grand Master shouted and pointed, his voice snapping everyone out of their horrified stupor.

Two men moved towards her but had gone no more than a couple of steps when they doubled up in agony. Around the room all save her and the Grand Master fell to their knees. At the altar, Sampson's body finally broke. It split wide and Gwen could see his muscle and bone shifting and transforming with a stomach churning movement. She looked up at the Grand Master who almost screamed at her.

'The Heralds of Carnothal! Look what you've done! We're not ready!'

He grabbed the book and backed away to the far wall as the thing that had been Sampson rose, unfolding wetly from the ruined corpse.

It was a truly terrifying sight. It stood taller than a man on cloven hooves with legs that bent the wrong way, as if its knees were backwards.

It had no skin so its movements flexed and wormed their way across its body. Long sinewy arms ended in vicious looking claws that still hung with the remnants of Sampson.

The thing turned its eyeless, long, dog like, head towards her. Rows and rows of sharp teeth filled an impossibly large mouth and it let out a chilling roar.

Gwen scrambled to her feet as to her left and right, there were more wet snapping sounds and a glance showed her the rest of the rooms occupants apart from the Grand Master were suffering the same fate as Sampson. She looked across the room and into the eyes of Albert. He managed a weak smile before his face contorted in pain and he threw his head back, roaring in agony.

Gwen dived for the door as the Sampson thing rounded on her completely. She threw it open and dived through, slamming it shut just as a heavy thud smacked from the other side.

She dropped the wooden bar across the door, securing it as fast as her still bound hands would allow before taking off down the corridor. Reaching the junction, she turned toward the smell of fresh air and ran for her life.

Chapter Eighteen

Dearly Beloved

The sun was high as the carriage rumbled towards the village. The birds were singing and everything seemed perfect. Molly was staring out across the rolling landscape, looking but not seeing. Brody patted her knee.
'Don't worry lass. We'll be at the church soon.'
She turned and gave him a half smile. She felt sick with nerves and on her back, her mark was beginning to itch.
'Here.'
He offered her the flask again but she shook her head.
'No. Thank you. I've had enough.'
He shrugged and took a sip.
'And so have you.' she said, taking flask off him. 'You're walking me down the aisle, not me carrying you.'
Brody laughed.
'You sound like Nancy! Bloody hell lass, it'll take more than this to get me to the stage where I can't walk.'
He grinned at the girls opposite and they blushed. They'd never met anyone like him before.
Ahead, the village was coming into view and they could hear the church bells sounding loud across the fields.

Gwen pelted along the corridor, not really taking much notice about where she was going. She just followed her instinct. A left here, a right there, the place was a maze. Several times she ran into a dead end and had to backtrack.
Eventually she found a corridor that ended with a set of rickety wooden steps leading up to a rotten looking trap door.
Her breath loud in her ears she cautiously climbed up, trying to ignore the horrible creaking sounds the stairs were making and listened. There was no noise on the other side.

Putting her shoulder to it she pushed and the rotten wood held for a second before splintering and falling back. Muted daylight flooded in as from somewhere below there came a series of chilling howls.

Fear leapt into her chest once more as she climbed out and slammed the trap door shut.

Finding herself in a rotten looking building with broken windows and holes in the roof she ran for the door. It was hanging off its hinges and she squeezed through a gap between it and the frame, then ran for all she was worth.

After a few minutes she had to stop, her lungs bursting. The sun was high and she glanced around, trying to get her bearings. She'd reached at the edge of a small wood and in the distance, she could see the village. The top of the church spire was plainly visible and she could hear the bells ringing. Not knowing what else to do, she headed for the church.

The carriages rolled to a halt outside the church and Victoria, James and Sarah dismounted and headed in.

Brody got out first and helped the girls out, followed by Molly. They slowly moved towards the door and Molly was surprised and glad that a group of well-wishers had gathered outside.

She smiled and thanked them, feeling slightly uncomfortable at the attention but pleased nevertheless. Aunt Sarah was waiting for them outside the doors.

'Captain.'

Brody bowed low with a theatrical sweep of his arms.

'Ma'am.'

She gave him a half smile.

'Don't let me see you leading my daughters astray.'

'I wouldn't dream of it my dear lady.'

'What was in the flask?'

Brody opened his mouth but shut it again quickly as she raised an eyebrow.

'I bet it's not a patch on this.'

She reached into her small bag, took out her hip flask, had a swig, and passed it to Brody. He took it and knocked back a measure.

'Bloody hellfire!' he exclaimed as the powerful liquid burnt his throat.

She took the flask back with a mischievous grin and turned to Molly.

'He's waiting inside. You'll do fine.'

'Thank you.' replied Molly nervously.

'You two. Behave yourselves.'

The two girls chorused a 'Yes Mother'.

With a wink at Brody, aunt Sarah went inside.

'Bloody hell. Who's she?' asked Brody loudly and behind him the girls giggled.

'She's Marcus aunt. She's nice.'

He took a deep breath, letting it out slowly.

'Bloody hell!'

Inside the church an organ began to play.

'Ready lass?'

'As ready as I'll ever be.'

The Captain offered her his arm and she took it with a smile. Brody looked over his shoulder.

'Ready girls?'

'Yes sir.'

He smiled.

'Thought I'd better check. Don't want to get on the wrong side of your mother.'

He led them inside. The church was by no means full. On one side sat Marcus family and on the other was Mr Davis and a few locals. The old sailor looked uncomfortable in a new suit but he smiled as she came in.

Molly grinned back at him, feeling a little pang of sadness that Nareema wasn't here and then another as she thought of Gwen. She hoped she was alright.

At the front of the church stood the vicar, flanked by Marcus and next to him was Richard.

Richard wore a blue velvet jacket with a white rose pinned to the lapel. Marcus took her breath away.

He was dressed in a white military uniform with thick gold braiding and he had his heavy sword at his side. A wide royal blue sash crossed his body from the right shoulder to his waist on which was pinned a silver, star shaped brooch. He grinned as Molly drew near.

'You look stunning.' he whispered.

'You don't look too bad yourself.' she replied.

'This? Nareema gave it to me. I'm a General, don't you know.'

Molly smiled.

'Shall we begin?' asked the vicar.

'I now call upon all persons here present to make it known if they have any just cause why this man and woman should not be joined in Holy matrimony.'

Molly faced Marcus and he had her hand in his. She looked scared and he risked a glance at his family. His father was stony faced but his mother and aunt Sarah looked happy. There was a tense silence which he felt the vicar dragged out far too long.

'Very well, by the power...'

At the back of the church, the doors burst open, the heavy wood slamming back and ringing loudly against the wall. All turned to see a dirty figure stumble in.

'Gwen!'

Molly snatched her hand back from Marcus and ran to the girl who all but collapsed in the entrance. She was filthy, covered in mud and blood and her hands were bound tightly together. Molly dropped to her knees in front of her.

'Gwen. What's happened? Are you alright?' she asked as she began to untie her wrists.

The girl looked up at her with wild eyes.
'They're coming.'
'Who?' asked Marcus as he joined Molly.
As if to answer Marcus question, the large stained-glass windows at the back of the church exploded inwards and three large and grotesque shapes landed heavily in the shattered glass. There was a scream and both Marcus and Molly turned quickly.
'Dear God!'
The shapes were skinless slabs of wet muscle standing seven feet tall with long clawed hands and lipless, dog like heads filled with teeth.
Everyone was madly scrambling backwards away from them. Molly hauled her dress up and drew the long knife she had strapped to her thigh. Marcus gave her a disapproving look.
'Really?'
She winked at him.
'A girl needs to be prepared.'
He shook his head but couldn't hide the grin. Brody reached the pair at the door.
'What the bloody hell are they?' he asked, pointing at the monstrosities.
'I don't know.'
Near the altar, Mr Glossop was stood trembling in front of one of the creatures. He raised his Bible in front of him as if trying to ward off the Devil. The thing opened its mouth wide, revealing rows of needle sharp teeth stained red from where it had bitten the inside of its own mouth.
He thrust the book forwards.
'Begone foul fiend…'
The thing looked at him for a second before it slapped the Bible away as if it were nothing. He whimpered piteously as the creature grabbed his head in one of its hands.
'Hey!'
It snapped round as a hymn book bounced off the back of

its head. Molly was there with her knife in one hand another book in the other.

With a low growl, it tossed the vicar to the side and advanced on Molly. She threw the book and it bounced off its nose.

'Come on then.'

She moved quickly away from the door where the wedding guests were scrabbling through. Richard was there, ashen faced but resolutely seeing the people safely away. Marcus had his sword drawn and was facing one of the others while Brody and Davis were circling the last one. They had armed themselves with a couple of heavy iron candle holders.

'What now?' called Marcus.

'Kill the buggers.' replied the Captain.

The thing facing Molly roared and in unison, all three surged forwards. Their speed was breath-taking and they were upon the wedding party before they realised what was happening.

Molly dived to the left as a clawed hand tore through the space she had been occupying while the others clattered into the men and sent Marcus flying backwards.

Molly rolled to her feet and the gem on her wrist blazed blue. The creature was enveloped in a swirling vortex which knocked it off its feet.

It hit the ground hard but began to rise again quickly. Molly jumped towards it and drove the blade in her hand through the top of its head.

The creature roared in pain and lashed out, sending her crashing back over the front row of pews. She scrambled back and managed to get a hand on the hilt of the knife.

With a twist, she ripped it out and the thing dropped to the floor. It tried to rise once more but its nervous system caught up with the damage to its brain and it slumped sideways to lie still.

Marcus had picked himself up and dodged a couple of wide swipes before he brought his blade up to sever a flailing arm. The monster jumped back but Marcus followed, the razor-sharp edge of his sword easily cleaving its head from its shoulders. Molly sat up, wincing at a flaring pain in her side where she had hit the pews. She glanced around.

'Mr Davis! Watch out!'

Brody and Davis were still circling the other creature. It lashed out at Davis, who stepped out if its way to go tumbling backwards over the vicar who was on his hands and knees, trying to crawl to the door. As Davis fell, the thing moved forwards, driving a clawed hand into the old man's chest.

'You bastard!' roared the Captain.

Brody dashed forward and caught the thing on the side of the head with the heavy candlestick. It staggered sideways and he followed it, battering it in a flurry of blows.

The creature tried to turn on him but he caught it under the chin and its head snapped violently backwards. It fell and he went with it, straddling it and beating it until its head was nothing more than a mashed pool of blood, brain and bone.

'It's dead.'

Brody felt a hand on his shoulder and looked up at Marcus before looking across at Molly. She was knelt next to the old man. Blood caked his lips and he was deathly pale. He quickly went over.

'Come on you daft old bugger. Get up. You've had worse.'

Davis smiled.

'Aye Cap'n. That I have, but this one's got me.'

'That's rubbish and you know it.'

'Aye Cap'n.'

His back arched and he was gone with a sigh. Brody sat back on his heels and took the old man's hand.

'You old bastard. You can't die.'

Molly saw tears running down the Captains' face.

'You can't die. You're my oldest friend.'

Gently she reached across and touched the captain. She was horrified. She wanted to cry. It was like she'd lost her father. But she couldn't cry. She bottled it up. Forced it down.

'Captain…'

Brody looked at her distantly.

'He was my friend.'

'Mine too.'

The Captain gently closed the old sailors' eyes.

'I'll have a drink for you later you, stupid old bugger.'

He wiped his face with the back of his hand, his sorrow falling away to be replaced by anger.

'What the hell are those things?'

Molly glanced at Marcus.

'I don't know.'

Brody's face narrowed as he saw Gwen by the door. Quickly he got up and stormed over to her, pushing her roughly against the wall.

'What were those things?' he demanded angrily. 'Where did they come from?'

Gwen looked at him with wild, terrified eyes.

'Where did they come from?' he shouted at her.

'Sir…'

'Leave her alone Captain.'

Brody span round, vengeance and murder in his eyes.

'My best friend is dead and she knows something. She's going to tell me…'

A blast of wind picked him up and slammed him into the wall. Molly strode towards him, her eyes glowing brightly.

'I've lost a friend too. Almost a father. I know how you're feeling and later we're going to get so drunk we can't stand up, but now, now you're going to leave her alone. She's scared. She's been through I don't know what and shouting at her isn't going to help. I won't let you hurt her.'

She held his gaze for a moment before she released him, her eyes dropping back to a dull white.

Brody slumped to his knees and Molly knelt in front of him.

'Captain... Owain... He's gone.' she said quietly. 'There isn't anything you can do but whoever did this will pay. I promise you.'

He looked at her, his face full of loss.

'Aye lass.'

She put a hand on his shoulder.

'Right now Captain, I want you to go into the village and find some men. Then you're going to come back here and burn those things.'

She pointed to the bloody corpses in the middle of the church. He followed her finger, not really seeing the bodies but staring at Davis.

'Captain!' snapped Molly.

He looked at her, something of his normal-self returning to his features. He pulled himself up.

'Aye lass. It'll be done.'

She smiled tightly.

'Go.'

He nodded and cast one final look at his friend.

Molly sighed and stood.

'Mr Crawford. Take Gwen and the others back to the house. Make sure they get there and are safe. Marcus and I will follow shortly.'

Richard nodded dumbly.

'Now!'

He snapped in to action. The horrified stupor slipping away.

'Right. Yes. Of course.'

He left, herding the others away. James had his arm around his wife's shoulders and Sarah was comforting Tilly and Hannah. Mr Glossop the vicar was ambling behind in a daze, muttering to himself.

'What were those things?' Marcus asked once was everyone was out of the church.

'How the hell do I know?' she snapped back.

Molly closed her eyes and pinched the bridge of her nose.

'I'm sorry. I don't know. I just don't know.'

He took her hand and smiled.

'One day, we'll be able to go into a church without a disaster.'

She smiled back and looked down at her blood and dirt stained dress.

'And one day I'll own a beautiful dress I don't ruin.'

Marcus looked down at his uniform. Blood was splattered across the jacket.

'I hope that will wash out.' he said absently.

'What're we going to do?'

Marcus shook his head and put his arm around her.

'Talk to Gwen. Find out what's going on.'

Molly looked at Davis one more time.

'And then we stop it.'

Chapter Nineteen

Uncomfortable Truths

They'd hurried from the church and taken Marcus' horse back to the house while Captain Brody had stayed in the village to supervise the burning of the bodies. The villagers had heard rumours about the church already and what with the dog thing at the dance, they were nervous and scared.

Molly had been met at the inn by a couple of young women who had offered her a dress to change into. It was simple but not covered in blood and dirt and she had gratefully accepted.

Back at the house, people were milling round in shock. Molly jumped off the horse and went to find Gwen while Marcus dealt with everything else.

Aunt Sarah had taken her and her daughters to the library and Gwen was sat in one of the armchairs near the fire. The older woman had just handed her a large brandy when Molly came in. She went straight over and knelt in front of the girl.

'Can you tell me what happened?'

Gwen looked at her for what seemed like an age before she burst into tears. Molly took the brandy glass and held her while she cried. It was a few minutes before she calmed down. Molly gave her the glass back.

'Drink this.'

She took a sip.

'What happened?'

'They killed Elsie.'

'Who? Those things?'

Gwen shook her head.

'No. The man did. He called himself the Grand Master. He cut her throat. It was horrible. They chained her up and...'

She started crying again.

Molly looked up at aunt Sarah and the girls.

'Will one of you go up to my room please. In the top drawer of the dresser there is a small bottle of clear liquid. Could you bring it down.'

Aunt Sarah nodded and despatched Tilly and Hannah to fetch it. Once they'd gone, she turned back to the girl in the chair.

'Gwen.' asked Molly softly. 'I need you to tell me what happened.'

Twenty minutes later she strode out of the library with aunt Sarah in tow. Gwen was asleep after having some of the bitter tasting draught that helped Molly. Tilly and Hannah were watching over her.

'Do you believe what she told you?' Aunt Sarah asked as they neared the drawing room.

Molly nodded.

'Yes. I do.'

She opened the door and was assaulted by a barrage of questions from the people inside.

'What were those things?'

'What happened?'

'What the hell is going on?'

The last was from James. He looked angry and directionless. She held up her hands for silence and then told them everything Gwen told her. From the beating in the kitchen, to the storm, to the sacrifice. Everything.

A disturbed silence fell across the room broken only by the ticking of the mantle clock.

'Are you sure she's telling the truth?' ventured Richard eventually.

Molly glared at him.

'Yes. I am. She wouldn't lie about something like this.'

'It's all nonsense. The girl has gone mad!' said James

angrily.

'What about those... Those things in the church?' asked Victoria.

'Wild dogs or something...' it was obvious that James didn't believe anything he was saying.

'What're we going to do?'

Molly glanced at Marcus who nodded sombrely.

'Marcus and I are going to have a look.'

'What? You can't. The guests will be arriving in a few hours...'

Marcus looked at his mother and she fell silent.

'If Gwen is right then there might be another eight or nine of those things out there. What sort of mess do you think they'd make if they made it to the ball? We have to stop them now.'

Molly looked around the room at each of the troubled faces. Her own insides were churning but she tried to maintain an air of detached calm.

'Mr Crawford. Can I trust you to look after things while we're gone?'

Richard swallowed dryly but nodded.

'Yes. You can trust me.'

'Thank you. Captain Brody will be back soon I expect. He'll help you. Whatever you do, don't let him come after us.'

Richard nodded once more.

'Marcus, I'm going to change. I'll meet you outside in a few minutes.'

She turned and headed out of the room. Victoria watched her go and held her hand to her chest.

'She's very calm.'

'Yes. I told you she was capable.'

'Capable of what?' said James grumpily.

'Father...'

'Are you going to let her walk into whatever it is? She should stay here. Stay safe...'

Marcus almost laughed.

'Father. I couldn't stop her even if I wanted to. It's a trait she's picked up from the Princess. They're both stubborn. And besides. Someone has ruined my wedding and hurt Gwen. She may be just a maid to you but to Molly she's a friend. I fear someone is going to regret that.'

Marcus was waiting outside on his horse when Molly strode out of the house. She was dressed in her black leather jumpsuit, sturdy knee length boots and her sword strapped to her back. There was another long knife on her thigh and her expression was grim. She jumped up on to her waiting horse.

'Ready?'

Marcus looked at her. His sword hung from the saddle and he had a grim look on his face. She smiled sadly, nodded once, wheeled the horse around and headed down the drive.

James, Victoria and the others watched them go.

'It's indecent!' said James.

'What is?' asked Aunt Sarah.

'What she's wearing.

'Well you could hardly expect her kill monsters in a dress, could you? And between you and I, I already feel sorry for whoever is responsible.'

James looked at her.

'Why couldn't he have married a nice normal girl?'

'And where, my dear James, would be the fun in that?' she replied with a grin.

Molly and Marcus thundered down the road, swinging off on to a worn and muddy path a mile or so away and heading towards the woods Gwen had given them directions to. After a while the path disappeared and they were forced to lead the horses. After a few more minutes they arrived at the edge of the trees.

'We'll have to leave the horses here.' said Marcus, dismounting.

Molly nodded and Marcus helped her from her horse. He held her for a second.

'I must say that this isn't the way I envisioned my wedding day to go.'

She smiled.

'Me either.'

'Be careful.' he said, giving her a quick kiss.

'You too.'

With some reluctance, they separated. Molly drew her sword while Marcus took a deep brass tube topped with a wicked looking serrated bladed hook out of his saddle bag. It had belonged to the man who had taken his hand. The evil oriental, Tong Li. The man they had fought to get the Stones of Gunjai.

She watched him slide it over the stump of his right arm and winced inwardly. That had been her fault. Tong Li had been after the Stones. Stones which Molly had possessed and he had hurt Marcus to send her a message. She shivered as she remembered the vision she had seen. The man had heated up a sword until it was glowing hot and then three men had held Marcus down...

'What's the matter?'

Molly snapped out of her revere.

'Nothing. Let's go.'

She turned away and headed into the trees. Another five minutes walking brought them to the ruined building. It looked as Gwen had described. Rotting wooden walls, sagging roof.

They crouched down behind some scrubby thorns and watched. The whole area was silent. Not a bird or insect was making a sound. It was unnerving.

'What now?'

Molly slowly rose and crept towards the building. It

looked like it was an old barn. The door on the front was smashed and lying in pieces scattered across the heavily trampled ground outside. They could see bloody patches on the grass and broken wood.

Marcus peered around the edge. Rusting farm equipment was roughly piled against the wall with a mouldy bale of straw to the left. In the far corner was a deeper shadow surrounded by broken wood. There were no signs of life.

They slipped inside, weapons ready and moved to the corner. Below them lay a dark hole with the remnants of a rotten wooden staircase visible at the top, the rest, they couldn't see. From somewhere below a foul smell was wafting up. It stuck in the backs of their throats like spoiled meat.

Molly bit her lip and looked around, selecting a piece of rusty iron which she dropped down the hole. It only fell for a second before hitting the bottom with a ringing clang. She slid her sword back into the scabbard on her back.

'It's not deep. Go and see if you can find some rope or something and catch me up.'

'You can't...'

Molly smiled at him.

'I won't go far.'

Before he could say anything else, she jumped down the hole.

The bottom was only ten feet down but she landed awkwardly, sprawling amongst a shattered staircase. She pulled herself up and dusted off her knees and hands. It always seemed so easy when Nareema had done things like that.

'Molly?'

'I'm fine.' she called back up to the square of light above her with Marcus silhouetted against it.

'I can't find any rope.'

'Then wait there. I'll need you to help me get out again.'

She heard Marcus tut loudly.
'Don't be like that.'
'You've put yourself in harm's way again.'
'I'm sure it'll be okay.'
'There might be another eight or nine of those things down there!'
His head disappeared from above and Molly suddenly realised what she'd done. One of those things had killed Mr Davis. How much of a chance did she stand against half a dozen? She drew her sword and looked around. A roughly cut tunnel headed away from her with a couple of torches in iron sconces that had been hammered into the wall.
'Marcus?'
His head appeared back at the hole.
'What?'
'Go and find help. I think we'll need some more people.'
'What? And leave you down there? Not likely.'
'I'll be fine...'
From down the corridor came a chilling wailing sound. A discordant noise that set Mollys teeth on edge.
'What was that?' called Marcus.
Molly turned slowly with her sword held out in front of her. A knot of fear began to twist in her stomach.

Marcus was on his knees, peering over the edge of the hole. He could just make out Molly at the bottom.
'I'll be fine...'
Her voice floated up but tailed off as an awful keening wail echoed from the tunnel.
'What was that?' he called.
She didn't answer straight away but when she did, there was no disguising the fear in her voice.
'Molly?'
'Marcus. Something's coming.'
The noise came again, closer this time.

'Molly?' he called again urgently.

There was a heavy thud and he heard her cry out in pain. That was too much. He sat on the edge of the hole and after a muttered prayer, he jumped.

Molly heard the noise and then the pounding of heavy foot falls. Marcus called down to her.

'Molly?'

Down the corridor she could see a shape rushing towards her. In the weak and smoky torch-light she could see it was like the other monsters at the church. It was stooped slightly as it was too tall to stand upright in the tunnel but something was wrong with it. She could see deep wounds in its side and it was bleeding heavily. She raised her sword.

'Marcus. Something's coming.'

The thing roared once more and picked up speed.

'Molly?' Marcus called down to her but the thing was close.

She held her blade out in front of her ready to strike but she didn't get a chance. The thing was fast but blundered blindly towards her, impaling itself on the outstretched sword. It didn't slow as the steel ran through its chest, instead crashing into her and sending her flying backwards into the wall. She hit it hard and her vision swam as she cracked her head against the stone.

With a movement that seemed to blur with speed, it lashed out, driving two wicked clawed fingers through her shoulder.

She screamed and struck out. Her eyes blazed blue, as did the sapphire on her bracelet, and a blast of wind picked it up and hurled it backwards. Molly dropped to her knees as its hand was torn free. Marcus landed a second later. He quickly checked her.

'Are you alright?'

She clutched her injured shoulder, blood flowing freely

from between her fingers. He turned back as from down the corridor came another unearthly wail.

He drew his sword as the creature came back. It was slower this time, lurching unsteadily toward them.

Its left arm hung at its side and it dragged itself along, left leg bent and an unnatural angle. With a shout, Marcus charged at it. Swinging his sword in a tight arc that had nothing to do with finesse but driven by anger.

The monster raised its right arm to ward off the blow but the heavy blade cut through, severing bone and muscle with ease. It fell back once more and Marcus reversed his weapon, driving it point first into the creatures' mouth.

The sword exploded out of the back of its head, almost cleaving it in two. As it dropped to the ground, he turned and hurried back to his wife. She had slumped back against the wall and had gone pale.

'Are you alright? Let me see.'

Gently he prised Mollys hand away from her shoulder. The leather of her suit was torn and there were two deep holes in her shoulder.

'It's pretty bad.'

He shrugged off his jacket and tore the sleeve off his shirt before wadding the cloth against the wound.

'Press tightly.'

Molly nodded and did as she was told.

'Right. Now we need to find a way to get out of here.'

Molly took a deep breath.

'I'll be fine. Don't fuss.'

'Don't fuss! Molly you're hurt. You could have got yourself killed! What were you thinking? You're not Nareema!'

She shot him a hard glance.

'I know.'

'Then start behaving like...'

'Like what?' snapped Molly angrily. 'Like the perfect wife? Be seen and not heard? Do exactly as my husband commands? Just as your father wants me to be?'

She stood, her legs were a little shaky but she walked away from him anyway.

'Molly!'

'No Marcus.'

She pulled her sword from the dead monster and headed off into the dark.

Marcus cursed under his breath. Why did she have to be so stubborn? He hurried after her, catching up as she stopped to relight one of the torches. She had dropped the makeshift bandage and her hands were shaking.

'Let me. You need to keep pressure on your shoulder.'

'Its fine.' she said, her words clipped and harsh.

'It isn't fine! You've got two holes in you the size of my thumb.'

He picked up the discarded shirt sleeve and tried to press it against her shoulder but she moved away.

'Leave it Marcus.'

'No.'

He stuck his arm out and stopped her as she tried to walk away.

'Molly. Please. You're hurt.'

She closed her eyes and sighed deeply.

'No.' she said softly with a shake of her head. 'No. I'm not. They fixed it.'

'Who?'

'Who do you think?' she snapped, her anger returning suddenly. 'The bloody Stones, that's who. They're still with me Marcus and I don't just mean Saali.' she held up her arm and the sapphire in her bracelet was glowing dimly.

Marcus stepped back as if she'd struck him.

'I don't understand. I thought that after India that was all over.'

'Well it isn't. I can hear Saali sometimes and the rest are there when she is. Half heard whispers in my head. I can hear them now. They fixed it. Fixed me. Again.'

'Again? How long have you...'

'Since before we got back from India. Since I cut myself on your shaving mirror and it healed almost straight away. Every time I've hurt myself since then. Sometimes it's by accident and...' she looked down, unable to meet his eyes, ashamed of what she was about to say '...and sometimes not. They get better every time. It always gets better. The pain is there but the wound is gone. It's the pain that reminds me I'm alive. That's why I...'

She stopped and shook her head. Marcus looked at her dumbfounded.

'You can do that to yourself. Why didn't you say anything?'

'And say what?' she shouted. 'That I'm more of a freak than you thought? The uneducated lady with the white eyes. The laughing stock. The monster!'

She sat down heavily with her back against the wall, anger suddenly spent.

'I so want to cry now.' she said sullenly. 'You wouldn't believe how much. But I can't. Another thing on the freak list.'

Marcus knelt in front of her.

'You should have told me.' he said softly.

Molly took a ragged breath.

'I know. But I couldn't.'

'Why not?'

She smiled weakly but still couldn't look at him.

'You'd have only fussed.'

'That's my job.'

They went silent for a moment and Molly looked at him, her face full of pain.

'He hurt me Marcus.' she said quietly. 'He hurt me for the fun of it. Laughing while I screamed.'

Marcus didn't say anything. He knew exactly who she was talking about.

'Then he took me. Forced himself on me. I didn't want to but I couldn't stop him. He hurt me so much.'

She pulled her knees into her chest and gave a dry sob.

Gently he reached out and took her hand.

'He's gone. Destroyed. He can't hurt you anymore. I'm here to protect you.'

She looked up, her eyes glowing in the dim light.

'Is he? I can hear the Stones so what if he can come back?'

'He's gone.' he repeated. 'I promise I won't let anything happen to you. But you have to let me help you.'

She rested her head back against the wall and closed her eyes.

'He scares me. He's gone. I know he's gone but he still scares me. I wake up at night with his laughter in my ears and the memory of the pain.'

Marcus squeezed her hand.

'I'm here.'

She looked at him and smiled but it didn't reach her eyes or dispel the sadness in her face.

'Let's go. We need to find another way out.'

'Let me check your shoulder first.'

She sighed but nodded. Marcus carefully moved the torn leather. Underneath was covered in drying blood but there was no sign of the deep wounds there had been. Only a couple of angry red marks.

'They'll bruise pretty bad in a day or two but I'll live.'

'I don't believe it.'

'Well you'd better. You're not going to get rid of me on our wedding day as easily as that.' she said, trying to lighten the mood.

Marcus shook his head in disbelief as she stood and picked up the torch.

'This way.'

She headed away and Marcus took a moment before he followed her. He hadn't known what Malor had done. Just

thinking about it made him angry. He pushed the thoughts away. He'd have to get her to talk about it more. She couldn't keep it bottled up. It'd kill her. It'd kill him too.
 'Are you coming or what?'
 He smiled. The tension of the last few minutes seemed to have vanished, or at least put away for now. He followed her down the corridor.

 Finding the room that Gwen had described was easy. There was a drying trail of blood that led them there. It was smeared on the floor and walls, covering everything with a dirty red sheen. They cautiously approached the heavy door, or at least what was left of it. It had been smashed to pieces. Bits of iron and thick, blood covered wood, were strewn all around.
 Molly wrinkled her nose at the foul smell that wafted from the room. It was heavy with incense and death. Holding their weapons in front of them they peered in. The roughly circular room was a charnel house. A stone table was in the middle and they could just make out the dull glint of steel chains and manacles hanging from the far side. Pieces of torn flesh were plastered all over the place. Molly put her hand across her mouth, fighting down sickness.
 'Good God.' muttered Marcus.
 They moved into the room and Marcus gingerly prodded some of the remains with the tip of his sword.
 'It looks like they tore each other apart.'
 Half a dog like head was smashed against the large stone block in the middle of the room. They couldn't tell where the rest of it was and frankly they didn't want to look.
 'Over here.'
 Molly walked carefully over to Marcus, hand still over her mouth. Using his boot, he rolled half a skinless torso over and beneath was Elsie. Her once white dress was stained with drying blood and her lifeless eyes stared at the ceiling.

'Poor girl.'

Marcus gently closed her eyes and covered her with his jacket. Molly had gone pale.

'Are you alright?'

She shook her head.

'Wait outside while I look around.'

Once more she shook her head.

'Molly please.'

She looked at him before screwing her eyes shut and nodding.

'I'll be just outside.'

Marcus watched her go before looking around. He'd seen some battlefield horrors in his time with the South Essex but they were nothing compared to this.

He could make out enough body parts for six of the monsters and Elsie. That meant there were only one or two left, what with the three in the church and one at the entrance. What had driven them to such ferocity? To tear their kin apart. He shook his head. It didn't make sense. And where were the others?

'What now? Is there any sign of the man Gwen spoke about?'

He looked up. Molly had some of her colour back but still looked a little sick.

'No. And I think there are only one or two of the creatures left.'

'That's something at least.'

They headed back out and down the corridor to a junction. Left would lead them back the way they had come, so they went right. After a few hundred feet, they emerged in a round room with three other tunnels branching off from it.

'Which way?'

Molly shrugged.

'I don't know.'

They examined the tunnels. Each was hand carved but in the middle one, they found traces of fresh blood. They glanced at each other then headed down it. After another hundred feet, the corridor ended in a heavy wooden door.

Molly slid her sword into its scabbard and examined it. It was made from a dark wood and had been heavily reinforced with iron bands. There was a large round handle and a lock. She gave it an experimental twist, pulling and pushing as hard as she could.

'It's locked.'

'We can't let him get away.'

She shook her head.

'No. We can't.'

With that, she closed her eyes and after a moment's hesitation she ran her hands across its surface.

'What're you going to do?' asked Marcus.

She gave him a tired grin.

'This.'

He felt the air around him change as a hurricane formed in Mollys hands and with a shove, the door exploded. Bits of iron and metal pinged off the walls. Marcus threw himself to the floor as the door handle whistled past his ear.

'Sorry.' she said with a smile.

'You really should be more careful.' he admonished as he picked himself up from the floor. Once the dust had settled they found a narrow tunnel lay beyond and as Marcus ineffectually tried to wipe the worst of the dust and dirt from his clothes, Molly felt her mark twinge painfully. She put out a hand and held on to the wall.

'Are you alright?'

She shook her head. There was something else, a deep unsettling feeling worming way through her stomach. It was rancid and she felt sick.

'I want to get out of here.'

Molly stepped towards the corridor, anxious to be away but Marcus put a hand out to stop her.

'Let me go first.'

She was going to argue but nodded instead.

He moved past her, sword held in his left hand. Molly followed closely. The tunnel was about four feet wide and stretched away into the dark ahead. The floor and walls were rough cut stone with an arched roof that barely gave Marcus room to stand upright.
　'Stay close to me.'
　Molly nodded and they headed slowly down the corridor.

Chapter Twenty

Sacrifices

Gwen woke up in a panic. She didn't know where she was. All she could remember were the monsters and Elsie. She sat up quickly.

'Don't worry. You're safe.'

The voice was kind and soft. Gwen blinked a few times and the room swam into focus. She was in a big bed and it took a moment before she realised it was Mollys.

She looked round to see both Tilly and Hannah stood at the end of the bed with their mother sat in a chair nearby.

'How're you feeling?'

Gwen rubbed her eyes, catching sight of the ugly bruises on her wrists from the rope that had bound her. She ached more than she ever had and had a huge headache. She smiled weakly.

'I'm fine ma'am. Thank you.'

'That's a lie.'

'No, ma'am. It isn't, I swear...'

Gwen pulled the sheets back and swung her legs out of bed. The older woman stood and pushed them back again, pulling the covers up.

'You're staying in bed. You've been through a lot in the last couple of days from what I hear.'

'I can't ma'am, I need to see to her ladyship. It's her wedding day, I've...'

'Be quiet girl and do as you're told. She isn't here and Tilly and Hannah can perform any duties that she may require until you are rested, isn't that right girls?'

'Yes mother.'

Gwen looked at them and then back at the older woman.

'Where is she? If you don't mind me asking ma'am.'

The woman sighed and sat on the edge of the bed.

'Trying to find out what's going on. Now you need to rest.'

'But ma'am...'

'You may call me aunt Sarah.'

There was a quickly smothered gasp from the girls. The older woman turned to look at them.

'What?'

'Nothing mother.'

She held their gaze for a moment until they both looked down.

'As I was saying. I know that your mistress dislikes the formality of her station and dislikes having servants even more. I have no doubt that you don't call her "Your Ladyship" in private. Am I right?'

Gwen looked down at her hands.

'She insisted ma'am. She...'

'Then what is good enough for her is good enough for me.'

She stood.

'Are you hungry?'

'Not really.'

'Get some sleep. I'll send the girls up to check on you in a little while and bring you something to eat. Girls. Come.'

She swept towards the door but Tilly and Hannah remained where they were. She looked at them critically.

'May we stay for a while mother? We... Um...'

'That is up to her.'

Gwen looked between the girls and their mother before shrugging. Their company was the last thing she wanted but she didn't think she had much choice.

'The company would be nice.' she replied weakly.

Aunt Sarah glared at the girls who were staring at the floor.

'Don't tire her out and don't forget there is a ball this evening. The invitations are sent and there's nothing we can do about it regardless of what's happened today. You two better be ready to greet the guests.'

'Yes mother.'

The older woman's face softened.

'I expect that goes for you too my girl. I have a suspicion that you were on the guest list as her maid of honour.'

Gwen flushed with dread, but aunt Sarah smiled and left, quietly closing the door behind her.

There was an embarrassed silence. Eventually Tilly came and sat on Gwen's left and Hannah on the right.

'We're sorry we were mean.' said Tilly.

'Yes. We didn't mean anything by it. It's just...'

'I'm a servant?' finished Gwen.

'Yes. No!' exclaimed Hannah.

Tilly glared at her sister.

'Yes. Because you are a servant. We thought that, well, we thought...'

'It doesn't matter.' said Gwen with a resigned sigh.

'It matters to the Princess. She was upset and very angry when she found what uncle James had done.' said Hannah. 'We've never seen anyone so mad. She was terrifying. She spent all night out looking for you.'

That made Gwen feel a little happier. At least someone cared.

'She gave us a talking to. Told us why we were wrong to treat you like we did.' said Tilly.

'So you're apologising because you're scared of her?'

'No.' said the girl with a shake of her head as she took Gwen's hand. 'We're sorry because she was right. Hannah and I have always had the best things that we could hope for. Mother and is strict and hard on us, and rightfully so, but since father died we've taken things for granted. And people. We're sorry.'

Gwen looked at the two girls and saw nothing but sincerity in their faces.

'Alright,' she said eventually. 'Apology accepted. Now can I get some sleep? I've never been to a ball and I don't think it's...'

'You've never been to a ball?' said Hannah, surprised.

Tilly glared at her and she backtracked quickly.

'Oh, yes, of course. Well we're going to make sure you have a good time.'

Gwen smiled weakly.

'Thank you.'

The girls got up.

'We'll be back in a few hours to help you get ready.'

Gwen nodded.

'It's going to be such fun.'

She watched them go and as soon as the door was closed she swung herself out of bed. Where were her clothes? She was dressed in a long nightgown that most definitely wasn't hers and a quick search brought up nothing.

She didn't know where any of her things were. Biting her bottom lip, she opened the wardrobe and took out one of Mollys dresses.

'I'm sure she won't mind if I borrow it.' she muttered to herself.

She slipped it on over the nightgown. It was a bit long but it was better than nothing. Picking up a pair of boots, she crept to the door.

Listening for a moment she opened it a crack and peered out. The hallway was deserted so she dashed out and down the stairs, treading carefully in her bare feet and trying not to make any noise. As she neared the bottom she could hear raised voices from the drawing room.

'Where've they gone?'

'I'm sorry Captain, they asked me not to...'

'I don't care what they said lad!' came the shouted answer. 'I've been through more shit with them than you could possibly believe.'

Gwen snuck to the doorway and risked a glance inside. The big man who had shouted at her in the church was facing Richard. He was dirty and she could smell acrid smoke hanging on his clothes from where she stood.

'What're you doing?'

Gwen almost jumped out of her skin. She span around to find Tilly and Hannah standing behind her.

'We thought you were going to sleep.'

There was some more angry shouting from the drawing room.

'Well I'll bloody go and ask her myself!'

Heavy footsteps sounded and Gwen pushed the girls back into a cupboard underneath the stairs and followed them in.

'What're we doing?'

'Shhh.'

Gwen pulled the door to as the Captain stormed past and then up the stairs.

As soon as the coast was clear, she dashed for the front door, closely followed by the girls. Outside, Gwen pulled the boots on and ran off down the driveway.

'Where are we going?'

Gwen shook her head.

'I'm off to find Molly. You two better go back.'

They looked at each other.

'No. We don't think so.'

Gwen stopped and moved back behind one of the trees that lined the drive so she couldn't be seen from the house.

'Look. Where I'm going isn't going to be nice. I'm not even sure I want to go there again but it's a dangerous place and, well I feel responsible that she's gone there. I'm going to help.'

'Then we're coming too. We promised mother that we'd keep an eye on you.'

'You can't!'

'We can.'

Each of the girls smiled and hooked an arm through one of Gwen's, turning her purposefully down the road.

'So where are we going?'

The tunnel ran straight for about a mile. It was chilly and

damp and Molly shivered despite herself. She'd seen death before but that room had been something else. It wasn't just the blood and carnage. There had been something else in the room. A presence. Something dark. The sick feeling was receding slowly, as was the pain from her mark. She shook her head, she wasn't sad to be away from that room, that's for sure.

'Molly?'

She blinked, snapping out of her daze.

'What?'

Marcus had stopped walking and it took her a moment to realise why. Ahead the tunnel ended in another heavy door.

'It looks pretty solid.' said Marcus, banging his fist on the wood.

'Let me see.'

She pushed past him, shoulders scraping the wall of the narrow space. Placing her hands on the door she closed her eyes and concentrated. On her arm, the bracelet glowed dimly.

'Why don't we see if it's locked first?' said Marcus with a smile.

He reached past her and turned the handle, the door swinging open easily on well-oiled hinges.

She smiled back embarrassedly and brushed the hair out of her eyes.

'That works too.'

The room beyond was square and quite small, made of dressed grey stone blocks which were at odds with the pale, hand cut, sandstone of the corridor they'd just left. Another iron bound door was on the opposite wall while to the left sat a small wooden cot bed and an upturned box.

'Someone was living here.' stated Marcus.

Molly nodded and walked to the sparse furniture. The box had a scrap of mirror and a small notebook on it, along with a razor and strop.

Inside the box was a tin plate and some cutlery. Molly picked up the notebook. It was filled with careful and neat handwriting. The letters were not in any language that she had seen before and couldn't read. Marcus took the book from her and flicked through the pages.

'I've never seen words like this before. Maybe it's some sort of code?'

Molly shrugged.

'I don't know but whoever it belongs to isn't about. Can we get out of here?'

Marcus nodded and put the book in his pocket before heading to the door. This was unlocked too and he pushed it open. Beyond lay another narrow tunnel made of the same dressed stone as the room. It ran for about ten feet before it was blocked by a cave in. Tumbled rubble and earth completely filled the space.

'A dead end.'

Molly smiled at him.

'My turn.'

She stepped up to the blockage and placed her hands on the rubble. Closing her eyes, she concentrated.

'There's something behind it. A large space. I can feel the air moving.'

'Is anyone there?'

'Don't know.' she replied, feeling the beginnings of a headache pulse at her temples.

She stopped concentrating and pinched the bridge of her nose.

'Are you alright?'

She nodded.

'I will be.'

She took a deep breath.

'I think I can clear us a path.'

'How much is that going to tire you out?'

She smiled humourlessly her white eyes almost glowing in the flickering torchlight.

'A fair bit I expect.'

Marcus frowned and opened his mouth to say something when from down the corridor came a long mournful wail that set their teeth on edge.

Molly looked at her husband hoping her own fear wasn't showing in her face.

She pressed her palms flat against the rubble and concentrated. Thinking of the wind, she shoved with all her might. The sapphire glowed brilliantly and the force of a howling storm erupted from her hands again. It hammered into the rock and it was all Molly could do to keep herself standing. The wail came again, audible even above the raging wind.

'Molly.'

Marcus turned and looked back into the darkness of the tunnel his sword drawn and ready, although in the narrow corridor, he wasn't sure how much help the heavy blade would be as there was little room to swing it.

'Almost there.'

She could feel the debris begin to move under her hands. Slowly it shifted and with a dull grinding, the pile gave way. Suddenly some of the heavy stones were sent flying into the room beyond. Molly dropped her concentration and the wind stopped.

'Marcus!'

Molly scrambled through the gap in the rockfall. Marcus turned and followed, squeezing through the hole as from the tunnel the horrible sound echoed around, bouncing off the walls.

He stood and turned around as a blood soaked fanged maw shot through the opening. Lines of razor sharp teeth snapped an inch from his face. The foetid stink of its breath washed over him and he closed his eyes at the smell. It was eye wateringly foul, full of rancid meat and other things too terrible to try and identify.

'Get down!'

He barely had time to open his eyes again when Molly tackled him to the ground. She hit him in the waist and sent them both crashing sideways. Marcus caught a glimpse of an over long arm tipped with razor sharp claws tear the air where he had been standing. Molly rolled off him and drew her sword.

'Leave us alone!' she screamed at the creature before she drove the point of the blade through its eye.

It shuddered madly, thrashing about and scoring a deep set of scratches across Mollys arms and chest. She cried out and twisted the sword viciously, pushing it hard until it erupted from the back of its head.

It fell backwards and almost wrenched the sword from Mollys hands but the blade stayed with her as the monster slipped back off the metal with a nasty sucking noise.

Cautiously she peered into the tunnel. The thing was laying on its back, twitching violently and making a piteous mewing sound. Marcus stood and looked through the hole, both watching the thing die and feeling nothing but revulsion.

'Are you alright?' he asked, taking in the bloody rents scored across her body.

Molly shook her head.

'No. I'm not. The sooner we get out of here the better.' She sounded tired and her face was pinched and drawn.

'Why don't you rest for a while?'

She shook her head again.

'I want to get out of here. Feel the sun and wind.'

He nodded.

'Alright but go carefully.' he looked around. 'Where are we?'

They looked around. The feeble light from their torch doing nothing to illuminate the space they stood in nor dispel the deep chill and dampness that pervaded the place. It was made of dressed grey stone with large pillars supporting a vaulted ceiling. Water dripped almost constantly from the roof and slimy moss covered the walls in spreading patches. There was a foul-smelling pile in the far corner and Molly wrinkled her nose.

'What is that?' she asked.

Marcus moved to the pile. It was waist high and covered with sackcloth. He poked it with his sword and jumped back with a curse as from beneath the cloth flopped an arm.

'What?' asked Molly.

'Stay there.' he told her.

Using the very tip of the blade, he lifted the edge and peered underneath.

'Good God.' he breathed.

'Marcus. What is it?'

He took a deep breath and let the cloth fall back.

'I think we should leave.'

Molly folded her arms.

'Marcus...' she began but he interrupted her.

'We're leaving now. You don't want to look under there.'

There was something in his voice that made her hesitate.

'What is it?'

She took a step towards the pile but he caught her arm.

'It's the girls. The ones they... they used.'

A dawning realisation crossed her face.

'Oh God.'

'Yes.'

Marcus dragged her away and across the room. In the far corner, they found a set of worn stone steps leading upwards.

'Let's get out of here.' he told her with a forced smile.

He was doing is best to keep his tone light, but he could see the pain and anxiety in his wife's face and didn't like it one bit. They'd been through a lot together and he'd seen her hurt before. That was something that didn't get any easier but this time, she looked scared too and that troubled him.

Molly took a deep breath and went up the stairs, sword in one hand and the guttering torch in the other.

'Don't fuss. I'll be fine.' said Molly quietly as if she'd read his mind, but she was as anxious as he to be away from the cloth covered pile and the monsters.

Marcus made a non-committal noise with his mouth in a tight line.

The stairs wound upwards steeply to end in a rusty iron door. Molly dropped the torch and heaved it open. Beyond lay a square room with another set of worn stone steps at the far end and a couple of inches of stagnant water covering the floor. This room had dank alcoves in it and in each was laid a mouldy looking skeleton.

'I don't like this place.' whispered Molly.

Marcus nodded his agreement.

The steps at the far end rose to a flat stone slab that blocked the stairs but a thin chink of light was peeking through. Molly joined him at the bottom.

'Up then I guess.'

Jeremy Glossop sat in a pew at the front of his church and surveyed the damage. The two-hundred year old stained glass windows lay shattered on the floor while three bloody stains marked where those… those "things" had been killed. He was angry but not as much as angry he should be. He was still trying to get over the fear that he'd felt at the time.

When the monster had knocked away his Bible with such casual disregard, it had also shaken his faith. What was it if his beliefs were not cast iron? What sort of priest would he be?

Two or three of the locals had come in to clear up but he'd chased them away. He needed some time alone to reflect and pray. He stood and brushed some of the broken glass out of the way and knelt in front of the altar. Clasping his chubby hands in front of him he looked up at the cross that hung above it, trying to summon the words that would steady his nerves and soul.

'Dear Lord...'

His words faltered as he heard voices coming from the sarcophagus of the blessed Saint George that stood near the back of the nave.

'Just push.'

'I'm trying.'

There was some exasperated huffing and puffing. He stood up, the fear returning but he stepped closer, heart pounding in his chest. His questing hand found a brass candlestick from the altar. The voices continued.

'It's too heavy.'

There was some cursing.

'Move out of the way.'

The vicar took one more step before the entire top of the sarcophagus exploded upwards. It cartwheeled in the air to come crashing down in the choir stalls, smashing them to pieces. He took a step backwards but raised the candlestick ready to strike whatever abomination dared raise its ugly head.

There was some more cursing as the dust settled and two people hauled themselves out of the stone box, both filthy and covered in blood. The vicar stood and stared at them as they argued.

'You really should stop doing that. You'll wear yourself out.'

'I know but how else would we have gotten out of there?'

The man tutted loudly and then looked around for the first time.

'Oh. Hello Mr Glossop.' he said, genuinely surprised.

The vicar stared at them, the candlestick still held above his head.

'Are you alright?' asked the woman.

He nodded dumbly. This wasn't how a woman should dress. Why did she have a sword strapped to her back?

His mind whirled. She smiled at him, her white eyes almost glowing.

'What? How?' he managed before his brain caught up with itself. 'Master Kane, Mrs Kane. What is going on?'

Marcus stepped forward and kindly took the candlestick from him, gently placing it on the floor before leading him to a seat.

'Sorry for the intrusion Mr Glossop but my wife and I are in a rush. Have you seen anyone else come this way recently?'

He shook his head before blurting out.

'Look at the state of my church!'

The pair looked around.

'I'll sort that out later.' said Molly dismissively. 'But for now, we've got to get going.'

He watched, dumbstruck, as they both drew swords and headed out of the building at a run.

Gwen, Tilly and Hannah walked down the road. The sisters were having a great time. They were on an adventure! Gwen on the other hand wasn't. She'd seen what had happened to Elsie and seen Sampson turn into one of the monsters.

She knew the girls had seen the things too, in the church, but they seemed to have forgotten or were just ignoring it. Either way they didn't appear concerned.

Gwen doubted that they even realised what was happening or the trouble they were walking towards. She had tried on several occasions to get them to go back but they weren't having any of it.

Tilly was slightly ahead, swinging a thin stick around with Hannah walking next to Gwen.

'If we see any of those things,' said Tilly, 'We'll show them.'

She made vague swishing motions with the stick, as if it were a sword. Hannah looked sideways at Gwen.

'We *are* sorry you know. We didn't mean it.'
Gwen went to say something but stopped when she heard hoof beats on the road.

'Horses! Quick. Hide.'

She darted off the road, dragging Hannah with her. Ahead, Tilly giggled and followed them. Gwen hid behind a wide tree while the sisters crouched behind some thorny bushes.

'Shhh.' hissed Gwen at the girls, who were trying not to laugh.

The hoof beats grew louder and two riders appeared on the road. One was Richard and the other, looking uncomfortable on a horse, was the large Captain. They reigned their mounts in and Richard stood up in the saddle.

'Tilly! Hannah! Miss Fisher!'

The girls covered their mouths, trying to hide their laughter. Gwen cursed inwardly. This was not a game! The Captain moved closer to Richard.

'They can't be too far.'

Richard made a face and wheeled his horse around.

'Tilly, Hannah, come out now!'

The sisters looked at each other and then slowly stood, their faces plastered with a mischievous grin. Gwen waved them back down but they ignored her. On the road, Brody tapped Richard on the arm and pointed to the girls. He looked round.

'What do you think you're playing at?' he snapped angrily. 'Where's Miss Fisher? Come on!'

Gwen sighed and stepped out from behind the tree. Richard dismounted.

'Come here at once, all of you. Mother is terribly worried. You saw those thing in the church. What would you have done if you'd met another? It was stupid and reckless to go running off like that.'

The sisters looked at the floor. Gwen moved forward.

'Don't be angry with them sir. They were only...'

Gwen saw movement in the trees on the other side of the road.

She didn't have time to shout a warning before three things burst out of the forest. They bounded through the undergrowth on all fours like some sort of feral dogs. Their skinless bodies glistened in the light and disjointed legs powering them forward.

The largest was in the middle, standing a good two feet taller than its companions even on all fours, and Gwen knew instantly that it was the thing that had come from Sampson.

Brody half turned in the saddle just as the creatures reached him. The big one in the middle bowled into the Captains' horse, sending it and its rider flying.

Gwen heard one of the girls scream as it ploughed on, smashing through Richards horse and knocking him flat beneath it.

One of the other two skirted the downed horses and headed for the girls, jumping forward to land heavily in front of Tilly and Hannah while the final one stopped to tear the throat out of the Captains' horse, drinking the blood of the downed animal greedily.

The girls backed away as far as they could. Subconsciously they found each other's hands and held on tightly, too scared now to scream at the slowly advancing monster.

Behind it, the larger beast slowed and began its own advance on them. Sensing the bigger monster coming up behind it the closest one snarled menacingly, turning to snap and growl.

Without warning the largest one pounced. It smashed into its companion and sent it crashing to the ground.

The fight was a flurry of slashing claws and snapping teeth. Despite her fear, Gwen gently pulled the sisters away from the monsters. If they could put some distance between them then they might be able to run.

'Enough!'

The shout stilled everything, even the chatter of birds and insects. Gwen looked up from the monsters to see a man striding towards them. He was dressed in a deep black robe and had a thick book clutched to his chest. Gwen recognised him immediately.

The Grand Master.

The hood of the robe was thrown back and she got a look at his face for the first time. He was quite young, with sandy brown hair but his face and neck were a mass of scar tissue. The scars weren't random either. They were a mixture of five pointed stars and concentric circles and were similar to those she had seen on his arm.

Gwen had a horrible suspicion that they covered his entire body and that they were self-inflicted. Tilly tightened her grip on Gwen's hand as he came closer. He held a hand out to Gwen.

'Come child. Let us finish what we started.'

'Not bloody likely.'

The snarled words were from the Captain. He had struggled to his feet and drawn a sword from the saddle of his downed horse which he slashed clumsy down.

The blade missed the scarred man and Brody straightened, shaking his head to clear it. He'd hit the ground quite hard and felt a bit dizzy but he'd be buggered if he'd let a bastard like that take the girls.

He raised the sword again but the robed man darted forward to hit him in the chest. The blow wasn't hard but he felt like he'd been hit by a sledgehammer.

His chest tightened and he dropped to his knees, the sword falling from his grip. He couldn't breathe. It felt like his heart and lungs were being crushed. Unable to stop himself he dropped onto his face in the undergrowth.

'Stop! You're killing him.'

The Grand Master turned to Gwen, an odd smile on his face as he slowly curled his hand into a fist.

'Maybe I am. Maybe I want to. Maybe he deserves it.'
  Gwen glanced at Tilly and Hannah and freed her hand, taking a step forward.
  'Please. Don't kill him. I'll go with you.'
  'What? No! You can't!'
  Gwen looked back at the girls.
  'Get back to the house. Find Molly.'
  On the ground, the Captain was turning purple. The veins on his neck pulsing visibly and his face was locked in a grimace of agony.
  'Please.'
  The Grand Master smiled and released his clenched fist.
  'As you wish.'
  On the ground Brody relaxed slightly but was still gasping for breath.
  'Take her.'
  The Sampson thing bounded forward and scooped Gwen up, holding her tightly under its arm. She screamed as it's claws touched her.
  Its smell was horrible, like a week-old corpse and she gagged. Behind it the smaller two things formed up and together they bounded down the road. The Grand Master swung himself up onto Richards horse and followed them.

  Marcus and Molly ran through the trees, following the scream before bursting out into the road. A horse lay dead, it's throat torn out and stomach ripped open wide. Richard lay in the road and nearby Brody was trying to get to his knees. His face was streaked with dirt and tears and he was struggling to breathe.
  Across the road stood the twins. They were rigid with fear and pale. Molly bent to check on the Captain while Marcus looked at Richard. Brody pushed her away.
  'Sort. The. Girls. Out.' he gasped, his voice was tense and words forced breathlessly through gritted teeth.
  Molly looked at him.

'Go.'

She nodded once and went to the sisters. They looked at her dumbly.

'What's going on?'

'He took her.'

'Who did? Took who?'

'The man. The scarred man with the monsters. She gave herself up. He was going to kill us.'

'Who?'

'Gwen.'

Molly had a sinking feeling in the pit of her stomach.

'Are you both alright?'

They nodded.

'Good. Go back to the house. Now. Run. Get them to bring a carriage.'

The girls hesitated.

'Now!'

They tore off up the road and Molly went to Marcus.

'He's badly hurt. Leg's broken and God knows what else. What happened?'

'Bastard took her. Him and his monsters.'

They looked up at a panting Brody. His colour was returning but he still looked sick.

'Said something about finishing what he started. Took your girl. She stopped him from killing me.'

'Where did they go?'

He pointed down the road.

'I'm going after them. Marcus, you wait here for the carriage. Get them all back to the house.'

Marcus put his hand on her arm.

'Molly, no!'

'You can't leave him in the road and Owain can barely sit up let alone stand. Come and find me when they're safe. I'll be careful. I promise.'

She didn't give him a chance to argue before she began running down the road.

Chapter Twenty-One

Summoning

Molly ran as hard as she could and as soon as she was out of sight of the others she began to speak the words.

Each dark syllable fell from her lips in a stream of black mist which grew and formed behind her.

She felt the cold of the Darkness calling as the mist overtook her and began to fill her body with the pain of the transition.

Agonising cold filled every nerve with icy fire and when she thought she couldn't take any more she jumped into the air.

Around her the mist dissipated as fast as it had come and where Molly had been, there was a huge, glorious eagle which soared high through the trees.

The eagle was her link to the Darkness. It could be called, and while her consciousness was in the mind of the bird, her body and soul floundered in the Darkness. It was a cold place where the souls went and it was full of fear and death.

She had been linked to it in India by the Daughters of Kali to try and save her friend. The tattoo on her back, her mark, gave her the power.

Transition between the Darkness and the real world was painful and always left her with bad dreams but the sheer joy of flight was something to behold. Molly hadn't called the eagle since India. She'd been afraid, but now she'd done it twice in one day.

She was still scared and knew that the price would be high later but now it was necessary. That thought triggered a memory of Nareema. She had always said that certain things were "Necessary" and Molly had never really understood what she meant until now. She pushed the thought from her head. She needed to concentrate.

The eagle climbed quickly, scanning the landscape catching sight of the loping forms of the monsters and the rider next to it.

They were really moving, eating up the ground below but the eagle was faster. Molly couldn't risk Gwen's safety so had wait to see where they were going before she could do anything.

They neared the turning for the abbey and stopped. The rider dismounted and signalled to the monsters. The smaller ones surged off to the left and the larger accompanied the rider towards the ruins.

Above them, Molly circled and prepared to leave the darkness.

The Sampson thing crashed into what had been the heart of the abbey and dropped Gwen heavily on the floor.

She sprawled on the flagstones and pulled herself to her knees before she slowly wiped her mouth. The smell of the creature and its rolling gait had been too much and she had been sick but had been unable to do anything about it.

'What are you going to do?' she asked weakly.

The Grand Master smiled. The warped tissue of his face turning it into something sinister.

'I'm going to finish what I started. Now come here.'

Gwen made no move.

'Why didn't the monsters kill you?' she demanded.

'They can't. I control them.'

He tapped the book in his hands.

'The blood spilled to feed the pages is the key. It opens the words and the power. Unfortunately, by the time I'd bound them to me, they had turned upon themselves and half had been destroyed by the others... but well, now they have a new master.'

'Why now? Why here?'

'There are lines of power across the country, girl. They intersect here. This is why the book was hidden here. Now they are at their peak. The wall to Hell is thin and with the words in this book and your blood, we will break through.'

He sneered grimly before snapping at her.

'Now come here now or I will have to use force.'

Near the door, the Sampson thing growled menacingly. It was a low sound that sent tremors of primordial fear through Gwen. The Grand Master turned to it.

'Keep watch.' he said forcefully.

The creature bounded up the ruined tower, easily climbing the stone as if it were level ground. He turned back to Gwen.

'Come here girl.'

She shook her head. He marched over and angrily pulled her to her feet.

'Let her go. Now!'

They both span to see Molly standing in the doorway. She had her sword held in her right hand and took a step into the ruined building.

'Who are you?'

'The person that's going to stop you.'

The Grand Master laughed.

'I don't think so girl.'

'You'd better not underestimate me.'

'I'm not going to underestimate you. I'm going to kill you.'

He muttered a few words that Gwen didn't understand but that sent a deep chill through her. The words were answered by a deep growling from the ruined tower.

'Your Ladyship. Look out!'

Molly heard the growling and was beginning to move even before Gwen's shouted warning. That saved her life.

The creature dropped out of the tower and smashed into the ground where she has been standing. Its claws shattered the flagstones and tore huge gouges in the earth beneath.

She rolled away, rising to a fighting stance without even thinking about it.

The creature shook itself, rolling its shoulders as it dropped onto all fours and turned to face her. It's skinless, dog like head, waved back and forth while bloody drool slavered from its lipless mouth.

Molly began to circle the monster, trying to draw it away from Gwen. She watched it as it tensed and pounced in one blistering movement, covering the distance between them with ease. She ducked and felt it's hot, foul breath as it passed over her.

It sensed it had jumped too far and struck out with its claws as it passed over, raking her back and knocking her on her face. It landed with a screech and turned back quickly.

The Grand Master was watching the fight intently with a sneering half smile on his lips. Gwen glanced up at him and then Molly.

She was on her back with blood pouring from some deep wounds across her neck and shoulder.

She had to help.

The man's attention wasn't on her but he still had hold of her arm. In one move she twisted in his grip and lashed out, kicking him as hard as she could between the legs. He crumpled and cried out in pain as she ran for it, trying to put some distance between them.

He swore and grabbed for her. His outstretched hand grabbing the trailing hem of her dress. She stumbled and went down to her knees, twisting around to try and kick him again. The book dropped from his hands and fell open on the floor.

'Come here!' he snarled before reeling her in by her dress.

Chapter Twenty-Two

Trouble at the House

Marcus rode in the carriage. Brody was sat next to him and still looked a little dazed. Propped up on the other seat was Richard. He had come around but was in a lot of pain. His left leg had been hastily strapped up with a couple of stout sticks in place of a splint.

The coach arrived at the house and Marcus was out before it had stopped moving. He dashed inside just as the clock in the hall struck five. The ball didn't start for another couple of hours and servants were busy preparing everything.

He ignored them and headed to the drawing room. A shocked looking Tilly and Hannah were sat together on the chaise lounge with their mother fussing around them. She looked up when Marcus came in.

'Well?'

'He's in the carriage, aunt Sarah. He's broken his leg and I dare say a few ribs. I'll get some of the servants to help me bring him in.'

Richard was brought in and taken to the library where he was laid out on the table. Brody sat down heavily in a chair nearby.

That had been a close thing.

He'd been in a few scrapes in his time but that had been the worst. He'd been sure he was going to die. It was a feeling that was going to keep him awake at night, of that he was certain.

He took out his hip flask and tried to take the top off but couldn't get his hands to stop shaking enough to get a proper grip.

'Here. Let me.'

He looked up into the face of aunt Sarah. She smiled kindly and took the flask from him. He watched as she opened it, took a swig and handed it back with a wry smile.

'Not bad. Cheer up. You're still alive, aren't you?'

Brody laughed sadly and knocked back a large measure.

'That I am.'

'Good. I'd hate to have to drink the bottle of rum I've got on my own.'

He looked at her in astonishment and she winked.

'You can tell me all about your adventures.'

Before he could say anything else, she turned and walked away to see to her children. He shook his head and took another swig as Marcus came in.

He had his heavy sword hung at his side while on his right arm he wore the bladed hook that was in place of his right hand.

Brody shuddered as he looked at the deep tube. It was evil and reminded him of the man that had owned it previously. He would always remember that serrated blade slashing towards his throat as they lay at anchor off the coast of Iceland.

His ship had been boarded and Tong Li wanted to know where Molly had gone. He'd taken a beating and it was only Nancy that stopped the bastard ripping his throat out. He looked down as Marcus came over.

'Are you alright Owain?'

The Captain took a drink.

'Aye lad. I will be.'

He offered the flask to Marcus.

'No. Thank you.'

Brody nodded.

'Go find your lass. I'd come with you but...'

'You did everything you could.' said Marcus, interrupting him.

'Did I?'

'You nearly died!'

'Nearly.' he sighed. 'Honestly. Next time you two have a party, I'm not coming.'
Marcus smiled.
'You wouldn't miss it for the world.'
The Captain laughed.
'Aye. Your probably right. If I didn't come then who will pull your backsides out of the fire? Now stop gassing with me and go find your lass.'
Marcus nodded and opened his mouth to say something else but was cut off by the sound of breaking glass and a chilling roar.

Mr Tanning shouted irritably at a couple of girls who were supposed to be helping get ready for the ball this evening. He'd had to enlist some help from the village and they just seemed to stand around gossiping rather than doing what they were being paid for. He strode purposefully across the ballroom towards them.
'Come on. Move yourselves. Down to the kitchen and help there.'
He clapped his hands and they scurried off. As if it wasn't bad enough that the girl Elsie had disappeared, that horrid woman that master Marcus had married had made such a mess of the kitchen last night.
He shuddered as he remembered the black look in her eyes as she held the knife in front of his face. Taking a deep breath, he pushed the thought away.
There was something going on today apart from the wedding and the ball but he didn't know what. And as if that wasn't enough to be dealing with, now Mr Crawford had been brought back with an injury.
Rumour was that it was a riding accident but he'd put money on the horrible woman and her poor excuse for a maid having something to do with it.
Honestly, he thought he'd seen the back of the wretched girl but no. He shook his head once more turning back

towards the sound of chatter from the servants busy in the ballroom.

They saw him coming and a look of abject fear crossed their faces. Good, he thought. About time someone showed some respect for his station.

'Well don't just stand there gawping...'

The look of terror in their faces grew and one of them pointed dumbly behind him. He knotted his brow in confusion and began to turn as the large French windows that led onto the terrace exploded inwards.

Glass flew in all directions as through the ruined windows bounded a "thing". It was on all fours with a snarling lipless mouth showing a row upon row of sharp teeth.

Behind him, someone screamed and the monster snapped into action. It leapt towards Mr Tanning, knocking him to the ground, pinning him down with its front legs and snapping at his face.

He thrust his arm up to try and ward off the creature. It smelt awful and he could see bloody pieces of flesh stuck in its teeth. It reared its head back and let out a chilling roar.

Marcus ran to the ballroom. Servants were flooding out and he grabbed one as she passed.

'What's going on?'

She looked at him as a terrible roar echoed from the room. He let her go and drew his sword.

The room was a mess. Broken glass littered the floor and in the centre, was one of the monsters from the tunnels and church. Glass glittered from its skinless body with large pieces embedded deeply in its back and shoulders.

There was a cry of fear and Marcus saw Mr Tanning trapped under the thing. He was desperately trying to fend it off, but as he watched, the monster grabbed his right arm between its razor-sharp teeth and shook viciously.

The man screamed in pain as his arm was torn from his body in a spray of blood. Marcus dashed across, swinging his sword in a wide arc.

The heavy blade drove deep into its back and it reared up in pain, dragging the butler along with it. Marcus yanked his weapon free and struck again but this time the thing managed to bat the blade aside, sending it skittering across the floor.

It snapped at Marcus who dived to the left, his hand closing on his sword once more. From somewhere else in the house he heard another scream but couldn't do anything about it.

The monster in front of him dropped the poor butler, his body now no more than a torn and bloody sack, and turned to face Marcus.

He crouched low and backed away as the monster rounded on him. It roared again and charged, Marcus swinging his sword to meet it. It dodged to the left at the last moment and the blade sailed past its head. With a growl, it launched itself at him.

Snapping teeth closed around the brass tube over his right arm and he could feel them puncture the metal. With a cry, he wrenched his arm out of the tube and brought his sword round as hard as he could.

The blade entered just above its left shoulder and carried on before erupting just above the right hip as the monster howled and surged forward, crashing into him and knocking him flat. Its claws scored a deep line across his chest before the thing realised it was dead and went stiff.

He lay there for a second and tried to get his breath back before rolling the carcass off him and picking up his sword as another roar echoed from somewhere else in the house.

Brody heaved himself up as Marcus dashed out of the room and his head span.

God! He'd never felt this rough in his life! Beneath him, his legs didn't want to work and he had to sit down again.

Another scream sounded from somewhere. Something was up and he'd be buggered if he let the lad face it on his own.

He went to try to stand once more when the large windows behind him shattered and in came one of those bastard things from the church.

He looked around as one of the girls screamed. The bloody thing turned towards them immediately. On the table, Richard was vainly trying to get up but could hardly move while their mother put herself between them and it.

With its back to Brody, it advanced on the women and the Captain was impressed by the way aunt Sarah stood her ground.

Nearby, Richard hauled himself up only to be swatted to the floor by a sweep of an overlong arm. Brody was sure he heard something else break as he went down, crashing hard into the side of the table.

'No you bloody don't.' muttered Brody as he summoned every ounce of strength he had before throwing himself at the creature.

He landed on its back with his fingers digging deeply into its exposed muscle. It roared and thrashed around violently, trying to dislodge him, but he hung on for dear life.

Grabbing a handful of sinews, he pulled for all he was worth, while beneath him the monster roared once more before rearing up and slamming him backwards into a bookcase.

His breath disappeared as it was driven from his lungs and he couldn't hold on any longer. With his vision swimming, he slipped off and into a pile on the floor.

He was dimly aware of it turning to face him and expected to feel its claws and teeth tear him apart.

But the attack didn't come.

Instead the monster reared up once more. Through cloudy and tear filled eyes he could see that behind it were stood the girls. One had an iron fire poker while the other was brandishing a small iron shovel.

As he watched, the poker was driven deeply into the monsters' leg while the other was whacked smartly against the back of its head. The poker was rammed in again and erupted from the other side in a welter of blood as it turned to face its new attackers.

Marcus burst into the library. Richard was on the floor and Captain Brody was nearby on his hands and knees. Another of the creatures was stood in the middle of the room and Tilly and Hannah were next to it.

Even as he watched, Tilly drove a two-foot long iron poker through its leg and it roared in pain. Marcus dashed over to them, hacking down on the creatures exposed spine and severing it completely.

It fell to the floor but still tried to turn on the girls who were backing away fearfully. Quickly reversing the blade, Marcus drove it point first into the back of the things' head and pinned it to the floor.

He stood and looked around the room. Aunt Sarah was shaken and the girls were looking on in disbelief after what they'd just done. Richard was sprawled on the floor near the table and Captain Brody was on his hands and knees, trying to stand up.

'Is everyone alright?' he asked.

'No I'm bloody not.' said the Captain grumpily.

Marcus smiled, despite himself as his father and mother came dashing in. Victoria saw the body of the monster in the middle of the room and had to sit down.

'What the hell is going on?'

'Father, there were two of these things. They're dead. So is Mr Tanning. I'm afraid they killed him.'

'What? He can't be dead. We've a ball this evening'

Marcus didn't know what to say.

'Honestly James. What are you thinking?' snapped aunt Sarah.

He tutted loudly as from outside came the rumble of an explosion. They all dashed to the shattered window to see a giant column of purple light erupt from the ruined abbey and spear towards the sky.

'My god. What is it?' asked aunt Sarah.

Marcus looked at her with true fear in his eyes.

'Molly.'

Chapter Twenty-Three

Carnothal

Molly rolled to the left as the monster sprang back towards her. Her back was a blur of pain but she pulled herself to her feet and readied her sword.

She glanced towards Gwen who was struggling to get away from the scarred man but landed a solid kick to his head and he let go of her.

Molly scrambled away as, with a growl, the thing leapt at her once more. She dodged to the right but it was faster than her. It clipped her and sent her thudding back down, her sword falling from her hand.

She managed to roll over, sending a shock of pain through her injured back as it jumped on top of her, its snarling lipless mouth inches from her face. Foul breath washed over her and blood tinged drool fell from its mouth.

She punched it in the head and grabbed its chin, trying to force its head away but it was too strong. Inexorably, it slowly brought its razor-sharp teeth back down.

'Molly!'

She turned her head to see the scarred man holding Gwen down. He had a long, curved knife in his hand and next to him was the book. Anger flooded her and deep inside she felt something shift. Something dark.

On top of her the creature sensed it and seemed to hesitate slightly. It was all the opening that Molly needed.

On her wrist, the bracelet blazed blue and the thing was thrown clear across the abbey. It slammed into the wall hard enough to crack the stone.

She stood slowly as the monster shook its head, dazed.

'Enough is enough.' she said softly.

She bent and picked up her sword before precise blasts of wind hammered the monster into the wall again and again.

Eventually she let it go and it fell to the floor, bones broken and the wall behind it smashed. It vainly tried to get up but was completely unable to stop her as she brought the blade down, severing its head from its shoulders.

As it slumped down she turned to the scarred man. Her eyes were glowing blue but with a hint of a swirling black shadow flitting in and out.

'Let her go.' she demanded, unable to keep the tiredness from her voice.

He dragged Gwen up and held the knife to her throat.

'You have power.'

It was a statement, not a question.

Molly took a couple of steps closer.

'We will not ask again. Let her go.'

Mollys voice sounded odd to Gwen. As if several people were talking at once.

'Her blood will open the gate.' he shouted in reply.

The next few seconds seemed to happen in slow motion. The scarred man raised the blade and Gwen tried to get away, ducking and pulling with all her might. As she moved, the knife slashed across her forearm rather than her throat, leaving a deep cut. She screamed and he threw her to the ground.

Molly ran forward, her sword raised and the man struck out with the palm of his hand. It hit her in the chest and instantly she felt as if someone had taken her lungs and heart and was squeezing them tightly. Her face paled and sweat popped out on her brow. In front of her the scarred man smiled darkly.

'I'm going to enjoy watching you die. Then I'm going to use her to free Carnothal and he will be my tool. My hammer to crack the world.'

He slowly curled his hand into a fist and Molly dropped to her hands and knees struggling to breathe. In her head, she heard a voice. One she hadn't heard properly since India. Saali. The spirit of the Air. One of the Stones of Gunjai.

'Breathe.'

The words washed over her and she could feel its power filling her.

'Breathe.'

Suddenly the pressure around her chest vanished. She looked up and the scarred man took a step backwards. He looked at his hand and squeezed his fist as hard as he could.

Molly pulled herself to her feet. Her body was protesting and every part of her hurt.

'Impossible!' the disbelief in his voice was undeniable and for the first time he looked scared.

Molly took a step towards him.

'You've hurt the people I care about. Now it's time for you to pay.'

'No. You cannot...'

He sensed movement behind him and turned just as Gwen swung the book as hard as she could. The two-inch thick tome was held in both hands and contacted sharply with his head, the blow hard enough to spin him clean around.

He dropped to his knees and then fell on his face. Gwen raised the book once more, as if she was going to use it to beat him to death.

'Gwen. Enough.'

Mollys voice was soft and the girl looked up. Her anger and adrenaline drained all at once and she sagged before dropping to her knees. The book fell open on the floor in front of her. Molly stiffly walked over and knelt down.

'Are you alright?' she asked wearily.

Gwen looked at her with haunted eyes and shook her head.

'Not really.'

There were no words of comfort that Molly could offer.

'Let me have a look at that cut.' she said eventually.

Carefully she took Gwen's arm. The wound was quite deep across the back of her arm and would probably leave a nasty scar. As Molly gently moved the limb, a thin line of blood ran down the girls' skin before dripping slowly onto the book. It hit the open pages and began to fizz violently.

'Molly...'

They jumped back as on the floor the book began to glow with a sickening purple light.

'He comes...'

They both looked at the man on the floor. He stared at them with wild eyes and a bloody smile on his lips. Molly began to put herself between Gwen and the book which had started to rise slowly from the floor, the purple light getting brighter and brighter.

'He comes!'

The light exploded outwards, knocking Molly and Gwen from their feet. It expanded quickly until it surrounded the abbey completely before punching upwards. Above, the clouds began to turn dark and swirl around in a growing vortex.

'What's happening?' shouted Gwen as the held on to Mollys hand.

'Stay behind me.'

She unceremoniously shoved the girl behind her and raised her sword, both of them backing away until they bumped into the wall.

The book at the centre of the abbey began to spin around, the purple light becoming almost white at the edges as it rotated faster and faster. Contrails of light whipped outwards, forming a circle, twenty feet across as in the centre the book turned.

Molly began to edge towards the door, all the time keeping Gwen behind her. The scarred man had stood. He was on the far side of the circle and he had to shout to be heard over the roaring wind.

'It's no use running. He'll find you. You will be the first mortals to give themselves to him. I'll make sure of it!'

He laughed manically as from inside the circle there was an explosion of sound. Molly and Gwen covered their ears as the book stopped spinning and a wave of pressure thundered across the ruins with heavy static charges flicking across the abbey and purple electricity crackled and arced around.

In the centre, the book hung in the air for a moment before dropping to the floor. It still glowed with the strange purple light but that was cast into shadow by the figure that was stood above it.

'What... What is it?' asked Gwen in the sudden silence, too scared to even scream at the monstrosity that was now before them.

It was huge. Standing at least thirty feet high, it was a foul amalgamation of nightmares. Its skinless body glistened, corded with thick muscle and glistening with wet blood. Three barbed horns rose from a head that was more mouth than anything else. Row upon row of razor sharp teeth glinted in the odd purple light.

It looked around and flexed its shoulders. Molly shuddered as the muscles moved and slid across one another. Long arms ended in hands tipped with claws as big as Mollys forearm.

'Carnothal.' said the scarred man. His voice was full of awe and he prostrated himself before the figure.

'Master. You have come. Our works were not in vain.'

It looked down at him with beady black eyes before it snatched him from the floor. Molly saw his expression change from adoration to abject terror in a second. It held him up effortlessly in one hand, bringing him up close.

'Master...'

There was a sound. Something disgusting that rang like wet leather being slapped against a rock and Molly realised that the thing was laughing.

It dropped the scarred man who fell awkwardly before it turned its attention to her and Gwen.

Molly brandished her sword. Across the room the man had pulled himself to a sitting position. His left leg stuck out at an odd angle from beneath him.

'Yes. Yes! They're the ones that you want. The ones that tried to stop you. They're the ones.'

Carnothal bent and regarded Molly and the terrified Gwen, its bloody maw inches from them. Its breath was foul and stank of death and blood.

'Gwen.' whispered Molly, not taking her eyes off the thing. 'When I say, I want you to run. Run for your life.'

The girl squeezed Mollys arm.

'No. I'll not...'

'You'll bloody well do as you're told! I'll be right behind you. I promise.'

She felt Gwen tense as the monster straightened and brought a hand, easily as big as Molly down towards them.

'Now!' shouted Molly as the slashed at the hand with her blade.

It cut a deep groove across the palm and the monster roared in anger and pain. Thick black blood spurted for a second before the wound closed.

Gwen turned and ran towards the door with Molly close behind. They were almost there when Carnothal caught Mollys leg with a lazily flicked finger and sent her sprawling. She hit the ground face first and felt blood begin to flow from her nose. Ahead, Gwen turned back.

'Keep going!' she shouted, but the girl came back to try and help Molly to her feet.

Their hands touched for a second before Molly was wrenched away and into the air, Carnothal holding her upside down in front of its face by one of her legs.

Molly struggled and managed to get her hand on the knife strapped to her thigh as she saw the mouth open and row upon row of teeth.

It swung her towards the gaping maw and she lashed out, both with the knife and the power in her bracelet.

Carnothal stepped back in surprise before roaring in anger. He threw Molly away and she hit the wall of the tower hard before falling the last ten or so feet to land in a crumpled pile.

Gwen rushed over, ecstatic to find Molly was breathing but unconscious.

Across the abbey, the scarred man had crawled to the book and was feverishly thumbing through the pages and muttering under his breath.

A sudden anger filled Gwen.

She'd had enough.

Enough of being hurt.

Enough of being scared.

Enough!

She picked up Mollys fallen knife as from above her came another mighty roar that shook the very stones themselves.

From the book were spilling ghostly chains made of the strange purple light. They began to wrap themselves around the limbs of the monster in front of them as the man spoke.

With a wordless cry, Gwen rushed forward. The scarred man saw her coming at the last second and raised his hand to strike her but she held the long knife out in front of her like a lance and the blade speared his palm.

He fell backwards, blood spurting from the wound as Gwen dragged the knife free. As he fell, the ghostly chains stopped forming.

'No! I need to bind him. I can't let him loose. I...'

She slashed the knife down again and this time he managed to get the book up to block the blade. It plunged deeply into the leather and behind her, Carnothal roared in agony.

Molly rolled over and the world swam into focus. Her right side was a blur of pain and she could taste blood.

She struggled to her knees, head swimming, as Gwen ran towards the Grand Master while in the middle of the room stood Carnothal. Semi formed, ethereal chains were looped around its arms and legs but these began to dissipate as the girl threw herself at the scarred man.

Molly crawled to her sword and shakily stood. The blade was heavy and she clutched her right side as inside her something grated painfully.

Across the abbey, Gwen attacked the man, viciously swinging the long knife around with power driven by anger.

He brought the book up in front of him to block a stab that would surely have gutted him, but the blade pierced the book, burying itself deeply in the pages.

Above her, Carnothal let out an agonised scream as a deep rent appeared in its chest. Dark blood poured from the wound which showed no sign of closing on its own this time. As she watched, Gwen pulled the knife free and slashed down again, cutting the leather on the outside.

Once more Carnothal let out a scream of pain and another deep rent appeared on its body. The chains around its right arm vanished and it thrashed around, black beady eyes focusing on Gwen and the scarred man.

Gwen was tiring. The rage and adrenaline that had fuelled her was ebbing quickly and the knife was getting heavier and heavier. She brought the blade down once more and it scraped along the cover, scoring a deep line in the leather.

'Gwen. Move!'

She looked around to see a huge fist swinging towards her. She fell to the side and it missed her by an inch, sending dust and debris in all directions. The scarred man fell backwards too, the book falling from his hands.

'Gwen. The book. Get me the book.'

She looked around to see Molly stumbling beneath the monster.

'The book. The book hurts it.'

She looked around and madly scrambled towards the fallen tome. Her hands touched it at the same time as the Grand Master.

'Let it go. I need to bind him...'

Gwen lashed out with the knife and cut a line across his cheek.

'Bitch!'

She pulled the book towards her and with all her might, threw it towards Molly as the scarred man shoved her backwards.

The book sailed through the air and Mollys eyes flashed a brilliant blue. A vortex of air caught it as the last chain around the monster disappeared.

It raised a cloven hoof and stamped down hard enough to crack the flagstones. Molly dived to the left and drew the book towards her.

The pages opened and the words and images were swirling and writhing as it came to her.

She readied herself and as the book came close she swung her sword. The sharp blade cutting it clean in two along the spine.

The two halves fell slowly to the floor as Carnothal let out a chilling scream. Molly looked up to see the demon raise its head to the sky as its features contorted and writhed before the world exploded in a brilliant flash of purple light.

Across the abbey, the scarred man dived on top of Gwen. He opened his hand and hit her in the chest, instantly she felt her lungs and heart tighten and her breath catch in her throat.

'You're going to pay for that.'

He squeezed his fist closed, blood from the knife wound pouring darkly from between his fingers. The pain was unbelievable and she couldn't breathe.

Her head lolled to the side and through cloudy eyes, she saw Molly bring her sword down and slice the book in half. There was a huge scream from the monster, loud enough to make the floor shake.

'No, no no!'

The scarred man looked up from Gwen and the pain lessened for a second before the entire abbey disappeared in wall of purple light and sound.

Marcus was still a mile away from the abbey when the column of purple light exploded outwards.

He had ridden hard since it appeared and it was bathing the entire landscape with strange purple tinged shadows. The swirling clouds above were churning with barely restrained fury. Lightening crackled in them, lighting up the sky with purple flashes as from the abbey there came a chilling noise like a scream but he was sure that no mortal mouth could have made such a sound.

His horse reared underneath him but he held on for dear life. Just as he brought the animal under control the purple column vanished in an explosion of pressure.

It flooded out like a ripple in a pond, flattening every tree and building within half a mile.

The trailing end of the blast washed over Marcus and brought with it the smell of death and decay. He quickly spurred his mount on towards the ruins.

Molly coughed and rolled over onto on her back. She was covered in dust and dirt and was completely exhausted. She tried to sit up but her head swam.

'Gwen?' her voice was hardly a whisper.

She coughed once more and tried to clear her throat.

'Lie still.'

A face appeared above her, a face she was glad to see. Marcus. He smiled.

'I can't leave you alone for a few minutes, can I?'

She smiled back tiredly.

'Where's Gwen?'

'I'm here.' the girl sounded like she felt.

Molly sat up suddenly, crying out as pain flared throughout her body.

'What about...'

Marcus shook his head.

'I can't find any trace of him. What happened?'

'I'll tell you later.'

He frowned but nodded before he helped her to her feet.

Around her, the abbey was now nothing more than a pile of jumbled masonry. Its tower and walls were smashed to pieces and the old flagstone floor was cracked. She found her sword and slotted it home in the scabbard on her back.

She looked around and then at Marcus who had his arm around Gwen. The girl looked awful, with dirt streaking her face and clothes and more cuts and bruises than she could count.

'Let's go home.'

Marcus led Gwen from the ruins and Molly followed. Stopping only to pick up two halves of a battered and scorched book.

Chapter Twenty-Four

Home again

They returned to London soon afterwards to rest and recuperate. Gwen had eschewed Mollys offer of leave, deciding to remain at the house rather that spend time with her family.

She had, she told Molly, a job to do and she was damn well going to do it.

Marcus' parents and staff had wished them well but Molly thought they were secretly glad to have her out of the house.

Aunt Sarah on the other hand had already arranged for she and the girls to visit in London while Captain Brody had headed back off to his fiancé Nancy in Gosport. He'd been uncharacteristically quiet but Molly had made him promise to visit soon.

That had been two weeks ago. The aches and pains were still there along with some stunning bruises on both her and Gwen.

The day was bright and clear and Molly sat in the garden, enjoying the summer sun.

'Your Lady… I mean, Molly, can I talk to you?'

She looked around at Gwen who was hovering nervously a few feet away.

'Of course. Sit down. Tea?'

Gwen shook her head as Molly poured herself a cup from a delicate china teapot.

'What do you want to talk about?'

Gwen wrung her hands and stared into her lap.

'Was it real?' she asked eventually.

Molly smiled sadly.

'Yes. There are dark things in the world. Things that we probably shouldn't ever see. It was real. It shouldn't have been, but it was.'

The girl nodded, still staring into her lap.

'Will you teach me?'

'Teach you what?'

'To fight and be brave and strong. Like you.'

'I'm not brave or strong. I've just got a habit of being in the wrong place at the wrong time. And… and sometimes, you must do what is necessary.'

'I was afraid.' The girl said after a long silence.

'So was I.'

'I don't want to feel like that again. When they…' she hesitated. 'When they killed Elsie, I felt so helpless. I couldn't stop them. I…'

'Enough.' said Molly forcefully before she sighed. 'I will teach you the little I know but I'm not a master at anything.'

The girl looked up and smiled sadly. Her skin was still marked by yellowing bruises on her face and wrists.

'Thank you.'

'You don't need to thank me. What're friends for if not to help one another?'

There was a polite cough from behind them and they both turned to see Simcox the butler standing a few feet away.

'Begging your pardon Your Ladyship, but you have a guest.'

'A guest?'

'Yes, Your Ladyship. He's waiting in the drawing room.'

Molly stood and Gwen followed her as Simcox led them inside. He paused at the door.

'I will bring some tea Your Ladyship. Gwen. Please help me.'

She nodded and followed him back to the kitchen. Molly opened the door.

Stood by the fireplace was a short man. He wore a grey wig that seemed to be too large for him but his clothes were cut well and made of expensive cloth. He turned and gave her a smile that wouldn't have been out of place on a toad.

'Ah, Your Ladyship.'

He ghosted over to her and took her hand, mashing his lips against it as he bowed low.

'Who are you?'

He straightened with another smile.

'Direct and, ah, to the point. I've heard that, ah, about you, as has my employer. In fact, he wishes to meet with you. Say for, ah, dinner? Your husband is more than welcome to, ah, attend as well.'

His speech was clipped and it had an odd tempo. He seemed to speed up towards the ends of sentences, as if in a rush to get the words out.

'I don't know…' Molly replied warily.

'Never the less, I have been instructed to, ah, insist. The Prince is desperate to meet the lady with the white eyes. All of, ah, London is abuzz with talk of you.'

'Prince?'

'Yes. The Prince Regent. He was most, ah, clear in his instruction.'

Molly didn't know what to say.

'Very good.' continued the man. 'I shall make the appropriate arrangements.'

He bowed again.

'Oh, and once you've dined, could I, ah, possibly trouble you for a moment or two of your time?' he smiled his reptilian smile again.

'I think you may be able to, ah, help me with a little problem…'

Printed in Poland
by Amazon Fulfillment
Poland Sp. z o.o., Wrocław